The COMFORT *of* FIGS

Simon Cleary was born in Toowoomba in 1968, and attended university in Brisbane. He lives in Melbourne with his wife and two sons. He is currently working on his next novel.

simon cleary

The
COMFORT
of FIGS

UQP

First published 2008 by University of Queensland Press
PO Box 6042, St Lucia, Queensland 4067 Australia

www.uqp.uq.edu.au

© Simon Cleary 2008

This book is copyright. Except for private study, research,
criticism or reviews, as permitted under the Copyright Act,
no part of this book may be reproduced, stored in a retrieval system,
or transmitted in any form or by any means without prior
written permission. Enquiries should be made to the publisher.

Typeset in 12.5/16 pt Bembo by Post Pre-press Group, Brisbane
Printed in Australia by McPherson's Printing Group

Sponsored by the Queensland Office of Arts
and Cultural Development.

This project has been assisted by the Commonwealth
Government through the Australia Council, its arts funding
and advisory body.

Cataloguing-in-Publication Data
National Library of Australia

Cleary, Simon.
The comfort of figs.

ISBN 978 0 7022 3643 3

I. Title.

A823.4

Front cover image: Panoramic view of Story Bridge, Brisbane,
under construction (46466), State Library of Queensland.
Back cover image: Story Bridge, general elevation and plan,
1935 (BCC–B120–31044), Brisbane City Council Archives.

For Alisa

*There is no difficulty in designing a bridge,
aesthetic and satisfying all interests.*

Dr J.J.C. Bradfield
December 1931

*And the eyes of them both were opened,
and they knew they were naked,
and they sewed fig leaves together and made themselves aprons.*

Book of Genesis

Prologue: January 1940

Beneath the steel bridge, a rowboat. Two oars come to rest, heavy drops of water sliding off the blades, falling into the river, falling deeper into night, slapping against both. The rower and his passenger drift on the river's tide, its slow ebb; the river-mouth and the bay so many winding miles to the east. They listen. The rower hears more, with his ear trained to the sounds of the river, and the sounds too of the air between bridge and water. He closes his eyes. He hears the river's inhalations, its exhalations, its soft suckings and slappings; the movement of water against the banks, against the wooden hull of the boat, against the massive concrete piers, so recently sunk deep into the riverbed.

The boat pulls towards the closest pier, an almost imperceptible shift in its drift; some unseen eddy at work, the rower thinks, some gravity. He corrects the boat. Not with his oars — which remain resting in his lap — but with his right hand, which he drops silently into the water, cups, and deftly rudders below the surface of the river till the bow of the boat turns, just enough. He lifts his hand from the water then, wet and dripping, and a little calmer. Closes his eyes again.

The still air reverberates above the rower as a lone flying fox beats its path upriver. He hears its wing-beats — faint but regular — and shifts the angle of his head to follow it without yet opening his eyes. Then, as it nears the bridge, he hears it suddenly falter. He hears it stall and turn sharply, abruptly, against the night sky. He hears its mid-flight panic of wing-beat and bodily contortion. It is, he knows, the bridge. Of this he is certain. That the new steel crossing of the river has surprised the flying fox, is still an interloper, is not yet part of its blood-memory. The flying fox changes course. It drops, and drops again, and with shorter, less certain beats, passes through the channel of air between bridge and river, and then it emerges and is gone in broad sweeps of wing.

But in the flying fox's wake, another sound. This, finally, is what the two men were listening for. Above them now they hear the sound of footsteps on the bridge.

It is the rower's passenger who first recognises the hollow thud of bootfall on planking. It may have been me, he thinks — an odd thought — who laid that planking, those temporary ironbark boards resonating in place until the time comes for the bitumen to be poured, and for the deck itself to be completed. In the night quiet he recognises, of course, the gait of the man above. It gives him comfort, but brief.

Prologue

Then they raise their heads suddenly – both – as they hear the clattering above them of more boots. They raise their eyes and the night sky is filled by the vast bridge and its rising, swelling, steelwork. There's a rugged, rising staccato of boot-on-plank, of more men on the bridge, of running men on the bridge, and of the gait they know being drowned by the others. They look. But it is too late. In the space above, in the space between bridge and river, a man is falling.

Ficus

One

He is waiting for her in the square outside City Hall. On one of the monumental pedestals at the front of the old sandstone building he sits. Beside him a bronze lion guards the Hall's entrance. A second maned figure crouches close by, impervious to the presence of its mate, the two stilled creatures staring tirelessly out at the square and the people who occupy it. He too waits. He has learnt to wait. Trees teach you this – that some things take time.

    A late afternoon storm passes, short and fierce. He doesn't move, feels instead the pelting rain on his scalp, on his shoulders, on the nape of his strong, bare neck. His clothes dampen, and begin to pull on him. The languorous gravity of them. But when the rain ceases, it is so abrupt it surprises him. And yet, he knows, it shouldn't. These February storms do this. He should expect it – the change – but he doesn't, and the suddenness of the sky's transformation is unsettling, comes to him as the death of something. The rain ceases and the light that follows is infused with sadness. And with humility.

Robbie O'Hara runs his hand through his long wet hair and muses. He imagines the eucalypt-edged waterhole that was once here: sees it filling with rain, then spilling over in growing rivulets to the next in a chain of waterholes, the ponds linking, one overflowing into another, to become a creek. The creek itself running slow and sure and rain-swollen across the soft sloping land, feeding the broad brown river beyond. A creek which, in the city's frontier years, provided drinking water for soldiers, convicts and free settlers in equal measure. A creek which then took its name from the grains they planted on its banks. But the Wheat Creek was soon sucked dry and buried by the town it had sustained, and in time the watercourse was covered over by the business district. The stream became merely an underground sewer, remembered now only by the street name, Creek Street. A silent lament, hidden.

Robbie watches people leaving the Hall, looks for her face among them. Feet splash on the ground as the square fills again, sunlit once more, shoes scuffing shallow puddles of rainwater and spraying arcs of water droplets into the air with each step.

Then, abrupt as the storm, she is there, bursting from the Hall portico with three others, all animated, into the light. She is taller than he remembered. He watches as she stops, sunbathed, and turns in to face the others, her back to him. She is slender and erect, this woman he has come for, the contour of her spine distinct through her loose dress, her shoulders purposeful, her neck long and adamant. And then there is her hair, that extraordinary hair. Short-cropped and silver, flecked with white. She is only in her twenties, but she is silver-haired and startling, charged with energy, mercurial.

The circle breaks and the four move in their different directions, this woman singular now, and no less bold. Robbie slides off the pedestal and catches her as she steps out of the square. He reaches, and his hand touches the side of her arm. She stops and turns, and for a moment he is a stranger, and this woman caught still in whatever it was she has just left.

'How did it go?'

'Bastards,' she replies, recognising him. 'Bastards, bastards, bastards.'

The touch of her skin lingers on his fingertips, crackling.

'Ten thousand signatures not enough?'

'It wouldn't have mattered if every man, woman and child in the city had signed it. They wouldn't have listened. They've made up their minds.'

'So what now?'

'A swim to clear my head. You?'

'Walking you to the pool,' he says. He is not normally this confident, surprises himself, doubts he has ever been confident like this before, wonders where it has come from. 'Where do you swim?'

'Centenary Pool,' she says, her smile grim, her accent North American. 'Where else? From the diving tower you can see the whole of Victoria Park. Who knows how much longer we'll have it.'

We, he thinks, *we*. The way she does this — her identification with his city — intrigues him.

The Comfort of Figs

From the square they walk up Ann Street, one of the girls' names, as it runs away from the river. His city is simple. Streets with boys' names run east–west, streets with girls' names run north–south. For many years much of his city had this uncomplicated view of the world. Boys and girls were different. Though their paths may intersect from time to time, their life trajectories were at right-angles to each other. He accepted it for a while, this order, when he first perceived it, but in time it began to unsettle him, to agitate him. It continued to disturb him until he found a way of making sense of it. Though never quite coming to love the grid of street names, he learnt to shape their pattern into his own story. To give them meaning. This was, he felt, something. *His* something.

'Each street, no matter which way it runs, starts at the river,' Robbie says to her as they walk. Or ends with it, he thinks. 'It's because the city was built in the crook of the river. Every street – boy or girl – eventually runs into the water.'

The river claiming both sexes as its own.

This grid of boy–girl names was broken, interrupted, by a single ragged, subversive street. Robbie enjoys that. How at the end of the boy axis, at the business end of town, Creek Street, angling across the grid, answering a different compass, claims its own place. A song from another time, a different order to things.

They turn off Ann, and start up a steep set of steps – Jacob's Ladder, a name his mother loves – cut hard into the hill. They climb through a little-used park, a swathe of rainforest plants hugging the long flight of steps. They reach Wickham Terrace on the ridge-line at the top of the hill, looking over the city and the bridge and snatches of river, and then they chart a course through the streets of Spring Hill until they reach Victoria Park.

Ficus

As they walk he points out the trees. Leopard trees and lilly-pillies and tulipwoods and tuckeroos. She is distracted at first, her mind replaying her meeting with the mayor over and over until it is distorted by the repetition. Gradually Robbie's voice asserts itself, and she finds she is listening as he describes their route, tree by tree, fig by fig. Silky oaks and hoop-pines and Moreton Bay chestnuts. Hill's figs and rock figs and sandpaper figs and nipple figs. As each new tree approaches he stretches out his hand and touches the trunk without breaking stride. It is a gesture of familiarity. And affection. It reminds her of the way a father puts a hand on his child's head.

At the pool he watches her swim, her long angular body reaching out stroke by stroke. The stillness of her close-cropped head between her rhythmically rotating shoulders. He watches her from the stand as she finishes her laps, climbs out of the pool, and towels herself down on the pool deck. He watches as she turns her head first to one side, then to the other, shaking water from her ears. She looks up at him, her head tilted, and meets his eyes for a moment. She enters the changing rooms, like a magician's assistant will enter a box, and comes out again some minutes later, dressed.

He offers to walk her home. He tells her his name. That he was born in Brisbane. That he is an only child. That his father was nearly twice his mother's age when they married. That his father was an engineer, cold and inflexible as his creations. That his parents still live here, in an apartment overlooking the river. That Robbie has been planting trees for the city council, the same council she has been lobbying. And that of all the trees in this city, it is the Moreton Bay fig which is the most remarkable.

★

The Comfort of Figs

A fig grows on the banks of a river flowing into a bay. 'Imagine it,' he says to her, his voice quiet. Or it stands like a lonely sentinel on a hinterland slope. Or lowers curtains of root onto a rainforest floor. *Ngoa-nga* to the Turrubul people, who wove its stringy bark fibres into scoop-nets for fishing. Then, on 17 May 1770 a ship made of wood from trees unknown passes by the vast bay, outside its long sheltering islands. Its men looking at the land of this country and seeing paddocks for grazing, trees for timber, rocks to extract from the earth; and measuring, always measuring, recording and capturing, drawing lead lines on paper made from yet other trees of that other place – and, when gone, naming the bay 'Morton Bay' after one of their people – one who was not even with them as their ship passed by. Morton, a patron of Captain James Cook, being James Douglas the 14th Earl of Morton, President of the Royal Society, lover of the stars, financier of Cook's voyage of discovery in the year of Venus' transit. Morton itself not a man's name but a title, a barony, a castle even then crumbling into the frigid waters of a Scottish loch.

And yet – Robbie pauses – in the first published version of Cook's journal account of his voyage, 'Morton' became 'Moreton' – an error in transcribing Cook's handwriting into type-set. By the time of publication, Cook is no longer alive to correct the error, speared on a distant Hawaiian beach. And the 14th Earl is no longer alive to be offended.

So this tree, this silent giant creature which is cousin to the trees across the seas who were present at the dawn of creation, becomes a 'Moreton Bay fig', after the bay, after the island, after a man who had never been here and never stood in its shade, and who was himself never known by that spelling.

★

Ficus

'Where does it come from?' she asks. 'This love of figs?'

He takes her hand and leads her through the park towards a nearby stand of trees. He picks a way through, weaving a path between their trunks.

'There,' he says, stopping, his voice hushed.

She turns a circle where they stand. The grass underfoot is thin and pale despite the afternoon's rain. Around them is a light eucalypt forest. Above, through the canopy of leaves, the sky is deepening quickly, falling into purple. She turns a second circle. Nothing rises from the landscape.

She shakes her head, confused.

'What do you mean?'

He gestures to the tree directly in front of them.

Then she sees it. Or rather, them. There is the light grey of the trunk. A fig of some sort, the smoothness of it flecked with thousands of tiny, dark grey nodules. On the trunk, level with her stomach, she sees a wave in its skin, a curving-under like a lip, full, and she notices what she thinks is a knot in its flesh – a break in its surface, large, the size of her thigh. She reaches for it. She runs her hand along the fig's skin, rougher than it appears. She reaches the knot, explores it with her fingers and the palm of her hand. And realises that it is not the fig's skin at all. The different texture, the new colours. This bark is ribbed: long undulating grooves running vertically upward, long deep crevices of something foreign.

She takes a step back and looks up. Then she understands: there are two trees here. The fig and another species, their leaves and their branches interweaving above her into one mottled canopy. A smile crosses her face and she turns to him, her pale blue eyes glittering.

'Silky oak,' he says.

Two trees growing side by side. Entwined, she thinks.

'How romantic,' she says – not a word she'd normally use. 'How . . . *connected*,' she corrects herself.

He hears the strangeness in her accent, some vague, inchoate danger.

She reaches out and takes his hand and pulls him with her towards the tree. Two small steps and she is against the fig, her shoulder blades coming to rest on its skin, her buttocks soft against the fig's hard trunk. She draws Robbie closer till he too is pressed against her.

Two

He brings her things. Gifts at the end of the day. He arrives at her place as the afternoon begins its fall into darkness. 'Close your eyes . . . Here.' He passes an object to her.

A leaf from a silky oak, like a page of Braille. Or a macadamia nut, embedded still in its soft sheath. A mopoke feather. A shard of schist. An old bolt rusted almost beyond recognition, a gentle test. A mangrove seed pod. A jacaranda flower.

Something different each day. He describes his days to her like this.

Or they meet in the afternoons when he has finished work and she her day at university. On a park bench overlooking a certain bend in the river, not a bridge in sight. Or at the base of a cliff-face. At a lookout, or the end of a jetty. By a doorway. In front of a block of pink porphyry in the façade of a colonial-era building. At the foot of a silky oak. Or a bunya pine. Inside the roots of a curtain fig. He describes his city to her like this.

Freya Adams listens. She watches. She touches. She feels. This city of his, her adopted town. That you can live in a place for so long and not see it. That you can pass across the surface of a city as you would skate across a frozen childhood lake, impervious to its currents. It has taken her by surprise that there is something more, other layers he can show her. She thought she had it, had the measure of the city, thought she had seen it true, unencumbered by having been born here.

A city of a million and a half, stretching, growing. A city reaching further outwards, towards the bays and the forests and the mountain ranges she'd glimpsed from the airplane window, but couldn't grasp when she first flew in. So much water, so many trees, so many ridge-lines. A developing city, and a place of rough politics, hard to detect. A city shaking off a past it seems half-embarrassed by. Here, she sensed immediately, there was work to be done, and there might be a place for her. Somewhere she might settle.

She sought out a university, a respite from the immediacy of the place, thinking-space. In this three-university city, the one she chose was outside the urban centre, perched on the crown of a hill, its buildings hidden among gum trees, lost among them – this the reason she'd selected it. It had the right attitude, the right relationship with the environment, the right respect for nature. And it didn't matter that she spent the first few weeks of that first hot summer lost – as it seemed half the students were –

Ficus

following tracks through the bush, seeking out lecture theatres among the trees, the sweat of February dripping down her legs, the scent of eucalyptus oil strong and disorienting. It didn't matter, because the politics of it was right, was everywhere, and in everything.

But here she is, listening, watching, touching, feeling, anew. She succumbs to Robbie's gentleness, to the force of each day's revelations.

Without her hearing, he enters the house she shares with other students. They are alone.

'Don't turn around,' he says, his body close behind hers, his chest against her shoulder blades. 'Close your eyes.'

With his left hand he covers her. She feels his palm and the hardened skin of his fingers. She smells his day, so different from hers, and can't name where he has been, what he has done.

'Are they closed?'

Her eyelids flitter against his fingers.

'Yes.'

He withdraws his hand.

'Keep them closed,' he says.

'I will.' There is playful resignation in her voice. A submission she is content to give to his world, his way of seeing it.

'Now,' he says, 'taste this.'

He lifts a silky oak blossom to her mouth. She senses the object near her face, and her hands rise instinctively from her sides. He catches them, presses them gently back against her body.

'Trust me.'

He holds the blossom and its long golden bristles before her.

She smells it, the perfume, and knows then it is a flower. Her body relaxes, begins to sink into his.

She reaches with her tongue into the dark, searching, tentative.

'Here.'

He brings it closer to her mouth. Her tongue finds the flower, the bristles with their tiny nodules. The sensation is strange, and she withdraws momentarily. Then she registers the taste, the trace of sweetness. She reaches again and runs her tongue along the head of bristles, feels them on the very tip of her tongue. Robbie releases her hands and Freya takes the flower from him, her eyes closed still. She runs her thumb and forefinger down the stalk, collecting the nectar. She raises her finger to her mouth and licks the sweet sticky nectar off. Opens her eyes. Turns her body into his. Kisses him so he tastes both her and the flower, intermingled.

The city changes before her eyes. She is not sure whether with each afternoon's gift, or each fig he points out to her, he is adding texture or stripping something away, some false image she had formed of the place. Or of herself. It unsettles her as it thrills. The deepening. That she is falling deeper into the city, and its life. This place she has made her home. Constructed from the stuff of its people, its geography, its politics. And the pieces of her own life – she shouldn't forget that. She is loyal to the place already.

And yet, here he is, quietly, showing her more. She has the sudden feeling – a surprise to her – that it is not yet home. The feeling that she has more to do. That she must do more to make it home. That she needs Robbie for this.

So she follows him. Watches from her own car as he loads a ute with tools, picks up a mate, heads for his day's work-site, a park in the suburbs. The two men split, to work different parts of the park, and Robbie sets down near a pond, an ana-branch of the river, filled with tall, waving marsh reeds. Water hens – short, red-beaked, blue-sheened, scrappy things – patrol the banks. Freya positions herself above him on a slope, close to some shrubs: shelter for her spying should she need it. An ibis stalks nearby, its beak scratching the ground, working the grass, before it lifts itself onto a picnic table, a tilted eye fixed on her all the while.

Freya watches as he swings a pick, drives a shovel, gets onto his hands and knees to pull weeds from out of the ground around garden beds. The steadiness of it all, the simple concentration. She sees him begin to sweat, the colour of his shirt darkening under his arms and down the centre of his back.

She feels the shifts in her own body.

She collects a handful of rocks from the ground beside her, then crouches, and aims one near him. It lands close, raises dust, tumbles to a stop. He lifts his head – a sharp reaction – then stands straight, trying to work it out, scanning his surroundings. After a while he gives up, and as he drops to his haunches again Freya tosses a second stone. But she miscalculates the distance, and the stone strikes him on the back, hard, and he curses.

Robbie rises. Freya watches him mouth words, makes out two of them – *bloody kids* – and then he is striding up the slope, determined. She stays low behind the shrub. Then, when he is almost upon her, she jumps out like a jack-in-the-box, hooting. Robbie whips back and around, startled by the yell, by the manic figure leaping out in front of him, his heart pounding till he recognises it is her. Freya laughs, doubled over, crying with it. The ibis takes to the air, silent but for wing-beat.

He shakes his head, his nerves not yet calmed.

'And what the hell are *you* doing here?'

'You should have seen yourself!'

He is not yet laughing with her, but he smiles.

'Freya – *what* are you doing out here?'

'Reconnoitring.'

'You followed me?'

'You can't take risks, you know. Not with men.'

'You're mad.'

She is still laughing as she reaches for him, and pulls him with her to the ground beside the shrub. Robbie isn't ready to give entirely, is not yet with her, is still tense. She hasn't yet encompassed him, not yet. He feels the grass hard against his elbows, hears it crunch under the weight of their bodies. There is a sharp crease of fallen eucalypt bark in the small of his back as Freya rests on top of him, her eyes closed.

But he pulls away from her kisses, suddenly.

'Snake!'

Freya snaps up onto her bottom, half-erect, then – pure reaction – begins to scramble away, desperately kicking at the earth, pushing against the ground, and then against Robbie in her urgency to get away. Then she is on her feet, and she is taking short backwards stumbles before she realises that Robbie has not moved. He is still sitting on the grass, his arms propping behind him, at ease. And now it is he who is laughing.

'You bastard,' she pants.

They remain like that for some time, looking at each other –

he reclined on the grass, she standing hands-on-hips, catching her breath. Eventually he rises.

'Been out here before?' he asks.

'I didn't know the park even existed.'

He takes her hand.

'Let me show you around.'

There is the weeping fig at the top of the Dutton Park cemetery hill. Its leaves shine translucent in the early morning. Then there are the figs in New Farm park, their branches growing into each other, the western sun setting through their enmeshed canopies, its rays sparkling through the small gaps in the foliage, the leaves themselves darker still, heavier, more solid before the lowering sun. Other days, on his way to a planting job, he drives down the avenue of figs on Kelvin Grove Road. Driving through them is like passing between two lines of elysian dancers, the twisting torso of each tree facing its partner opposite. Moving through them he feels the tug of their dance, and his blood quickens. On Saturday afternoons there are the figs of Davies Park ringing the football oval, throwing a shade so deep it dizzies. And then there are those along the river nearby which glow phosphorescent when winter mists rise off the water, engulfing them. He takes her, also, to the banyan at the fig tree reserve in the city's financial district. Traffic routes around this vast-buttressed monumental fig. It is like the stationary centre of a moving traffic-mandala, and though it is an exotic, it still moves him.

When Robbie first understood the figs, he saw the city anew, unbuilt. It became a place populated not with people and buildings, but with plant life. After *seeing* the trees, he noticed the contours of the landscape. Beyond the buildings and railways and roads, the land, he'd come to realise, is one of ridges and rises and ranges and low valleys. Of creeks and catchments. When he opens the street directory now, it is not the streets, but the threads of water-blue and the green patches of park he reads. And it is the rise and fall of the land beneath the bitumen and buildings that becomes his terrain.

She wakes, late one Sunday afternoon, disoriented by the sound of some bird she cannot name calling outside. She rolls to observe him. The long deep breathing of his sleep, his chest rising and falling, the seams of muscle running beneath his skin and the symmetrical sloping of his pectorals down into the shallow gully running along his centre from his stomach to the boned ridges collaring his throat, otherwise so vulnerable. She takes in his long brown hair, the stubbled jaw, the leanness in his cheeks. She purses her lips and blows a stream of air onto his eyelids, watches them flutter, and blows again, harder, till they open. Earth-brown.

'How long have you lived like this?'

'Like what?'

'Alone.'

'I don't feel alone.' He shifts, turning to her.

'Why am I here then?' she smiles.

'Why *are* you here, Frey?'

She gets up to explore his house, her lithe body naked in the still, soft light. A weatherboard cottage with a roof of corrugated iron – 'workers' cottages', they call them here. A handful of steps off the street up to a narrow front verandah, the floorboards dry and grey where they are daily exposed to the afternoon sun. His large bedroom, and opposite it, across the corridor which splits the house, a second bedroom, used for storage. He is at her shoulder as she peers inside.

'Go on.' He kisses her on the back of the neck. 'Tell me what you find.'

'Don't rush me.'

He follows her around the house. The living room is lined with old, unpainted chipboard bookcases reaching to the ceilings – bookcase set upon bookcase obscuring the walls, each shelf swollen with books, buckling in the centre from their weight. The collection of books tells him that his university years – the half-completed degrees in literature and art-history he'd built as a shield against his father – were not entirely wasted. She circumnavigates the dark room and the sweep of books, close, womb-like.

Beyond the living room and the bathroom there is the small kitchen and the dining room with a long timber table. Freya sits on a straight-backed chair, her body cool against the seat. She runs her hand along the boards of the table.

'You made this yourself?'

'Recycled hoop-pine floorboards.'

'And this?' She touches the wooden bowl set in the centre of the table, her fingers playing with two fine symmetrical arcs of grain on opposite lips of the bowl.

'Hand-turned jacaranda.'

'Mmmm,' she says.

She points to the rows of framed photos on the wall. Black-and-white eucalypts, a series of solitary pines on hills, colour photographs of fierce blue native flowers from the granite belt, a collection of figs in shadow.

'No people,' she observes.

'Mmmm,' he answers.

French doors open onto the deck at the back of the house. She steps out and finds it cooler than inside. She rests her elbows on the railing and looks down at the land falling away sharply into a deep gully beyond the house, before bottoming out and sloping up the hill opposite.

'Does the creek run?'

'Not for years,' he says.

Rainforest trees rise up from the gully, a black bean and a colony of umbrella trees, but it is a fig tree which dominates.

'Let me guess,' she says. 'A Moreton Bay fig?'

'*Ficus macrophylla*. It's why I took this place. You just don't find these in your average backyard.'

Though there was more to it than that. There had been the tremor of recognition at the precise moment he'd seen the fig, some violent, ungraspable memory. A vestige of his childhood he hadn't yet erased. When he was a child he'd carved his initials into a tree just like this one, which might have been a fig – a tree anyway which had offered him shelter, sanctuary from his unyielding father. The protean memory had stopped him, seized him, touched him; he took the house because he wanted to know this feeling, to get at it, to understand it. To bury it. Finally.

He climbs down the back stairs. She watches him slip on a pair of sandshoes and descend into the deep cool beneath the fig in the gully, his own nakedness luminescent in a shade the afternoon sun never penetrates. He climbs into the fig, his shape ghosting through the tree. He climbs up far enough to tear a leaf off a branch, then makes his way backwards down the trunk, feeling chords of muscle stretch along the soles of his shoe-enclosed feet.

When he returns, panting lightly, he passes her the leaf, large as a hand, soft as leather to the touch. Its sap is crystallising at the end of the stalk when he gives it to her, its milky bleeding just slowing. She takes it between thumb and forefinger, raises the leaf and rolls the stalk between her fingers. The leaf turns slow rotations before their eyes. A dancer on a music box; or a dervish, not yet ecstatic. She sees the glossy dark green of its face turn into the rust brown of its back, turn to green and then brown again. Green, brown, green and brown.

'Shiny on the surface,' he says, 'but sombre underneath.'

'Strange,' Freya says, 'and beautiful.'

'It's an honest tree. You can see its dark side.'

They laugh together and return inside.

'So,' he says, 'what did you find?'

'A passionate man who likes his solitude,' she says.

'I can be an activist too,' he says. 'Move in with me.'

Three

Each morning he leaves her. He slides from the bed they now share and dresses quietly in the dark. Then he tiptoes out of the house in his thick socks, sits on the front steps, pulls on his boots, and enters the day before it has yet become solid.

Aloneness. Solitude. Singularity. He thinks about the way he is, the way he has become. About his relationship to things, to the world, to people, to women. Growing up an only child he'd wondered often enough, but he'd learnt there were competing theories, rival explanations, none of which seemed to allow each other.

Genes – one of the theories, the word he'd first heard from his year-eight science teacher. Genes now, it seems, an explanation for everything, stripping mystery from things, emasculating

Ficus

will, blind to the decisions you make. Robbie doesn't doubt their power — in fact likes the solace of being able to surrender to them — but he believes there are other masters too. Such as experience.

What people do to you.

As a fourteen-year-old, envious of those kids with easy friendships, he'd tried hard to join them. For months he tried: exposing too much of himself, or too little, trying *too* hard, outrageous boasts about him and his family that even he didn't understand. He suffered the endless little humiliations of not being accepted. Then, suddenly, he was one of them. Suddenly, without warning, the boys from one of the gangs at school invited him to join them on a night-time escapade. Even as he climbed out his bedroom window near midnight, he saw himself as the fifth member of the gang, had already become a part of the group, was one of them.

They meet in the street, all upturned collars, bent heads, and bravado. Robbie doesn't know where they are going — the details of the adventure don't matter. Just moving with them through the night, together, is enough. After five or ten minutes Robbie hears one of the boys say the name of the bridge, and he guesses it's their destination. The thought excites him. The bridge at night: the lights, the noise, cars and trucks and motorbikes roaring past, the height, the view. The things you can do, the things you can get up to.

Robbie's mind races with possibilities as they leave the dark side streets and reach the approach to the bridge: six lanes, three each way, though the traffic thinned now at this late hour.

The Comfort of Figs

They take the footpath. Soon it leaves the roadway, and they are on the decking of the bridge itself, and can feel through their sandshoes — through every nerve of their bodies — the vibrations of vehicles on the deck. He thinks of the stories he's heard about older boys, the things he's heard they do on the bridge. Throwing stones from the approach-ways onto the rooves of houses, or flicking bottle tops at ferries. Laying throw-downs or cap-gun caps or empty soft-drink cans on the road for car-tyres to set off. Brown-eyes from the top of the staircases.

One of the boys — Nick Kettle, the oldest of them — stops, and turns to the railings. They all halt, waiting for him. Kettle unzips his jeans, leans close to the railings, and takes a piss — the arc of urine immediately pushed out of shape by the breeze up here. When he is done they continue. The steelwork of the bridge is now directly overhead. They are not just on the bridge, Robbie thinks, they are *in* it.

He'd heard rumours of boys climbing the bridge at night, scaling it all the way to the top, and he thinks, *yes*, that's what this is about, an *initiation*! The thought carries both excitement and fear. Robbie looks up at the tunnel of intersecting steel beams, the different angles, and wonders how you could select a route through all that.

About a third of the way across the deck they stop, he the last of them. The other boys part for him, and somehow he is at the centre of the group. They all turn to face the traffic, taking Kettle's lead, resting their elbows on the safety barrier separating them from the vehicles flashing past. Robbie also looks across the bitumened deck. There is only the odd car or the lone truck now. Kettle points. He says something that Robbie cannot hear over the engine and the tyre noise of a semi-trailer that passes in front of them at just that moment. One or two of the other boys turn to look at him, and Robbie thinks, yes, they are here for him, an initiation. A boy breaks from the group and walks back down the footpath, facing the oncoming traffic. He is fifty metres away before he stops. There is more talk between Kettle and the others that Robbie cannot pick up.

A long gap appears in the traffic. Kettle climbs over the barrier and steps out onto the bitumen, looking back at him. Ah, Robbie thinks, this is what the test is then: not to climb, but to *cross* the bridge on foot, to run across the six lanes, to dodge six lanes of traffic. Yet, it seems almost too easy — with so little traffic, with only midnight traffic. Robbie waits, his heart beating with excitement, for more.

Then he feels a hand on his shoulder blade. Then arms around his legs, followed by a ferocious shove in the back, and Robbie is over the barricade and on the ground, on the bitumen of the deck itself. There are two boys on top of him, their full weight pinning him to the deck. Kettle has his right arm, and is stretching it out in front of him. Robbie is pinned, impotent, doesn't understand, feels only terror. He struggles and kicks, but they have him. He yells out but his voice seems so small, muffled by the bodies on top of him, and the expanse of bitumen against his cheek, traces of warmth still remaining in the deck from the day's heat.

As he fights against them he sees, far down the slope of the deck, the other boy, standing in the middle of this closest lane of traffic, directing cars away, waving them out of the lane they're in, towards the centre lanes. Nothing makes sense. Nothing is real, nothing right.

It is all he can do to swing his head around to see what they are doing with his arm. They have it over an expansion joint. A fresh wave of fear. *Almost!* he can hear them. He feels the steel of the expansion joint, then, against the palm of his hand. *Almost got it!* they're yelling to each other, forcing his fingers down. *Just about got 'em in!* He hasn't got the strength any more, and he feels his fingers thrust between the steel teeth of the expansion joint, as far as they can go, stopping at the third row of knuckles. Robbie is no longer resisting, is weak beneath the weight of the boys, the fingers of his hand jammed down into the steel-toothed gap.

'All we have to do now,' whispers Kettle, the meanest of whispered teenage taunts in Robbie's ear, 'is wait till the bridge cools down for the night.' As if there is some cruel delight to be had out of it. Some mature evil, beyond Robbie's conception, issuing from Kettle's lips.

Robbie vomits.

'Fuck me!' Kettle yells. 'Aaaww fuck!'

'He's fucking spewed!' another shouts, and they release their grip on him, and they are standing up now, and wiping vomit off their shirts.

'Can't take no fucking joke, can ya?'

He kneels on the earth, the day breaking open around him. The dampness of the ground comes through his trousers at the knees, and the wetness of the dewy earth reaches his skin. He is solitary. A man kneeling alone on unwanted land by a railway, in a sleepy suburb in his city. An early mist seems to glow with its own even light. Broad day has not yet come, and the cry of a single crow swirls around him through the fog.

Ficus

He kneels with his gloves tucked into his belt and, barehanded, scoops out shallow cups in the earth. He keeps his fingernails bitten short, but the soil still wedges between skin and nail, strains against the quick. He cups his hands and scrapes the sides of them against the ground, enjoying the abrasion of it. Enjoying the feeling of the earth gently giving way. A train whistle sounds through the mist and Robbie stops to listen. He straightens and rocks back on his haunches, the muscles in his thighs tightening, filling out his legs. His toes push against the ends of his boots, and he feels the blood beating there. Robbie brushes his hands against his thighs, shaking off some of the soil. The sounds of the train's coming get louder: the *whooshing* of the displaced air, the *ka-thicking* of the wheels passing over the joints in the track, then the breaking as it slows for the station. He counts his heartbeats, and feels heart and count quicken, till the train passes and recedes.

Robbie dips his hands into the soft earth again. At the bottom of their scooping the two hands meet under a shallow cover of soil. He pauses and gazes down for a moment at his arms which look strange, handless, disappearing into the earth at the wrists. He thinks of childhood holidays at the beach and being buried in the sand by his father, his small body lying in a trench of his own digging and his father scooping the sand over him so it is only his head which is above-ground. Sand. Clean and pure and rinsed and glistening. *Sanitised*, he thinks. *Suffocating*. It is the earth, the lived-in, broken, secret-keeping earth which comforts him these days. He has grown away from sand, grown from sand into soil.

The earth hollowed, Robbie reaches for a seedling he has brought. He takes the potted fig and tips it upside down, loosening the roots and the soil by squeezing, then tapping. The plant slides out and Robbie cradles it gently in his outspread fingers before righting it and lowering it into its place in the earth. He fills the hole around the young fig with the soil and pats it down, the first of his day's plantings complete.

He does this in the early mornings – planting figs in the city before it wakes, sewing them into the city's fabric before it rises, dropping them like dream-seeds into the city's repose.

It saddens him that the Moreton Bay fig is not respected in Brisbane, not celebrated. That it is just one of the fig species populating the city's parks. That free, nineteenth-century Brisbane-town should have uprooted its figs, the colony's flogging trees. Should raze them as it sought to erase the memories of its convict beginnings. In Sydney, to the south, the Royal Botanic Gardens promoted Moreton Bay figs for its grand avenues and parks. They are found in so many public gardens, so many churchyards. It irritates him. It irritates him that Brett Whiteley, who had such glorious licence to paint Sydney Harbour, would presume to sketch the Moreton Bay fig, as if to claim it too, for Sydney.

He hates it. He hates it that the fig is forgotten in Brisbane.

So he leaves her each morning to plant. Somewhere in his city, in some corner, he finds earth to kneel upon and open with his hands. Each morning he places a tiny Moreton Bay fig into the earth, to settle, to take root. Each morning this private ritual, this quiet offering.

When it is done he returns to the house. To Freya, stirring.

The first time she is confused.

'Where have you been?'

'Planting.'

Her head is tilted in query, needing more.

'The first tree of the day is mine,' he says. 'The rest of the day is the council's.'

She doesn't push him, her strange lover, doesn't ask to accompany him, lets him be.

He lifts the sash window one morning at the end of their first week together in the house. Freya is used to this already – his return, her daily alarm. The sound of the timber frame clattering up its grooves, and then when she opens her eyes the muscles in Robbie's back and shoulders tensing and relaxing with the effort of lifting, then the fresh air from outside swallowing the remains of the night, the shifting air carrying Robbie's scent to her as she lies in bed. It is the freshness of the day, and Robbie brings it new each morning. She is growing to like this. She rises and joins him at the window. For a moment they embrace, then she draws away, lightly, her day too now begun.

She pulls the thin grey blanket from the bed. Keeping hold of one end in her fists, she launches it towards him.

'Here, help me out.'

Robbie snatches at it, misses, and then bends to collect it, fumbling till finally he has an edge, then he straightens and they both take backward steps and the blanket becomes taut between them.

Freya leads. She makes the first fold, from right to left – but

Robbie doesn't follow, and when she looks up she sees his brow knotted, gaze lost and breathing gone shallow.

'Hey,' she says.

He looks at her and shakes his head, as if wrestling something free.

'What?' she asks.

'A memory. A deja vu.'

'Have we done this before?' she says. 'In another life?'

Robbie smiles.

'No. My father. A bad memory.'

'Go on.'

'It's nothing... the last time I folded a blanket... it's nothing.'

They stand there, awkward, the blanket between them sagging.

Despite himself, he remembers. A camping trip. Allows the memory to swell, and holds it in. He was in year ten, and his father had just returned from overseas. How long had he been away that time? Robbie can't remember. Two or three months, more. Robbie can't remember the project, can't remember the country. Something important, whatever it was, something grand.

But by year ten Robbie had begun not to care, had begun to resent his father, and his golden returns to Brisbane and their home. This time, he'd pulled Robbie out of school for a camping trip on Stradbroke Island. By the final morning when they were packing up – *decamping*, his father called it, some remnant from the war – and his father demanded he help

Ficus

fold the blankets, Robbie's resentment had become fierce and unanswerable.

It was prickly, sloppy, adolescent resistance at first. Then, when his father hardened, and grew irritated – *Stop being bloody difficult. You know how it's done, Robert, now just do it. Don't push me!* – Robbie had shrugged his shoulders, dropped his end of the blanket to the ground, and turned away. He had only taken three steps – he was going nowhere in particular, just away – when he heard his father's heavy step and *Hey boy, what do you think you're doing?* Robbie stopped, turned square, set himself as solid as he could, arms straight down, tightening, ready now, ready.

Who do you think you are? Robbie challenged – the rest of it, the whole of it, was no less clear for being unspoken: *Who do you think you are to turn up like this? By what authority? By what right?* His father did not yet see the resolve, did not see it shift and become fury, youthful, expanding and unpredictable. His father came closer.

By then Robbie had just one thought. It was simple and clear, not even a thought – truer than that. It was the sound of his blood, the rhythm of its very beating: Go on, touch me, just touch me, just touch me.

Robbie's hands became fists as his father leant closer, and said again, *What the hell do you think you're doing?* The rhythm of Robbie's blood began thumping in his brain, regular as the beating in his chest. Just touch me. Robbie wishing now his father would press a finger into his chest, hoping it would happen, desperately willing it to happen.

But his father saw it, at last, and stepped back, retreated. And Robbie's chance was gone.

★

'My father was into control,' he says to Freya. 'Folding blankets as much as everything else. He thought there was only one way to fold a blanket. Seriously – that there was one way that was better than all others, one perfect way. He was an engineer, this stuff mattered to him. And if you challenged him he'd tell you why – he'd list his criteria: speed, compactness, number of folds, efficiency of process. He'd insist you did it the *right* way. There was no alternative. He'd force you to bend. He was a bastard of a father.'

'Will I meet him one day?' Freya says, slowing him down.

'No, Freya ... He's not half what a father should aim for.'

'Even so,' Freya says, 'I'd like to meet him one day – so I can learn more about *you*.'

'That'd be a poor deal, seeing as I'd have to leave the country to meet *yours*. No way.'

'Come on ...'

'No chance. He's gone, Frey. Gone.'

'Gone?'

'As good as. He's not part of my life, and hasn't been for ages.'

Robbie had done the sums once, what part of his childhood his father had spent away: well over two-thirds. Now he thinks of the false returns, all those quick trips back into the country. Visits. His father sneaking home for a few days or a week or a month, coming home to suffocate Robbie. And his mother – dutiful, obedient, allowing it to happen.

'Anyway, forget my father, Frey.' He touches her shoulder, strokes it with his thumb. 'Here, let me help you with that thing.'

Robbie takes up the grey wool blanket again, arms raised,

Ficus

outstretched along the edge. He waits until Freya mirrors him, till she faces him with open arms, then he steps towards her, one step, two, gravity drawing the blanket down, halving it between them. He leans forward and takes her edge from her, his fists filled with the tight woollen knit. Then he steps back, so she — her hands now free — can reach down and take the blanket along its new fold. So they can begin the second movement.

Four

A private equilibrium emerges. While the mornings are his, the evenings are Freya's.

As the months pass, she settles each night, after university, at the long hoop-pine table, to work. In the centre of the table, always, is the jacaranda wood bowl she is filling with his gifts to her: the leaves and seed pods and feathers, his descriptions of the city. Surrounding it, papers are strewn: rough minutes from campaign meetings, newsletters, council pamphlets, a copy of the city's planning regulations, hand-written notes, doodles sketched in the top right-hand corner of a writing-pad. The evidence of her labour – thoughts, wishes, will – all that she is trying to do reduced to words.

Once a week she and her campaign colleagues gather around

the hoop-pine table. It's a disparate group — students and scientists and teachers; professional environmentalists and locals. Among them is a legal aid lawyer, Bec, dark-eyed, firm-jawed: Freya's friend, the reason she settled here in the first place all those years ago. They muster here, full of anger or justice unrequited, to plan how they will stop the highway through the park.

Each week Freya starts the discussion, shapes it, directs it, shifts it when it stalls. She extracts hard facts from the talk, records what they've decided, what each of them has committed to, when each of them must accomplish their own contribution to the campaign.

In the room, or passing through, Robbie will watch as her hands move to emphasise some point she is making, rest for the shortest of moments on the table, then take up a pen to write. He sees the incline of her head over the laptop as she types, sees her rock back on her chair when she is done to listen to someone else's argument, her hands behind her head, her fingers intertwined. Sometimes she will feel the intensity of his gaze and swivel in her chair. She will smile at him, wink, and smile again before returning to her meeting.

It's not that he doubts her. It's not that he doubts the worth of the campaign, the rightness of it, the impulse behind it. It's just that he can't entirely bring himself to *believe* in it. He feels that it is beyond him, too big for him to grasp, beyond his capacity to understand and trust. The planning, the strategising, having to think two, three, four steps in advance. He watches Freya at work, watches as she sets upon a course, meets some obstacle, changes tack. Watches her herd and corral, lead and inspire people. Or identify their weaknesses, and exploit them. It's not that he doubts *her* – it attracts him, intrigues him. But he feels it is beyond *his* capacity to know. There are too many people involved, so many different motivations, too difficult to fathom.

'Freya?'

'What?' she says, the house dark, her friends gone, the two of them in bed, winter outside now. This the season the city denies. The cold is probing to get in through the cracks in the floorboards, the gaps in the sash windows.

'Where is the accent from?'

As if the question has only now occurred to him.

'Toronto.'

'Toronto . . .' he sounds it out. Then, 'My grandmother was Canadian.'

The maternal grandmother, a woman he'd never known. Her nationality was a dry fact fallen long ago from the family tree.

'And your name?'

'Freya?'

'Yes.'

'A Norse goddess.'

'Of?'

'Love . . . fertility . . . sex.' She smiles, reaches for him under the blankets. 'A phase my mother was going through. If I was a boy I would have been Thor.'

She laughs.

'Why do you do it, Frey?'

Ficus

'What?'

'The ... campaigning.' A strange word, one that sits awkwardly on his tongue.

'Because someone has to.'

He is silent, unsatisfied. She gives a little more.

'Because I believe in it.'

'Yes, but ...'

'And because I enjoy it. Because I need it.'

'But why here, Frey?' he asks. 'Why are you satisfying your need here? Why not ... in Canada?' And then, 'Why did you leave?'

She laughs again, playful.

'Why must it be a leaving? Isn't it just possible,' she says, teasing, 'that all I've done is arrive?'

'Every arrival is a leaving,' he says, but immediately feels he has gone too far, in his own preoccupation with leavings.

She shrugs. 'This is where I am.' Where I've chosen to be.

After a while she resumes, narrating into the dark.

'When I was a young girl I packed a bag and put on my warmest clothes. I took all the money from my bank account, and hitchhiked across the country ... I wasn't scared, because my parents were travellers – we were used to it. And I knew that people were generous. That they'd feed me and drive me a little further along the way, or arrange lifts with people they knew who were travelling that way. I just knew things would work out.'

She remembers long journeys with her parents in their Kombi van. South, for days on end, for weeks, a flight from winter. She remembers evenings spent in broken, darkened rooms, in Guatemala or Salvador or Nicaragua. Childhood seasons on the move, her mother a centre she could never quite hold onto, but the constancy of discovery.

'When I got to the edge of the mainland, a ferryman took me across – so I reached the west coast of Vancouver Island, where oil was washing onto the beaches with each new tide. A tanker had been punctured off the States, pouring thousands of gallons of oil into the ocean, the oil sweeping north on the currents. And when I saw that oil, I cried. I'd seen it on TV, the volunteers and the sea otters and murres and bald eagles . . . But still.'

Robbie lies in the night beside her.

'Is this better than what you left?' he says after a while.

'Different,' Freya flashes.

Freya looks out the window at the Brisbane night, her home now, the chosen city. The world beckons, and you answer. But it irritates her that the question keeps returning. That she is marked: by her accent, by other things imperceptible to her.

You leave because you stand at the edge of possibility. You scan the horizon. See what you can. You look, you choose. You hug your decision close while you're making it, but you discard it when it's done. You move.

Five

In the square outside City Hall there is the whir of a June westerly, swirling around, pulling at the branches of trees. Tiny jacaranda leaves, stripped and seized by the wind, eddy at their ankles. The wind hustles people inside, where the councillors are voting.

Protesters crowd the chambers, smuggle placards into the gallery. A touch of madness in them, Robbie thinks. Some are evicted, struggling against the security guards.

The voting is disrupted, but the decision is taken anyway, the choice made. The highway through Victoria Park to proceed.

'Is it over?' he asks.

She doesn't falter.

'There are council elections next year,' she says. 'We'll make this an election issue. Reverse the decision.'

'That's optimistic, isn't it?'

'You've got to have faith,' she says, and she is indefatigable.

Faith?

It's as if he discovers the word for the first time. Or rediscovers it, from childhood. He bounces it back at her, testing.

'Faith is planting a tree you'll never see grow to maturity,' he says.

She looks at him, at the unexpected gap between them, difficult to measure.

'That's what *I'm* saying. Think of the people who planted all those trees in Vic Park a hundred years ago,' she replies, and then grows angry. 'All those trees, all those figs. Those people, how do you think *they* would feel?'

He wonders about them, for the first time. The sudden realisation they were like him. Tree-planters. He remembers things, the things you pick up as a kid, half-listening, wishing you were somewhere else. Pieces of story. The street-sweeper who planted the weeping fig in Lutwyche Road at Windsor – he was given the fig and told to take it to the dump in the back of his cart, but couldn't bear to throw it away. Planted it instead. And the women who planted the figs of Bulimba Park, to remember their sons killed in the war. The kids from Milton State School who planted the Haig Road fig, on Arbour Day 1914. He wonders about their city, the quality of their faith.

Freya continues to campaign, tireless, thinking always of new angles. A tent embassy protest in the park, in winter. Community

Ficus

broadsheets circulated to the city's inner suburbs, each broadsheet with a piece about the local history, Aboriginal and settler, deepening the ties, learning herself. Lobbying the politicians, setting them against each other where she can. Nurturing the media. As the weather grows warmer, she campaigns to pull back the council decision, to slow the momentum, to force a retreat. You can't relax. Having given so much, you must continue, redouble your efforts. Have faith.

He watches her, wants to ask but dares not: What, Freya, if this is all in vain?

Robbie reaches into the pantry for the tin of green tea she bought him last week. *Fairly traded*, she'd called it, harvested by hand from a cooperative in Sri Lanka, the profits returned to the labourers. As if she was saying to him, *See, you can make things happen. You can do things, you can change the structure of things, you can make a difference.* He pries open the lid with his thumbnail.

At the table he places a hand on the back of Freya's neck, touching a ridge of muscle with his thumb. She looks up, startled. He sees the lick of her silver hair above her forehead curling over, kinetic.

'Something to drink?' he says to her. She smiles, receives this, turns to her friends.

'Who wants a tea?'

Robbie returns to the kitchen bench. He fills the steel kettle at the sink, then places it back on the stove. Reaches for the box of matches on the window ledge, turns a dial until he hears the hiss of gas, then strikes a match and holds it to the gas till it catches, transforms into a small blue flame, the first flare burning off the drops of water which have dripped down the outside of the kettle.

He looks out of the window while the voices swirl and catch and double back behind him. He looks to the north and the night-time hillside covered with houses like his, stilts propping them off the steep sloping ground. Slight wooden frames with caps of corrugated-iron roofing. And above the hill and the roof-line there is the glow of the city lights reflected in the September night-cloud.

The water boils, and Robbie takes it off the stove a moment before the kettle can whistle. He spoons twisted dry tea-leaves into a large ceramic art-deco teapot, and pours the water. Hot steam rises out of the kettle's spout in a vapour which slides across the back of his hand as he pours, scalding him a little.

Gazing out the window once more while the fair tea draws, he listens to the sound of Freya's voice, insistent, urgent, marshalling. Though she is behind him at the table, he leans out of the window to find her, thrusting his head and shoulders into the night where cicadas purr in the gully. He plays with the sounds. He listens for her again, and now the crescent of her voice passes out the French doors and through the night before arcing around to him craning out the window. The damp skin on the back of his hand tingles. Of all the words, about the freeway cutting through Vic Park and chewing up public domain for highway, about the waterholes filled in and the ancient Aboriginal camping grounds desecrated, it is only Freya's voice which leaves an impress in him. Of all the words of opposition, all the strategies for generating community support and media attention, there is only the sound of Freya's voice.

'Robbie,' he hears her say, her voice raised, the group hushed, waiting for his answer, 'what do you know about the Normanby figs?'

Six

He leads her along the ridge between the two hills overlooking the city centre, walking along the bones beneath the city's skin, hill to hill.

Brisbane is a city of hills. It undulates, Brisbane, is never level. As they walk, Robbie strips it of its buildings in his imagination, of its roads and its footpaths and its train tracks. The land rises and falls from hill to hill in sweeping waves: Red Hill and Spring Hill, Duncan's Hill, Windmill Hill, Cook's Hill, Bowen Hills, Hamilton Hill, Constitution Hill, Wilston Hill, Sparke's Hill, Highgate Hill, White's Hill, Camp Hill, Weller's Hill. Then, further out, Seven Hills and Alexandra Hills. And rising above them all to the west, sheltering them from the setting sun as if from a sorrow, is the city's mountain, Aboriginal Mt Coot-tha.

Ficus

From its summit you can observe the hills like a brood of children squatting on the landscape below. You also see, curving its way through this rising falling resting forgetting remembering landscape, the river. Or rather, you see segments of it. The city's hills conceal it, so it is never more than a series of ribbon strips as it appears and disappears among the graduating landscape. The river is actually more hidden than visible, and Brisbane is a city of hills and the trees which cover them.

A monochrome cloud obscures the spring sun. Along the ridge-line the road thrums with afternoon traffic as they near the Normanby fiveways. Running off the ridge to the north, this road shovels traffic between the suburbs and the city. A row of massive weeping figs, *Ficus hillii*, separates the inward and outward lanes, and then curves around the pub on the corner. In 1909 the publican paid ten pounds for the figs. In return the town council asphalted the footpath outside the hotel. Robbie and Freya stand outside the pub, gazing at the trees across the road, asphalt under their feet.

'They're stressed,' Robbie says, his voice raised above the traffic noise. 'But they have been for years.'

'How can you tell?'

'They drop their leaves when they're struggling.'

Freya notices their patchy canopies, as much branch-stalk as leaf.

'So . . . with major construction here, Robbie – road widening, tunnelling – the figs may not make it?'

They wait for a break in the traffic before hurrying across the road to where the figs stand in the median strip. Robbie reaches out, running his palm around the girth of the largest of the trees as he slowly circles it. He stops at a waist-high horizontal gash, and touches the wound left in the trunk where a car has gouged the fig's flesh, brutal. A day-old wound, two days at most. Sap has run and congealed over the cut.

They feel the pull of the traffic – the sheer mass of the stream of vehicles tugging at them, the constant trembling of the earth, the fig vibrating under his fingers, cars rushing back and forth on either side, the blaring of horns, the braking, music beating from open windows, fumes scratching at the back of his throat. Robbie feels momentarily exhausted.

The tree's inner-flesh has darkened where it was opened. The wound is closing already, healing.

'Figs are tough,' he says to her. 'They can take a lot. They fight their own fights. They can endure.'

Usually you miss these moments. They pass and you are unaware they paused before you, humble, waiting. The hollowing of the air before a breeze changes direction; the touch of a jacaranda flower on your shoulder as it falls; the suspended moment between dark and light when dawn emerges, infinite, uncertain.

One October day, summer's long ascendancy close, his morning's private planting complete, he moves across the city and something catches him: the rising sun illuminating a bunch of purple fruit in the canopy of a huge Moreton Bay fig, the fruit – the figs – candescent in the sun's rays. The tree's size comes from its trunk with its enormous tangled, twisting, buttress-rooted girth. And from the canopy, scraggy and uneven and vast. Its large leaves growing in hands, green-dark like giant upward-pointing fingers, and each bunch of figs resting in the palm

Ficus

of a hand of leaves. The underside of some of the leaves – the younger, adolescent leaves – is dusty brown, looking prematurely aged.

Robbie climbs this tree on impulse, drawn to the figs as if they are jewels, as if he is a boy again, as if he is suddenly ten years of age and fleeing his father, seeking refuge. Southern figbirds compete with him inside the canopy for branch space and for a share of the fig treasure. A bird sets down on a branch at his shoulder, and plucks a fig from the tree, the fig pincered in its beak as Robbie watches. The bird raises its head to drop the fruit down its throat, and then pauses for a moment at the top of this motion, as if to savour it. Head tilted back, round fruit silhouetted in the beak, breast puffed out. Like an Anzac Day bugler at the dawn services his father took him to, stilled at the moment between raising the instrument to his lips and blowing. Then the fig is tossed back, and the squawking, flighty bird returns to its feeding, darts towards another piece of fruit.

He collects the figs, as many as he can, snapping them off between finger and thumb, rubbing each purple globe against his shirt, polishing them. When his pockets are full, Robbie descends, surrendering the tree to the birds.

On the ground, he wonders if he might make something of them for Freya, some gift. Somehow he needs to tell her about the figs, how these trees had given him direction – how, in a flash of understanding, in the stencilled shadow of steel girders, he'd seen that where his father had erected bridges he would plant trees. He wants to tell Freya that he was saved by these fig trees, their solidity, their toughness.

The birds only finish their feeding when the tree is stripped of ripe fruit. They chatter, slur and whistle, and finally, as a flock, move on, sated. They bustle in flight, taking short hops from tree to tree. Robbie sees one of them break from the colony and land in the branches of a silky oak, resting while the swarm cackles through the air ahead. The lone figbird shifts on its branch and passes a loose bundle of tiny undigested seeds, depositing them in the high crook of the limb.

In time those seeds will germinate, will break open into roots: adaptable, patient, tree-hugging, cunning, soil-bound – roots which will sink into the earth for the fig to take its water and its minerals from the soil rather than the sky. For its girth to swell. For its broad shiny leaves to cast their shadows on the trunk of the silky oak. For its embrace to strengthen, tighten, suffocate.

For it to stand alone.

Seven

Sometimes Freya feels alone. Sometimes there is the whisper of doubt. That nothing arrives, no clear way forward, no obvious answer.

Perhaps it is not *faith* she had meant at all, but *hope*, the distinction only now coming to her. Faith, and the blindness you need. She'd be prepared to be blinded, if it would help. But neither faith nor hope accommodates the anger that sometimes pools in her stomach, her sense of injustice. Sometimes she loses herself between the two, feels a weight, solid and unwanted.

The year ends. They sit at the hoop-pine table, Freya and friends – acolytes, Robbie thinks – Bec and half a dozen others,

The Comfort of Figs

just a few hours of the millennium remaining. They measure the progress of their campaign – someone's idea, to take stock. But the victories are so small, so ephemeral. There's no outcome certain, and the park is still destined for ruin. The disappointments build like Freya's childhood snowballs, growing till they are presences which loom like avalanches. She is not the only one. They all doubt, in a hard slow trajectory: at year's end there is little to show. Optimism is muted. Their zeal is stretched thin, gone melancholy.

Robbie, sitting with them, plays with the stubble on his jaw. He thinks of his own year and compares it with theirs, measures it in the trees he has planted. Especially his private plantings, one a day. His city tangibly greater by three hundred and sixty-five figs.

He looks upon them. They slouch at the hoop-pine table, drinking, listening to the low murmur of protest songs, till eventually the music begins to mock them.

'Let's go,' Bec says suddenly, standing from the table.

'The fireworks,' someone else suggests. A distraction.

They all enter the night, piling into someone's station-wagon, Robbie somehow at the wheel. The city is shifting, as if rolling into a more comfortable position, its centre of gravity altering. Everywhere people are looking for vantage points – places to watch the millennial fireworks as they light up the river. There will be thousands of people on the high-ground of the Kangaroo Point cliffs with their views of the city and the vein of water sweeping both left and right, and the bridges which leap across the river. The Southbank parkland will be choked. Mt Coot-tha too far away.

'The Botanic Gardens,' Robbie says to Freya beside him in the passenger seat. Just right for the fireworks, the city Gardens

Ficus

shelter in the crook of the river, as if driven there by the march of buildings and the traffic which roars up to the ornate memorial gates.

It is less than two hundred years since John Oxley's expedition first rowed up the river, first looked out from their whale-boats at the pocket of land which is now the Botanic Gardens, first rounded what is now Gardens Point. The point was thick then with rainforest: crows ash, yellow wood, tulipwood, figs, hoop-pines rising tall on the edges of the forest, silky oak and cedar. Staghorns and elkhorns nestled in tree branches, luxuriant flowering vines draped across the forest. On the water's fringe, perfumed lilies grew. A Garden of Eden, as Robbie imagines it.

Since then this patch of ground has lived half a dozen lives, has metamorphosed again and again. It was the first country to fall: the hoop-pines for masts and shipping timber, cedar for the first crude shelters. Next the land inside the elbow of river became the farm for the white settlement, the first crops of wheat and the hopeful plantings of fruits in that rainforest soil. Then it was the playground of the colony's first botanist, an early tree-planter. Here Walter Hill mused over vegetative possibilities. Experimented with mangoes and sugar cane. Collected specimens of subtropical plants and grew them, all together, in this garden of his. The rainforest strip along the river with its Moreton Bay chestnut is Hill's, first planted in the 1860s. Thus the Gardens were born, and among the vast lawns fig trees were sown – to suffocate mosquitoes with their canopies of shade, in accordance with the wisdom of the day. Then, in the 1930s, the Gardens became a zoo, a menagerie of exotic birds and animals, cages of monkeys and parrots, and a bear pit for mothers to lean over with their children. A fascinating – but alien – exhibit in the city's heart. Eventually the bear pit was filled in, and lagoons returned, swollen with fish.

People respectfully describe this dark rainforest stretch along the river as a *remnant*. As though it's a thing which cannot be killed off and which, by surviving, has earned a begrudging right to stay. As if there is honour in surviving. But although it appears to be a remnant rainforest, it is not. This sliver of rainforest in the tightest corner pocket of the Brisbane River, in the middle of the city, is not a remnant but a replica.

There is an unmistakable *pop*, pregnant with what sounds to Robbie like malevolence. A flying fox above them jags sharply mid-flight, an instinctive change of direction. Waves of sound they cannot hear pulse through the air and press against the bat's body in warning. Robbie watches it wheel uncertainly away, one beat, two beats, three, wings driving. In his peripheral vision he sees the first white flash-pop of a firework rising, a reversed celestial body. At the height of its trajectory, in the long suspended moment of hanging there, this small white light explodes into coloured tracery, the sky a fluorescent swirl of red and green, the bat's coat wet with a red-green sheen.

And in the short pause between light and sound the flying fox drives away through the air, then there is the explosive bang and the night shattering. And the sky, for all the sound and light, is empty.

Freya breathes into his craned neck, looking up again at the torrents of colour, the breaking of white into orange and purple, the outward-spreading blankets of green, the falling curtains of red and blue mesh.

'Come on!' she motions with her hand, and he follows her. She makes for the footpath that runs along the river bank. As they get closer to the river he sees the water and the view of the Story Bridge opening before them, and some light in him goes out, fizzles and dies like a firework fallen too early to the water.

The bridge is decorated, dressed for the evening. It has a beguiling delicacy, as if wearing its finest gown. A chain of enormous globes hangs like a string of pearls across the bridge's shoulders. Its steel-grey frame is luminescent in the glow.

'Beautiful,' she whispers, and Robbie is aware of others around them murmuring the same hushed sentiment, pointing.

An old weight is forming inside him, as grey and heavy as the looming girders.

The fireworks in the sky shrink. The explosions abate, one by one, until there is only smoke drifting silently across the sky on a faint wind, and people wondering if it is over, the pause long enough for friends to turn one to the other, on the verge of voicing their regret. Then from the bottom of the stillness another burst – this time it is as if the bridge itself is exploding. Rockets of light erupt from its twin shoulder platforms, rushing out into the night sky before exploding. Outwards and upwards there is a mass of explosion and light, as if a tripwire has been triggered and a munitions store in the bridge has been set uncontrollably alight. There is a mad cluster of fire-burst and sound, domino runs of small light-bursts along the arms, neck and shoulders of the bridge. First one way and then returning, and before the blazing extravaganza has ended, two massive explosions launch from the bridge's shoulders once more and the entire structure is showered in light and debris and for a moment the bridge is gone, and there is only a shroud of smoke, ringing ears and the blur of over-strained eyes.

Gradually the wind draws the curtain of gunpowder-cloud from the bridge and it is there again, calm and solid. Steely. The bridge triumphant. Beauty flung wide.

'Impressive,' Freya says, her gaze fixed still on the bridge settling back into itself.

Then she looks at him.

'What?' she says.

His silence prickles. It is almost sullenness, almost petulance. She has never seen this in him before.

'What is it?' she says again.

He is resistant, in a mood beyond embarrassment now, beyond talk. He wishes they could just leave.

The smoke from the fireworks is at his nostrils, sharp with acrid bite. He says to her, as if throwing something away –

'My father built it.'

'Your father?' she turns to him, incredulous. 'What? Your father built the Story Bridge?'

'That's how they always told it.'

Eight

'They built it in the Depression to give blokes something to do. To stop them from starving. Or causing trouble. Or killing themselves. It was a distraction. From unemployment, from the war which was just around the corner . . . An attempt to make a town feel good about itself. But what's worse, it's a try-hard bridge. If Sydney has a Harbour Bridge, then Brisbane can have its own steel and concrete version. A sad bloody trophy!'

A fresh salvo of fireworks begins, a series of single popping sounds, like anti-aircraft flak shot into the sky.

'My father was just an apprentice boilermaker on the bridge at the time, but he claims it as his. That's the family story . . . Anyway, the bridge showed a boilermaker he could become an engineer. The bridge made him proud, gave him a reputation, set him on his way. Made a Brisbane boy believe he could walk the world.'

'Did he?' She's tender, giving herself a chance to work this out.

'He was overseas half the year. He was always overseas. Home ... Brisbane, it was just a base for him while he worked on projects around the world. Bridges, dams, roads ...'

He stops for a long moment, the words inadequate, his agitation growing, until a new thought propels him forward once more.

'He was away so much that, when I was young, he was someone I learnt about through Lily –'

'Lily?'

'My mother.'

'Go on.'

'Lily would put me to bed with my father on a construction project in India. "Your father's helping the poor people," she'd say. Or he'd be in Africa, or in New Guinea. And we'd have the atlas out and she'd be pointing to cities. And every day we'd cross the Story Bridge and Lily would say, "Your father built this bridge," as if he was mythic, more than just a boilermaker punching rivets ... as if I should be grateful for the bridge –'

'Anyway ... now there's nothing there.'

'What do you mean?'

'He's a statue.'

'What are you talking about?'

'Paralysed with stroke a few years ago. He can't move, can't speak. He spends his time staring out the window like a statue.

Ficus

The engineer who turned iron ore into bridges has himself become stone!'

It began with a gift.

It is his tenth birthday, his double-figures birthday. As if he is doubling in age overnight, graduating from one to two digits in a single sleep. A gravely important event. The next quantum birthday leap — from two figures to three — usually doesn't happen. His mother has told him that in the Bible Methuselah lived to nearly a thousand years, but Robbie knows people die before they reach three figures. Robbie knows this from his own experience, from weeks of tugging on his mother's dresses, and pointing to people with their walking sticks or on their benches and asking, *Is he a hundred Mum?* And the answer always: *Not quite, love.* Once you enter two digits, that is where you stay, nine-year-old Robbie sees. This is the only birthday of such magnitude he will ever experience. It has to be special.

And for a while after waking it is. There at the end of his bed, resting on his brightly coloured quilt, is an enormous box covered in newspaper. It is heavy too, Robbie finds, as he carries it down the corridor to his parents' bedroom. He stands outside their closed door and shakes the box, hears it rattle inside. Robbie puts it down to knock, then waits till he hears his father's voice calling him in, before he turns the handle and pushes the door open. The expectation is almost too much, not just for him. His father motions him to come round to his side of the bed, a strange urgency, and Robbie is vaguely aware this is different from previous birthdays, when it was his mother he gravitated to at the moment of unwrapping.

Robbie peels off the layers of newspaper, the wrapping falling to the floor on either side of him like shed skin, or bark. At last he reaches the box, sheathed in a tight, thin plastic film, transparent so he can see the picture on it – a crane. Robbie pauses to try and understand, and in the moment of his pausing – the shortest of moments – his father reaches across, and with the back of his man's fingernail slices open the plastic film. In years to come it will be the violence of this moment Robbie remembers, the sureness of it. But for now Robbie watches as his father lifts the box into his own lap and opens it, watches how his father lifts the cardboard flaps one by one, with something like reverence. How he does it slowly, deliberately, heightening Robbie's anticipation.

Robbie is confused at first, by what is there in the box. Or what is not there. There is no crane at all. Just a plastic moulding with lots of metal bits and pieces sitting in separated tubs. Parts.

Then Robbie begins to understand.

A surge of disappointment rises in him, swamping the happiness of only moments before. Robbie doesn't understand the disappointment – it is too big, and too new – but he knows that what is in the box isn't a present at all. He wanted a gift that was ready to use. Like a bike, or a game, or even a book. Not something that isn't even finished. He is going to have to make his own present. Robbie looks down at his fingers, black with newsprint. He is ten years old now. He will not cry.

Despite his disappointment he is aware of his father's excitement, feels his father's energy overcome him. His powerful father unfolding the instruction booklet and pointing out the diagrams of things you can make. A crane and a truck and a car. The buildings. A bridge. Robbie is shrinking already as his

Ficus

father opens the little plastic satchels which separate the differently shaped tin struts and panels, and the tiny nuts and bolts. The little spanner. Through eyes small and distant Robbie follows his father's finger as it points out the neat photos on the underside of the box – little meccano structures standing lonely on a table. A crane without a weight to shift, a truck without a highway, a car without passengers, buildings without a city, a bridge without water.

Robbie's disappointment lingers for weeks. His father refuses to let it to go away, magnifies it. Each night after school, and then on weekends, Robbie's father has them sit together over the verandah table and make things out of the meccano pieces. He feels powerless. It is not the first time, but this is absolute. How could a father not know his child hated this? How is it that Robbie can't make his father see? Evening after evening Robbie excuses himself to go to the toilet where he stays for long minutes with his father barely noticing he isn't there, or hasn't come back at all, or returns with a runny nose from where he has cried, despite himself.

At the end of every evening there is a new creation. A different structure his father has built while Robbie looks on. And every evening, when the structure is complete, his father claps his hands together and says, *There we have it!* And his mother is summoned to see whatever it is they've built. Evening after evening she will smile and congratulate them and say how nice it is and fail to see the greater part of it – Robbie's horror. A boy without a present.

In the end he tries burying the meccano set in the backyard. Not all at once, but over time. He comes home from school and, when his mother's busy in the kitchen preparing dinner, he takes one or two pieces of tin from the set which is strewn over the verandah table. Or some nuts, or a few bolts, and with no one looking he tosses them off the verandah into the backyard, where they disappear in the tangle of overgrown bush beyond the boundary between the mown and the unmown.

His father realises eventually, of course. He counts the parts one evening, so there is no doubt. Pieces have gone. He writes out an inventory of what is missing, or rather calls out the numbers for Robbie to write them down in an exercise book. How many long struts, how many short ones. How many nuts, how many bolts.

Robbie halts his sabotage after this reckoning. It is too dangerous. But the meccano construction continues relentlessly, worsens. As if now there is a new lesson in this for his father to teach him, a lesson about persistence in the face of obstacles. With fewer pieces it means they spend even longer each evening designing and building their meccano pushbikes or their tin-and-nut clothes lines.

Sometimes Robbie cannot bear the not-understanding. The failure of it. That a collection of small narrow, hole-punched pieces of tin is somehow responsible. That his mother can look through him not seeing. Is there nothing there for his mother to see? Or is her sight, her mother-sight, somehow failing? Or does mother-sight compete with other things, like wife-sight?

But this story fails to capture what went before. Robbie knows this. The dark spaces of his father's life, the shadowed chasms filled with experience and being which cause a father to reject a son. The gift that petrified their relationship was only the thing that opened Robbie's eyes. Not the thing that hardened his father. There are moments when he allows his father this, that his father may once have been a different man.

Nine

He has slumped into silence under the stars. Freya waits, in case some new fragments of him break off.

'I've got an idea,' he says. 'Come on.'

He pulls her arm, a rough, impulsive movement. Away from the crowds, away from where they had left her friends, towards the rainforest, his grip on her arm over-firm. There is an opening in the wall of trees in front of them. He makes for this path into the forest, but when they reach it – the close, tangled trees and the track burrowing into darkness – Freya baulks.

'Robbie, where are you going?'

'Fireworks by forest light,' he says.

There is no enthusiasm in his voice. She hesitates.

Ficus

'The others are expecting us,' she says. 'They're waiting. They won't know where we've gone.'

He shrugs his shoulders.

'They'll be *worried*,' she says, still unsure.

He shrugs again, turns and disappears alone into the darkness of the forest, leaving her at the edge of the crowd.

The murmur of human-noise fades, drops as sharply as the temperature. He enters a different world, tight and thick and dank and dark with trees. He pauses, lets his eyes become accustomed.

Buttressed roots like enormous stabilising fins holding firm to the earth, spread like experiments across the ground. Strangler figs entwined around box trees, intimate in suffocation or surrender. Supplejack vines thick as an arm drape from tree to tree. In forked limbs, crows nest ferns and staghorns nestle, their broad-tongued leaves radiating outwards in sensuous falling arcs from centres wet and deep.

Above the forest the fireworks continue. But in here the colours' metamorphosis is slow, a gradual moving through the spectrum of light. A passing of strange sunsets through the thick canopy.

He follows the footpath through the fan palms and the cabbage tree palms, tall and smooth like posts. The path takes a turn towards the water and drops to steps cut into the slope. The steps are rough-cut basalt, with tar slapped over them, dark and greasy, to even the roughness of the stone. The basalt blocks are damp with moisture seeping from cracks in the aging mortar, cracks which the tar has not covered. Robbie loses his footing as he descends, and thrusts his hand out towards the basalt steps, instinctive. He rights himself, his hand stinging from a cut caused by the sharp rock. The dampness of blood and rainforest moisture mix in his palm before he wipes them both off on the side of his trousers.

He takes the path as it runs through the forest, until he comes across a second set of steps, pink sandstone this time and cut into the embankment itself. The steps lead down to the river bank, and Robbie finds himself on a path running along the edge of the river. He turns upriver, the dark water and the mangroves on his left. To the right is the flood embankment which withstands all but the largest floods: an 1893, or a 1974. Beyond the embankment is the cover of forest he has just left.

Mangroves. Once, they extended no further than Breakfast Creek, miles downriver. Now thick and protected, the mangroves have crept further and further upriver from the bay, colonising new country, sustained by the soil flooding downstream from the cultivations in the Brisbane River Valley. You pass through mangroves now where once forest grew to the water's edge. Silver-grey trunks and branches reaching like arms from the tidal mud, limbs of what could be half-buried bodies stretching out imploringly from the mud, hands and fingers of leaves brushing against each other in the canopy. Surrounding these undead limbs are swathes of black tap-roots rising a few inches from the mud: thousands of oxidised quills, rusted black and caked with the flakes of accumulated tidal residue.

The path merges into a boardwalk. What had been packed earth under his feet gives way to timber, and his footsteps now echo. Water is below and beside him, washing around the base

Ficus

of the mangroves which spread out for metres as a buffer from the open currents of the river.

He pauses on the boardwalk, and leans over the railing, looking into the dark river-water eddying around the base of each tree, creeping across the mangrove mud with the rising tide. He watches the tide slide over the mud like a dark veil.

Above the low creeping sound of the water Robbie hears another: the quick-step of feet on the boardwalk, and alert, he waits.

'Robbie?' It is Freya's voice. 'Robbie?'

'Here,' he calls, the shape of her becoming distinct as she nears. She draws beside him, only an uneven echo of feet on timber lingering.

She is panting and has to catch her breath. 'Thanks for waiting,' she says eventually, agitated.

'I didn't think you wanted to come.' But he is smiling now and Freya sees his mood has lightened. Has the forest done this? The river? The solitude? She nestles her shoulder against his and for a time they look out through the mangroves together.

'Here,' Robbie says after a while, taking a coin from his pocket. He rests it for a long moment on the back of his thumb before flicking it out from the boardwalk. The coin spins hard through the air as it leaves his hand. Its trajectory vanishes into the dark, and they listen. There is a *plop-suck* noise when it hits the mud.

'Now you,' Robbie says, taking out another coin. 'For luck. The river can be our wishing well.' Freya tosses her coin into the darkness, and together they hear the double-sound of the coin rebounding off something solid before landing with its *plop* in the mud.

They walk together. The river finishes its ninety-degree arc and swings out of the Botanic Gardens and into the long stretch of the city reach. The path hugs the riverbank, mangroves still fringing the water. The sound of traffic enters their consciousness and the ceiling of plant life in the forest gives way to concrete, as the riverside expressway, hanging off the side of the city like a ledge over the water, stakes its claim to the riverbank. Soon the suck of the water against the bank is gone, and the forest-muffled sounds of the fireworks are swallowed by the noise of traffic. Robbie and Freya emerge from the dominion of plants and are back in the city, a canopy of highway above their heads.

This path rolls out along the riverbank for miles, skirting the water, following upriver the route of the broad watercourse. They're tempted to believe they could walk to the source somewhere high in the range far to the west.

They stride out now along the path, concrete hard and unforgiving under their feet, the noise and light of the city harsh after the forest. They stay at river-level, following the path. Beside them as they walk, the river's embankment rises steeply close by, and the path begins to narrow. The concrete underbelly of the expressway rumbles above them, and suddenly they are not alone.

In front of them a figure emerges from behind a concrete pillar, and behind they hear the sudden sound of running footsteps, and the moment Robbie turns is the moment he is knocked to the ground. The cracking sound of his head hitting the pavement merges with Freya's cry, terrified.

Robbie finds himself stumbling and rolling across the ground in an uncoordinated attempt to rise again. He is barely aware he is taking kicks – fierce, bruising boot-strikes – and that it is the kicks keeping him off balance. He gets to his feet in a swirl of elbows and forearms, and finds he has cleared a space around himself. He steadies. One of the figures is dancing in front of him with something Robbie can't make out in his hand, spitting as he screams:

'Your wallet, man. Your fucking wallet. Give us your fucking wallet, man!'

Robbie knows he should be trying to meet the man's frenzied eyes, should attempt to defuse him, should protect himself. But he can't help looking for Freya as he says 'it's cool, it's cool' over and over again, as if the words alone might somehow keep this all at bay.

'Your fucking wallet!' the man shrieks again, before Robbie is able to find her. 'Your fucking wallet!' and the man feints a lunge at Robbie who sees now the contorted face and the eyes, wild under a baseball cap.

'Okay, okay, okay,' Robbie yells back, urgent, desperate, and reaches for his back-pocket, the wallet held tight there, and winces with the pain.

'Here you go, here it is,' and he holds out his wallet. The man grabs it from his hand, and Robbie is immediately pushed to the ground again from behind, this time with a knee driven hard into the small of his back. And again. And again.

'Where's yours?' the voice screams again. 'Where's yours?' and Robbie knows it is Freya the voice means. From where he is lying on the ground, he hears Freya sobbing *no, no, no* and Robbie is craning his neck to see what is happening, and he hears again Freya's distraught *no*, and he thinks he might be yelling at Freya himself: 'Give it to him, give it to him.'

The Comfort of Figs

But above it all the voice reaches a new pitch of hysteria:

'Is this what you want, bitch? Is this what you want?' And Robbie knows it is going to be a needle, and there is enough light when he finally angles his head so he can see, and it is. 'Is this what you want?' But the crazed words are coming too quickly, and there is no time, and the needle is being jabbed into her stomach even as she recoils.

'Bitch, dumb bitch,' the man says when it is done, but almost to himself. As if it is a muttered, inevitable Amen.

Things slow. There is Freya doubled over like a crumpled marionette. There is the river. And the needle being thrown into the water. Robbie watches it. He follows its dark, serene trajectory as it is flung off the path, wheeling slowly end on end, till it drops in the air and falls silently against the water, the surface of the river disturbed already by the wake of a ferry that has passed just moments before. The pulse of the ferry's engine is suddenly audible. The thought crosses Robbie's mind that perhaps he should be diving into the water after the needle. As if it had been a snakebite: you kill the snake if you can. Bring it in. You need to identify it to know what antivenene to administer.

Freya's screaming disturbs some fruit bats feeding in a fig somewhere distant, and as Robbie blacks out he hears the bats screeching, as if mocking his impotence.

Ten

He finds himself in hospital, and remembers, later, the colours of the trip in. Freya's face and voice in the back of the ambulance with him. The blur of hazy red and green lights through the windows of the vehicle. The colours switching on and off in strange concert with his flickering consciousness. The pull on his organs as the ambulance brakes for traffic lights before passing through intersections. Sounds of doors slamming shut or open, of a concertina-legged stretcher snapping into place. Freya and the night so far away.

Freya is unhurt, with only the smallest prick-mark where the needle entered her abdomen. And whatever else entered her with the needle. Nothing punctured, no organs damaged, no muscle torn. 'Fortunate,' the doctor says. 'Not like a knife wound.'

The doctor speaks to her in words without shape. *Baseline tests. Post-exposure prophylaxis. Antiretroviral.* She sips water from a disposable plastic cup and signs a consent form. She wants to laugh but is too alone. A nurse enters the room. Pathology take a biopsy, will test her blood. She closes her eyes with the new needle, is overcome with nausea, vomits over the lino floor, long and violent.

Freya asks the nurse later: 'How long until I know the results?'

'What did the doctor say?'

'I can't remember.'

'I'll walk you back there, after we're done here,' the nurse says.

'HIV, Hep B, Hep C, tetanus.' Her mind grasps at the words but they won't stick.

He begins to speak in percentages and she thinks he is trying to reassure her.

'I want to write this down,' she says. He offers a pen, and a notepad with a drug company's name printed on each sheet. She records what he says, folds the sheet of paper slowly, neatly, and puts it in her jeans pocket. As if sealing something, some moment, some fact, some truth.

The doctor walks her to Robbie's room. She leans over Robbie and rubs her nose gently against his unbruised cheek. The doctor waits.

'He's sedated. He'll sleep for hours. Do you have someone you can be with?'

'I think so.'

An orange light comes off the east, already burnt.

She calls Bec, and her friend picks her up from the hospital and takes her back to the house. Bec makes a bath for her. She tells Freya not to talk unless she wants to, and Freya feels the kindness, the gentleness of it. Freya is tired and needs to sleep, but the day is too bright. Bec stays with her till being in the house makes no sense any more, and drives her back to the hospital mid-morning, New Year's Day.

When Freya arrives, a woman is settled in Robbie's room, a solid small-faced sixty-year-old woman in a dress which falls heavily against her legs when she rises in greeting.

'You must be Robbie's girlfriend.'

Freya looks blankly at the woman.

'The nurses told me what happened. Awful. Awful, awful.' Then, remembering, 'I'm Robbie's mother.'

Freya turns from the woman, a distraction, and moves over to Robbie, sleeping heavily still in the bed. He is serene. His hair is wild and stuck back, and though there are abrasions on his cheek, and cuts on his forehead, it is the serenity that takes her. Freya reaches for him, but her arm begins to quiver as she stretches it out from her own body. The tiny tremors become shakes that refuse to stop. She drops her arm to her side, and remembers the other woman in the room.

'How is he?' Freya says.

Lily repeats verbatim what the nurses have told her and

pronounces with authority what she remembers from the charts hanging at the end of the bed. Freya nods as she speaks.

'I'm sorry, who are you again?'

'His mother.'

'Ah. So he'll be alright?'

'In time. And how are *you*, love?' Lily asks, her voice round and gentle, as if trained by the softest of accents.

'Fine.'

'Of course you'll need *your* rest too, dear. Robbie will appreciate the visits but you need to look after yourself too now.'

'There's nothing that can be done for me, Lily,' Freya says, disengaged, unconnected, but remembering her name. 'It's just waiting for the test results.'

'Rest. Rest is what you'll need, love. Don't spare yourself. Get your sleep. And don't worry if you can't be here, because I can sit with him. And the good Lord is watching over him too, of course.'

Lily O'Hara is an accomplished carer. She can remember nothing else. Though, if asked, she might retrieve a faint memory of herself as a young girl straining against the role. It is the merest echo of a struggle between some other vision of her life and the demands of sacrifice which came with being the only child of an ailing single parent. And yet even so she wonders if this half-memory is real, or if it is something she creates. The truth is, she simply does not know whether she ever did make a decision years ago to do one thing over another. To stay rather than to go. To look after her mother rather than look after herself.

Ficus

She prefers to see it as a calling, that God has called her to be a carer. Like the priestly vocations the church would sometimes ask people to pray for – those young Catholic men whom God had so mysteriously called to be priests but who were resisting, out of folly or pride or some private motivation no less mysterious. She, however, has heard and answered her calling. There is solace in this. And certainty. The sureness of one's place in the greater scheme. The comfort that comes from doing God's will. She thinks of the Bible stories, the women of history. A history of daughters, and wives, and mothers, and God forever opening and closing women's wombs. It is always the Old Testament women she thinks of – Sarah and Ruth and Hannah and the others – who did God's will and attained their place in history. A great, robust, unpredictable, imperfect, forgiving history. Comfort in this.

However it happened, nursing her mother when she was just a girl set the course of her life. Just a few months after her mother died she married Robbie's father, Jack, and soon after that came Robbie, and the years of raising him while Jack was away. Keeping him at her breast, on her lap, and then by her side. Like Old Testament Sarah, she had just the one child, a son. Unlike Sarah, God granted him to her when she was still young. That was enough. It was good. She has been blessed. In recent years there has been the task of caring for her incapacitated husband, the hours of each day now shaped by his needs, and there is a blessing in this too.

And yet how fortunate, Lily thinks, waiting by her son's bedside, that she is still available when Robbie needs her now. That she is strong enough still to care for them both. Again.

★

Robbie wakes after half a dozen starts. He wakes into a clean white-lit world. In the whiteness his mother takes shape, close by. His mother. He is conscious enough to wonder where Freya is, and whether the figure leaning with her back against the white wall of his room, behind his mother, beyond his blurred eyesight, is her. His thinking becomes swamped by the ache of the blood and sinew and muscle of his back, and the rippling pains across his chest and stomach, and the headache at the back of his skull.

He coughs to loosen his dry throat and the coughing sets off a domino train of thumping aches down his spine, the pain bringing flashes of the attack back to him. He lies still and resists the urge to cough again. His mother brings a glass of water to his mouth and he sips. With her other hand she strokes his head. He feels her eyes, penetrating.

Caring is not all caring either. You have to be tough to care. People don't realise this. You see it in nurses. They are crisp, starched. They have to be hard, disciplined, know better than the patient what they need to recover. Lily has learned exactly this: that there are times, often, when you have to be firm. On these occasions she inclines her head and looks down from her tilted-head angle and says *noooo*, long-drawn and rising. The low-pitch of it, the way she holds the sound for a second or more like a meditational chant, her eyes unmoving. It signals that she will endure, that she will stand firm, that she will outlast whatever passing objection her mother or her husband or her son might have.

★

Ficus

Robbie's injuries aren't serious: superficial wounds mainly, though the bruising is extensive. He can walk, but it is stiff and painful. His lower back has been tenderised from the beating. It will take time for him to become fully mobile, longer still for the strength to return.

On the second day he is discharged. Bed rest – this is his mother's prescription as he leaves the hospital ward. She repeats it like a mantra. *Bed rest*. It is this simple. And yet what a strange term, he thinks when he first hears it, stirring into consciousness. A term from another era.

Lily drives them home, Robbie and Freya, after he is discharged, though in the car it's as if she is aware only of her son. She fits the key into the ignition and then, about to turn it, pauses.

'You know, love, it's like taking you home after you were born.'

Robbie winces. The nostalgia in her voice is dangerous, a seductive purr which would draw him back to his childhood. Not now, he hopes, tired and weak, not now.

'Soon as we got in the car you started up – crying I mean. It was probably the sound of the engine that you didn't like after the quiet of the ward. You started up, Robbie, and you just didn't stop. Not for me, no matter how I rocked you, and Jack was driving and he was trying to soothe you too. But no, Robbie, you kept crying and crying. You were almost choking, you were that upset. And you'd been so good in the hospital.'

Robbie has heard the story before, knows it intimately. It is one of his blood-stories. He wants to interrupt her, wants to stiffen his response and include Freya somehow. To pull the talk off this past, and onto something else, but he is too weary. Lily is concentrating on the story, lost in another time. The car keys swing in the ignition still, the engine waiting to be started.

'We didn't know what to do. Do we take you back into the hospital where you might calm down? Do we go get a nurse to help? Do we wait until you tire yourself out? Do we just go? On the one hand it was nothing, Robbie, but it was awful. I didn't know what to do. And you were crying so loud, so upset. And why were you crying? I mean, why *were* you crying? I didn't know what to do . . .'

He cannot let it continue. But just as he resolves to summon the energy to stifle this conversation, Lily trails off, remembers the car and turns the key. The engine starts and she guides the car, ramp by ramp, down the levels of the hospital carpark. She stops at the entrance boom-gate, pays the attendant and pulls out onto the wide terrace with its lanes of traffic in and out of the city. When they enter it they find the traffic slow, the city muffled and uneasy. Itself hungover or injured.

'We left eventually,' she recommences. 'I don't think it was a decision to go – Jack just started driving. He had to do something. But the driving didn't stop you. You got louder. You were telling us something, love. Louder and louder you got with your wailing. And I was almost beside myself and neither of us were saying anything, we didn't know what was going on. The first time and all. We just wanted to get home.'

Her story wearies him, dulls him, shrinks him. He reaches for Freya's hand, and it is all the effort he has left to grasp it.

They drive past the old museum building on Gregory Terrace, sanctuary for reconstructed dinosaurs and German First War biplanes which thrilled Robbie as a visiting schoolboy. Past

Ficus

the first of the Valley pubs – the Shamrock – and the red light district deeper in, pausing at an intersection before swinging down the hill into a slight depression which was once a shallow valley. And then up again to Kemp Place and onto the approach to the bridge.

'Screaming and screaming, Robbie, you just wouldn't stop, and the car was full of your crying. You were so distressed, Robbie, and what was I to do? And Jack in the front – by this time he wasn't even looking around, he'd fixed himself on the road ahead. He'd left us, in a way ...'

The car presses forward, All Hallows' girls' school with its convict wall on the right, the firestation with its viewing tower on the left, and the mouth of the bridge with its open-throated tunnel of interlocking silver girders immediately ahead of them.

'And then we got here, Robbie. Right here where we are now. And as we pulled onto the bridge and started to drive across it, the car tyres began hitting the expansion joints in the road, and you began to quieten.'

Despite himself, Robbie is listening now for the sound: the car travelling over the bridge deck, the wheels hitting the regular breaks in the black bitumen.

'It was the thumping of the joints, rhythmic they were. The bridge itself was beating out a rhythm for you, love.'

Thump-thump. Thump-thump. Thump-thump.

'And then you stopped your crying. About here, about three-quarters of the way across.' *Thump-thump. Thump-thump.* 'You just plain stopped. The bridge had put you to sleep. True.'

Robbie wants to weep.

★

Steel and vibrations. Bridges are fragile constructions. This is what his science teacher told them, the shaven-headed priest who'd once been a chaplain during the war in New Guinea, and who'd stayed on as a missionary. An army platoon must break step as it crosses a bridge. If the vibrations of the platoon's marching is the same as the natural frequency of the bridge, it will sway. Bridges have been known to shake so violently with those vibrations, that they have been destroyed simply by a group of soldiers marching across.

Robbie had stared at the priest in disbelief. Bridges are immovable. That is the truth.

Eleven

Days pass. Robbie rises. Freya falls.
She begins by looking after him, settles him into the house, prepares his meals, helps him in and out of bed, cushioning the movements of his sore body. She takes calls from Lily, calls which make her strangely jealous. Lily visits unannounced one of the first days, and the two women sit awkwardly on the verandah drinking tea while they wait for Robbie to wake.

Robbie strengthens with rest, with Freya's care, and with the long quiet hours alone looking out over the rainforest gully at the back of the house.

She worries about him. It tires her. The lack of sleep. The shock of the assault which comes creeping back to her. The trauma of it revisiting her unexpectedly, unwanted, peeling back her dreams, forcing its way in. Finally, finally, she is exhausted. She succumbs and takes the valium the doctor prescribed at the hospital, and sleeps for the best part of a day and a half. When she wakes it is Robbie leaning over her, concerned.

It is as if they have changed places, have swapped ends of a playground see-saw, some invisible fulcrum between them.

'What's wrong, Frey?' Robbie asks, his vitality returning. 'What's happening?'

The routine these early days is an uneasy one, the awkwardness of their different trajectories. The ennui that has enveloped Freya, Robbie's confidence returning.

He plants again. He is ready, wants it: the touch of the earth, its reassurance and conviction. But he requires the alarm to wake, his body shunted off its rhythms by the drugs, its deep need to repair itself and pull in close for a while. He slides out of bed, and dresses, his clothes ready from the evening before. At the doorway he turns and looks back at Freya in the night. She has not stirred, but her eyes are wide open, flat in the dark, following him. He returns to her and puts a hand on her cheek.

'I won't be long.'

He brushes her eyes closed. Looks back again and she is staring at him once more. Some sleepless sphinx, her gaze blank and impenetrable.

The first fig is tiny. He selects it from among the figs he's potted, under the house, which take light in shafts through the boards of the deck. It is a gesture of belief. For this first fig he plants after the attack he deliberately chooses the smallest.

He plants it by the river. Not too close to the city centre, to the bikeway, or the riverside expressway – he is not ready for that – but by the river. The same river.

He finds a place beside a boat ramp, with its ribbed concrete sloping away towards the water. Already there are rowers on the river, light filtering their hollowed voices and oar-slap. The bulk of an abandoned power station rises in the dawnlight, upriver. Robbie selects his spot, squats, kneels, opens the earth.

Robbie takes to walking during the day, to exercise.

One morning the phone is ringing as he returns from the corner store. Freya's calico bag is slung over his shoulder. In it are bread and milk, some fruit. He doesn't hurry as he unlatches the gate and walks up the front stairs. He lets the phone ring as he turns the key and enters the house. In time the ringing stops, and the answering machine clicks in. He hears Freya's voice on the recording, *just leave a message, we'll get back to you as soon as we can*. He wonders whether Freya, lying in bed, is awake to hear herself speak. There is enthusiasm in her recorded voice, and he remembers, when she first moved in, the tickling and the faces he made as she recorded the message. Does she remember too? Then the machine beeps, there is a rush of static, and Robbie expects someone to speak as he carries the bread and the fruit down the hallway. But there is nothing, not for long seconds is there anything other than a mangle of background noise. Submerged in the static Robbie wonders if he hears a voice, muffled and indistinct, but the line goes dead and there is only hollowness.

Minutes later the phone rings again. Still Robbie lets it run.

Just to hear Freya's voice, to hear her before she entered the cocoon of her bed a week ago. She speaks again: *just leave a message, we'll get back to you as soon as we can.* He is not sure what more he can say to her, whether there is any message he can leave that will get to her.

Freya's voice is followed by another this time: a young, uncertain voice.

'Hello ... Look ... We've found your wallet – ummm ... Is that Robert O'Hara? If that's Robert O'Hara then, ummm, we've found your wallet. So, if you want it, then –' and at this point the child's voice turns away to talk to someone else, and Robbie strains to hear but the voice is too distant and the other voice might be just Robbie's imagining. Robbie makes no move to pick up the phone. His quickened breathing and the beating in his chest fill him, and he is transported in blood-pulse waves to the night two weeks ago on the path by the river.

'We just thought that you might want it back, okay? Well, you're not there so we'll call back.'

The message ends with a click.

Robbie stares at the phone for long moments before he realises Freya is behind him, standing at the threshold. It is the first time he has seen her out of bed for days, and she is weak from the effort, leaning against the door jamb in her bedclothes and dulled, dishevelled hair. Her eyes are wild as she looks at him, and there is something other than fear or weariness in them.

Hunger.

As if her spirit has seeped out of the puncture hole where the needle entered her stomach, Freya is withering while Robbie heals. The space where her spirit once was is filled now with the fear of what the blood tests might bring.

Ficus

Robbie replays the message, and they listen to the boy's voice. He is sure it is a boy's voice.

'He's more certain about hanging up than speaking.'

'*Will* he call back?' Freya says, mainly to herself.

'Don't know.'

'He has to call back,' she says, willing it to happen.

'Yes.'

'If he does, answer it.'

'Yes.'

'You must answer it,' Freya says, fierce. 'You must.'

They remain together in the solidifying, mid-morning light. He makes tea and they sit in easy chairs in the room off the kitchen, within sight of the phone. They are silent. It was a boy's voice, and yet there was no child there that night, two weeks ago. Their minds turn over the possibilities.

It is afternoon before the phone rings again. Robbie picks it up.

'Robbie O'Hara.'

'Ohh.' There is a half-startle in the boy's voice, as if he wasn't expecting Robbie to answer. When he recovers himself the boy says, 'We've got your wallet.'

'Who's we?' Robbie asks, cautious but calm.

'What?' the boy says. How old is he, Robbie wonders – ten? Twelve? Then the boy's confusion shifts to anger: 'Look, mate, do you want your wallet or not?'

Mate. The great distancer. Where had the boy learnt that from? It buys space. The boy might be older than he sounds.

'Yes,' Robbie says, 'I did lose my wallet, and yes, I would like it back.' He resists the urge to say that it was stolen from him, that he didn't lose it at all, but he pushes on. 'How did you get it?'

There is a pause at the other end – a pause ridden, imagines Robbie, with guilt.

But the boy says simply, 'I found it.'

'Of course,' Robbie replies. He was always going to say that. 'So, how do I get it back?' he asks.

'We can meet you,' the boy says. It is practised, or at least considered.

'You keep saying "we", who's the "we"?' Robbie tries again.

'Me and a friend.' And then the boy says, an afterthought turned into a speech, 'Look, mate, no worries. We found your wallet, we thought you might want it, and so we called, that's all. Don't be scared. Do you want your wallet or not?'

But Robbie *is* scared.

'Why don't you post it? I can give you an address.'

Freya is close beside him now, thrusting her face into his and shaking her head, her eyes wide, almost threatening. '*No*,' she hisses into his free ear, 'no!'

Robbie hears the boy mutter a curse to himself, and senses him turning away from the mouthpiece. Then, after a break, the boy returns to the phone, irritated.

'Look, Mr O'Hara. We don't have any money, okay? It costs to post things, okay? All we wanted to do was give your wallet back, if you wanted it. Your address was on your licence and the telephone directory gave me your number. Shit, I'm just trying to do the right thing.'

Robbie is losing the boy.

'Okay, okay, okay,' Robbie rushes to calm him. 'Thanks, yeah, thanks very much. I appreciate it. I do. So where's a good place? Where will we meet?'

The boy answers after a long silence, but reluctantly, as if he is no longer engaged in the conversation, as if he doesn't care. As if he has left.

'It doesn't matter,' he says.

'No, no. I appreciate the effort, mate.' *Mate*, the great equaliser. 'I'll come and pick it up.'

There is a long pause.

'Alright then. We can meet in the park at the top of the cliff. You know the one near the bridge?'

'The New Farm side? Wilson's Park?' Robbie asks.

'You expect me to know the name do you?' the boy replies sarcastically, and then stops.

'The park near the bridge?' Robbie repeats quickly, to keep him, then adds, 'On Bowen Terrace?'

'I don't know names, I told you,' the boy says with growing irritation.

'I think I know it,' Robbie says, fearing now the boy is close to hanging up. 'It's the one with grass, and a couple of benches, and there's a cliff and the river in front of you, with the Story Bridge there on your right as you're looking out over the river?'

'Yeah.'

'Okay, I know it. Well, what's a good time? What about later this afternoon? Five?'

'Yeah, okay then.' The boy's voice strengthens again. 'See ya.' And he hangs up.

Twelve

The day has hardened, and there is glare coming off everything. The polished car bonnets, house windows, television aerials. The clouds have been burnt away, excised from the day. The blue above hollows out into black with too much looking.

As the long day draws towards five o'clock they leave the house. Heat pours out of the car when they unlock it, as if they've opened the doors of a furnace. They wait a minute or so for the air to escape and Freya, revitalised, checks the film in the camera around her neck. His camera. They wind the windows down then get in, gasping still at the hot stale air scalding their throats. Robbie starts up and pulls the car into the street, steering through the narrow gap between cars parked on either curb, and then turning left into the major road.

'Where are you going?' Freya asks.

'The park,' he says.

'You're going the wrong way, Robbie.'

'No, this is fine.'

He is firm, will countenance nothing else. A river city is held together by its bridges, collects them like sutures across a wound. Freya retreats, and gazes out as he takes the car towards the city rather than to Kangaroo Point and over the Story Bridge, which crosses the river near the park which is their destination at New Farm. She keeps her silence, her hands playing with the camera in her lap until she is sure, until the car has passed out of West End and is about to cross another bridge – the Grey Street Bridge – and enter the city itself with its choking traffic and one-way streets.

'Robbie,' she says, 'it would've been much quicker to go over the Story Bridge.'

'I don't drive over that bridge,' he says, dropping gears, crunching them. Short, firm, factual. He is not joking.

'You don't go over the Story Bridge?' she repeats, amazed.

'Superstition.'

'Yeah, right,' she says with sarcasm. 'Come on, Robbie – *what*?'

'Superstition. For some people it's star signs. For me it's that bridge.'

Freya twists in her seat, the safety-belt pulling hard against her body as she looks at him and tries to penetrate what he is saying. Robbie's gaze remains fixed on the road and traffic all around. In the distance, beyond him, between the office buildings, she sees the steelwork of the Story Bridge. His father's bridge. The one his mother drove them across.

They enter the Ivory Street tunnel and flash back into sunlight, emerging near Brunswick Street. At the change of lights Robbie turns up Brunswick, and then right into Harcourt, lined with its boarding-houses. At the end of this road the bridge is visible, filling the short horizon, so huge it appears to link the houses on either side. He drives slowly, the bridge growing as the houses fall away. The steel-girdered cross-work pulls him up the street. Magnetic. As if, despite everything, the bridge itself is his destination.

At the end of Harcourt Street is Bowen Terrace and the park. Robbie stops the car by the side of the road and, still with some discomfort, pulls himself out.

Freya remains in her seat, leaning forward, fingers tapping against the dashboard. She watches as Robbie crosses the terrace and sits down on one of the park benches. Shivering despite the heat, she reaches for the camera. She attaches the zoom lens, turns the camera on and trains it on Robbie, ready to photograph the scene. This is all she can do: make this attempt at certainty. Try to reclaim something. Everything is leeching away, draining from her. She reasons: if this is one of the men from the attack trying to extort money, I'll photograph him. If it is *the* one, the mad one, then I'll remember, I'll call the police.

They should have done that already, she thinks suddenly, and checks she has her mobile phone in her bag. What risks are they taking? Why are they here? To plug a hole, staunch a wound?

★

Ficus

The afternoon light is still strong, and evening is an hour or more away. Behind him people jog past along the footpath, or walk home from work. Others, he hopes, look down from their apartment balconies. It is light and it is open and it is public. And Freya is watching from the car. Robbie waits, anxious.

The park is small, a thin slice of rich-green grass sloping away from the street to the sheer drop of the cliff. There is a near undisturbed view from the park down to the river, and across it to the city. The cliff is fenced off, the bridge too.

The bridge stands at his shoulder, to the right, filling the western sky, leaping off the cliff and into the space above the river. But he gives it nothing, looks away as he surveys the view.

Below him the river. Always the river. Solid and muscular, carving its way through the city. Curling around the office towers of the business district, each of the houses of commerce marked by vast lettering, each tower placed into the city as if it were a piece on a board game. And the river makes its own claim, an old, slow, strong claim.

A group of black shapes curves through the large sky before him; their mid-flight carping pierces the insidious din of traffic crossing the bridge. The crows pick their way through the air towards the bridge before dropping, and then dropping again, until they land in the high branches of a eucalypt in the park at the tip of Kangaroo Point, over the river.

Across there, where the bridge sets itself down on the other side, the land has been moulded into a point by the river's coursing. Over the millennia the river has deposited up-valley sand and soil on this point, as it has swept its way downstream to the ocean, so that now a sandy beach has grown there. As a child

Robbie played on the flats of this beach, his feet squelching in the damp grey sands in search of small-boy treasures. Often the beach, and the river, would offer up bottles or pieces of tin or fishing net, and he would argue with school friends over these spoils. One year the beach became a camp for an army of blue soldier crabs, and none of the boys would venture onto it for fear the crabs would rise as one out of the myriad holes that dotted the beach, and surround them.

Downriver from the point, long-abandoned jetties linger off the bank of the river, planks grey-bleached over darkened wooden pylons. They appear to him now like strange water-spiders standing deathly still in the shallows, waiting for prey. Beyond these, a marina has sprouted from the bank, and scores of sleek white yachts are moored at pontoons which rise and fall with the water.

Above the gleaming white of these hulls and masts and yachtsmen's leisurewear, the land on this eastern side of the point is now crowded with apartment buildings, a growing cluster of high-rise towers which compete with each other for river views. From where Robbie sits he can see the building where his parents live. If he were to look, if he were to count the floors from the bottom up, he could pick out their apartment, their balcony, their sliding glass doors, open or closed.

Instead he looks, as always, for his figs. Brush strokes of green, emerald through lime through grey, speckled across the city below. He counts them off – the canopies in the streets and parks below – as if checking the health of the city, checking that everything is in place. Surveying his garden. He begins to lose himself, fig by fig, seeking them out in expanding circles.

Ficus

Interrupting the sweep of this vision, a camphor laurel has taken root on the edge of the cliff, just beyond the metal fencing. He stops at the tree, its solid girth, its roots tentacled over the cliff, its glossy pointed leaves. Across the deep grooves of its barked trunk, kids have sprayed their initials in black paint. *BS* and *JC*. He admires it reluctantly: tough and magnificent, imported from China via the Kew Botanic Gardens in London in the early years of the colonies. A landscape tree, an ornamental. But the gardeners lost control very early on. Now its colonisation of the east coast is unceasing: tireless, it has become a weed, poisonous to birdlife and fauna, narcotic, addictive.

The wind shifts. The traffic noise on the bridge pulses louder and Robbie is drawn to the thudding of car tyres as they hit the expansion joints. He shudders, involuntarily, and has to catch his breath. The wind shifts once more and the traffic noise fades into its steady thrum.

A small ferry makes its way upriver, against the tide.

At the end of the park, there's movement in his peripheral vision. A figure emerges, an adolescent boy. He has probably been watching Robbie for a while. As the boy approaches, Robbie inspects him, guesses he is twelve, thirteen at most. He wears a dark t-shirt, with fading blue jeans stained in places, bleached pale in others. A canvas army-disposal bag is slung over his shoulder, the strap crossing his chest. On his feet, where Robbie expected to see Nikes or thongs, the boy wears black school shoes, heavily scuffed. The leather toe of one shoe has sliced open where the boy has kicked against something sharp, and Robbie can see the soft white under-leather there. The boy's hair is straight and brown and stuck together in clumps. His eyes are hooded, darkness squinting out from sunned skin.

He is not yet pubescent, but there is sureness in his jaw. The boy is alone.

'Heya,' Robbie calls over, his voice rising gently, rather than in challenge.

'Hey,' the boy responds, cautiously coming closer. 'You Robert O'Hara?'

'Yep.'

The boy stops a few paces from the bench and swings the bag around to his front without taking it off. He unfastens the clip, reaches in and produces Robbie's wallet. He does not hand it over immediately, but opens it and shuffles through the plastic cards. The night of the assault rises inside Robbie again. This intrusion by the boy, this liberty taken, this power exercised.

'It looks like you alright,' the boy says, inspecting the photo on Robbie's drivers licence. His shudder-laugh sounds wooden. 'Here you go,' and then he takes a step forward and offers it to Robbie in a small outstretched hand.

'Thanks.'

Robbie takes it, his eyes on the black wallet now rather than on the boy. He opens it. No cash, though the cards seem to be there. The two credit cards, the licence, the telephone card, work identification that gets him into the council building in the city when he needs to. A photo of him and Freya. A fig leaf, dried and cracked.

'Where did you find it?' Robbie asks.

'In the city,' the boy responds.

'But where exactly?'

'In the park.'

'The Botanic Gardens?'

'Dunno the name. Down the end.' The boy turns around

Ficus

and points at the dark green mesh of the Gardens, as much as they can see of it from here.

'There's money missing,' Robbie says while the boy's head is still turned, looking across the river to the Gardens and the city. This jerks him back.

'Huh?'

'There was a hundred bucks there,' Robbie says.

'Well, there wasn't a hundred bucks there when I found it,' the boy shoots back. His hands are on his hips now, his mouth pouted.

'Right,' Robbie says, nodding his head. And then, after a long pause, 'Thanks for calling . . . Thanks for letting me know.' Robbie's mind is whirring with possibilities. After another pause, 'So, tell me . . .' and Robbie figures he has nothing to lose, 'I don't know your name?' But what is the point? Why does he want to know? Is this for Freya?

The boy just stares at him blankly. Stares through him. Says nothing. As if he is stupid.

'Look, you know my name, you may as well let me know yours.'

But the boy is unmoved. The boy can hold this silence. A crow pulls in out of the sky and lands on the cliff-fence. It cranes its neck at the two of them, inspecting them with a single white eye for long moments. Then it drops to the ground and picks at something embedded in the grass, its hard black beak making a cracking sound as it works at whatever has caught its attention. Robbie looks back at the boy, who has barely moved, and tries again.

'So, you found it in the park. Like, where was it? Just on the ground, or in a bush, or in the water or something?'

He feels the leading questions coming out, the plaintive note to his voice, the likelihood they will flounder. But the boy is still here.

'We found it in a bin,' the boy says, his head lifting, his forehead creasing and his eyes lit, before rushing on. 'We were looking for food and found it in a bin, okay. There was nothing in it, okay. We just found it, saw the cards and stuff and thought you might want it back, you know?'

Robbie looks at the boy with his unkempt hair and clothes and broken shoes, and the little hardnesses about him despite his age, and thinks that all this may be true. He constructs a narrative, simple: the attackers are junkies, interested in one thing only — cash — they take the money, discard the wallet in a rubbish bin, and a homeless boy foraging for food scraps left by New Year's Eve revellers finds it. Yes, Robbie thinks, this may be all that has happened, there may be nothing more.

The sun is dropping below the level of the city skyline. Pulsating corridors of orange light push through the city towers beyond the bridge.

Robbie is tiring, is being pulled towards the end of this meeting.

'Thanks again, mate. Thanks for getting it back to me.' Robbie pulls a fifty dollar note from his pocket and holds it out. The boy steps up and takes it, the transaction done.

'Lucky, hey?' the boy says.

'What do you mean?'

'Lucky I found it before the bin was emptied. You'd never have got it back then.'

There is another moment of uncomfortable silence, as if Robbie has overstayed a welcome. He pushes himself off the

Ficus

bench with his right hand and gets to his feet. He goes to thank the boy once more, but nods instead in the boy's direction without meeting his eyes.

Robbie starts up the grassy incline to his car. There are scores of marble-sized palm seeds lying scattered on the grass, dislodged from the cocos palms above by night upon night of flying fox feeding. The smooth orange seeds are hard under the soles of his shoes, and his weight presses the seeds deeper into the earth with each footfall.

'What do you think?' Freya demands.

'He's just the kid who found the wallet.'

'There might be fingerprints,' she says, 'of the attackers.'

They look at the wallet, greasy from the bin and the boy's pocket, and Robbie's own hands. Inert and greasy.

'I think we've reached a dead-end, Frey,' he says gently, resting his hand on her shoulder.

She looks away, turns her shoulder, drops it and sinks into the seat, says almost to herself, 'I've taken some photos anyway.'

Robbie opens his wallet, flicking again through the cards and receipts he'd stored there. He comes to the photograph she'd given him months ago: the two of them after a bushwalk at Tamborine, exhausted but beaming, the angle of the photo askew from where she'd propped the camera in the fork of a gum to take the self-timed shot.

'Here,' he says, 'remember this?'

She turns back to him, takes the photograph in her hands, studies it for a moment. It is not just the captured split-second she remembers, but her entire life till then. Dread comes upon her — that she has changed, that her old life has ended, and nothing will be the same again.

The Comfort of Figs

'It's good to get this back anyway,' he says.

She sighs, and the photo, with her hands, the blood draining from them, drops lifeless into her lap.

Thirteen

The next day is different. It is early when Robbie rises. He doesn't look, as he drives through the pre-dawn grey, for an empty patch of ground in which to plant a fig. This morning, instead, it is a camphor laurel he seeks.

He makes for an avenue in Chelmer, a street he knows is shaded by the camphors, their thick-barked limbs, their deep canopies, their perfumed leaves. Parking in the avenue of trees, Robbie gets out and walks the length of the street, inspecting each of the camphors by streetlight, scanning their branches, their forks. When he is done and has selected one, he pauses at its foot, eyes raised, as if paying respects. He returns to his car and drives closer, till he's underneath the chosen tree. Out of the car boot he takes a fig sapling, some twine, a bag of soil and an old wooden fruit box, a small one made from thin slats of plantation pine.

Robbie climbs onto the car roof and quickly swings up and onto the overhanging branch. The sky is lightening, but suddenly, deep in the tree, it is darker. He will find no birds' nests, he knows this. He looks for possums instead, sated on leaves and berries, but there are none. He slides down the branch towards the trunk, and when he reaches the fork, he nestles the box in the crook between trunk and branch. He secures it by digging its edges into the bark with a pocket knife, fixing it there, then running twine around it and under the branch before tying it off. Into the box he plants his sapling, tipping the soil and roots in, patting it down, adding soil. He checks it, that the fig is firm and comfortable in its epiphytic nest.

Back along the branch, he swings from the tree onto his car, and then slides down again onto the road. The pine box is barely visible from the road.

He looks down the long avenue of camphor laurels, unwelcome now. Looks at the mornings before him, the task of reclamation. The camphors that will need to die. The slow, necessary stranglings.

Hardened by this, he sets out on the second journey of the morning. He drives through Rocklea, past the fruit markets where he will collect more boxes in the weeks to come, along Ipswich Road to Woolloongabba. He crosses the marsh of freeway entrances and exits and, once clear of them, pulls up onto the long cliff-top road at Kangaroo Point which will take him to his parents' apartment at the end of the peninsula.

A flash of dawn light reflects off one of the city towers across the river to his left. Robbie has never seen the city from this angle at this time of day. On impulse he pulls into a parking bay looking out from the Kangaroo Point cliffs, over the river to the city. He walks the few metres to the chest-high granite wall at the top of the precipice. Across the river are the Botanic Gardens, settled dark in their river nook. He sees Freya and himself down there, just two weeks ago, looking up at the cliff where he now stands.

Three dozen yachts are moored off the Gardens, the white of their masts rising tall from their decks and outlined sharp against the dark of the forest behind them. To the right of the Gardens the city begins, the transition from forest to skyscrapers abrupt. Robbie watches the reflection of the sun rising in a blue-glass tower by the river. The curved glass is burnt orange near the ground as the new sun's radiance first strikes it, fading upwards into blue-black reflections. Moment by moment the building catches fire, until the entire structure is alight.

The cliff-top street joins the main flow of vehicles which merge into the Bradfield Highway to cross the bridge. The 'Bradfield Highway' is little more than an on-ramp; named after the bridge's designer, it would have remained unnamed if there weren't so many people to publicly reward. I wonder if he was embarrassed, Robbie thinks to himself.

As usual, rather than cross the bridge Robbie pulls off the approach-ramp at the last opportunity and curves back around and under it, the traffic above sounding a dull roar through his window. 'Riverview' comes into sight: twenty-four levels of apartments populated by business executives, wealthy retirees, young couples – and his parents.

At the entry he presses the buzzer beside their apartment number.

'Hello?' His mother's voice.

'Morning,' he says. 'It's me.'

'Robbie!' she exclaims. 'I'll let you up –'

'Lily –' Robbie speaks quickly, before she has time to disconnect – 'Is he ... will he ... ?'

'I haven't forgotten,' she says, her delight dulled. 'Don't fret.'

In the foyer Robbie crosses to the lift, presses and waits. He waits, and feels, for the first time this morning, anxious. He watches the numbers descend, watches the lift counting backwards in small red digits. A sensation of going backwards, of falling into the past, comes over him. He begins to doubt. But when it arrives, he forces himself to enter the small space, to press the button for the twentieth floor. He starts the slow rise.

His mother is there when the lift arrives, waiting for him at the entrance of her apartment.

'Is everything alright, love?' she asks.

He bends, her voice close to his ear as she kisses his cheek, and with the kiss comes the sweet memory of his mother leaning over him in childhood, in bed, to bid him goodnight.

'Everything's fine,' he says.

'And Freya?'

'She's fine too. I just thought it'd be nice to visit. To thank you for looking after us at the hospital.'

He passes in front of her and enters the apartment.

Ficus

It is years since he has been here. And yet it is unchanged. Everything is unchanged: he enters the apartment feeling – and the realisation of it disappoints him – as much a stranger as he ever did. No stronger, no surer. Is this just foolishness? he asks himself, unsettled now. He is aware, suddenly, of all that he does not want to see.

This place appears to him, as it always did, to be in conflict with itself, wrestling between that which is open and that which has been closed, between illumination and shadow. Robbie steps forward, steps into silence and secret and memory.

Off either side of the dim, darkly carpeted entrance hall are the two bedrooms. The doors are both shut, as his mother assured him they would be. Yet Robbie feels a pang in his stomach, sharp as if he's been stabbed. He steps past the doors, looking fixedly ahead. He is conscious of his mother's footsteps brushing the carpet behind him. He walks quickly, unbreathing, down the hall to the living room, which is bathed in sparkling sun.

Standing there, he's dizzy from the brightness. A sliding glass door opens onto a balcony, and out further onto the world beyond. The apartment faces north across the river, down the line of the bridge, level with it. That was, after all, why his mother had moved them here after his father's stroke. But Robbie doesn't yet look out through the glass. It is not a conscious decision to ignore the bridge, rather what is inside the apartment has seized him.

All around, competing with the light and the windows and the air and the space and the very modernity of the apartment itself, are the mementos of his parents' life. In the middle of the living room he turns a slow circle, taking in the museum of his parents' existence and all its exhibits. He gasps with fresh surprise, and with a flood of misgiving.

The souvenirs of his father's journeys are all still there: the hand-carved furniture; the ceremonial masks; statue after statue carved of timber or ivory or bone, from Goa, or Ghana or Guinea Bissau. Carpets and kilims hanging from walls. Feathers and shells and beads. A chest-high shield propped in a corner. Paintings on bark, on hand-made paper, on hide, scenes of village life from three continents. Primitive histories that his father's modern engineering constructions must have swept away. Robbie thinks of these as his father's guilty record of those places, those times.

His mother's keepsakes are here too. Her vases stacked on shelves, above cupboards, as centrepieces on tables or benches. On the dining room table is a single large white vase – more bowl than vase – filled with water, on top of which float frangipanis, their scent fading, their soft tips beginning to brown. They will be changed today, he knows – his mother is fastidious about old blossoms. And beside the porcelain vase, his mother's King James Bible has been recently laid aside. The first half – the *Old* half, the thirty-nine books of the Old Testament – is well-thumbed, but the second half, the *New* half, has barely been touched. Even so, a waist-high plaster statue of Mary stands in a corner of the room, her blue robes chipped, her left hand amputated at the wrist.

'I remember this,' Robbie says.

'The parish gave it to me. It was lovely of them. For arranging the altar flowers. After I couldn't do it any more – after your father . . .' She trails off, but Robbie doesn't notice.

He's wondering rather, as he looks at it, if the gift was more than a simple thankyou, if the parish priest may also have been trying to counterbalance Lily's unusual interest in the Old Testament with a statue of the Queen of the New. Robbie's gaze lingers on it. He recalls the Sunday masses of his childhood. Back then, the statue held a golden orb in its outstretched hand. Robbie wonders when it was disfigured. He wonders almost idly: Was she an imperfect gift, or has she been damaged under my mother's care? Eventually his mother says, 'What is it, love?'

There is something else in the room. The thing Robbie has been ignoring, conscious of all along – the gravitational centre of the apartment.

He turns to it eventually. Against its own wall is a low silky-oak bookcase. 'The Story Bridge bookcase', his mother calls it. Old tensions knot his stomach when he finally faces it, their Story Bridge shrine.

The books on the shelves are histories with old black-and-white or colour-plated photos of the bridge, chapters about its importance to the city, about its iconic status. The bridge kitsch is there too: souvenir teaspoons with tiny images of the bridge captured on their handles, china plates with delicate paintings of the bridge in gold paint, postcards, a Story Bridge inside a plastic liquid hemisphere which you can shake to see snowflakes fall on this land for the first time since the ice age. There are the scrapbooks with fifty years of newspaper clippings, his mother diligent about her collection of articles. Every news item about the bridge from the local newspapers has been cut out, kept and catalogued in the scrapbooks. And on the walls above the bookcase are paintings of the bridge, prints or sketches, dulled from years of sunlight.

Then there are her private keepsakes. The biscuit tin with its treasure of pay-slips and notices from the 1930s. The ceremonial booklet from the Opening Ceremony. Old photos in old frames, propped on the shelves. The bridge-workers posing for the camera, strong and proud and sure.

One of the posing workers his father, Robert John O'Hara. Jack.

Robbie turns towards the windows, and the bridge, vast, sweeping across the river. An unusual movement out there catches his eye, something apart from the bridge. In the early light, a lone flying fox – the last of the night – is making its way across the sky. The others have all returned to their roosts. What has kept this one? Robbie watches the bat as it staggers across the sky, lost, injured, or, Robbie wonders, simply frail. The bat – turned dark gold in the sun – navigates itself around the bridge, then drops out of sight, a mile yet from the nearest roosting ground, a long way yet from home.

BRIDGE

One

October 1939. A drop of rain falls heavily from the sky, bursts against a steel girder, explodes into fragments. A man feels the splash on the back of his neck, and straightens from his work. Looks to the sky, the grey cloud swelling now above him.

'Wet steel!' he cries. 'Wet steel!'

The cry catches. First one man, then another, till the bridge rings with the sound of men calling. The steel hums with the vibrations of rain and men's cries. They secure their tools and descend from their stagings and their platforms. Out of their harnesses and bosun-belts. The men desert the bridge like ants before a storm. Surrender it to the weather. The slippery, wet, dangerous steel. They abandon it and converge on the dressing sheds, one on either side of the river. They drip with moisture – their sweat and the rain and the particles of raindrops which have detonated against the steelwork in their falling, fragments ricocheting onto girders and cross-pieces and men.

The doorway to the shed on the Kangaroo Point peninsula is a bottleneck. Jack O'Hara and the other men jostle against each other to get through the door and out of the rain. O'Hara enjoys the closeness, the roughness and suddenness of the intimacy, the shared purpose. Inside the men sit on benches and catch their breath while the rain falls through the open doorway and hammers on the corrugated-iron sheeting above them.

In time the downpour softens, lightens, and talk becomes possible.

'What would you do if you slipped, Jack?' one of the men asks O'Hara.

'I'd be looking for you to catch me, mate,' he replies.

'Well, I'd be looking the other way, so that'd do you no good.'

'You'd be a bastard of a mate then, wouldn't you,' O'Hara snorts.

'What would you do though?' the man persists.

O'Hara is young, twenty, and already his word counts. But he knows the limits of his influence. He will not be drawn into giving an opinion on this, which he senses is beyond him.

'Look at that thing around Irish's throat,' he says, pointing to the metal cross hanging from Patrick Flanagan's neck. 'There's your answer. I'd get in as many Hail Marys as I could.'

Flanagan the Irishman laughs with the other men. He'd have growled if it was anyone else who'd said it. Though none but

Bridge

O'Hara would have risked it. Flanagan cuts O'Hara slack, sees something of himself in the younger man's spirit, something beyond the tribal bond of their names.

'Would you live if you fell, but?' Peter Carleton asks, breathless, arriving late after tying up his boat under the wharf. Carleton is the youngest, still a boy at sixteen, this question the thing, right now, he wants to know. 'Would you live, but?' he says again, his head thrust forward off his chest at an awkward angle, adolescent and intense. The question is anyone's to answer, though he longs for O'Hara to take it up.

'It depends on how you fell, lad,' someone says.

They debate ways of falling. One of them proposes rolling into a ball.

'Stupid,' heavy, square-shouldered William Hodges challenges. 'It's like concrete, the river is, when you hit it. If you rolled yourself up into a ball, you'd bounce like one too.'

'Feet first,' someone else offers. 'Like you're pencil-diving.'

'Break your legs.' Hodges again.

'You might break your legs but they'll mend. And if they don't, then you're losing your legs to save the rest of you.'

'What do you reckon, Irish?' O'Hara puts the question.

They turn towards the dark-haired, grizzled, bull of a Celt. There is nothing he does not know about bridge construction. He's travelled the world following them. The Harbour Bridge in Sydney, the Golden Gate in San Francisco, migrating from bridge to bridge following some hidden compass. Now Brisbane. He has seen the world, is their link to the greater part of it. If there is a way to fall, the Irishman will know.

'Boys, there's no one way,' he says at the end of an expectant silence. He plays it, the silence, his accent finding the time of the rain falling soft now on the roof. 'I've seen a man pissed as a newt walk right off the end of the decking without knowing it. He fell near a hundred feet. Still strolling, he was, putting one foot in front of the other when he hit and sure enough he walked away without a bruise. I've seen another man take a thirty-foot fall and never walk again. Paralysed for life, the poor bastard, his legs driven up either side of his spine. There's no one way,' he concludes. 'You could do worse than pray.'

'But what would *you* do?' O'Hara asks him.

Irish looks none of them in the eyes now, his glance his own. He understands, at moments like this, he is a seer to them. He is reluctant but feels their need.

'I'd dive in head first. The prettiest swan dive you ever saw.'

'And have your skull pushed through your shoulders?' Hodges shakes his head, unconvinced, emboldened.

'You weren't listening, Billy-boy, were you?' Irish says. 'You're a slow one. There's no sure-fire way. But I figure it like this,' and Irish looks around the tight room, meets their eyes one by one, as many as he can. 'If you pull the dive off, if you slide into the water – fingers hands arms head shoulders torso,' he touches the parts of his body as he names them, elevating them into things of beauty. 'If you get it right, then you walk away. If you don't, then I figure this. The impact of your head on the water will kill you.'

'Or knock you out,' says Carleton spontaneously.

'Or knock you out, boy,' Irish concedes. 'But if you're unconscious you drown. Look, boys, I'm not saying you'd survive. You may not. But there's no middle ground if you dive, there's no lifetime of sitting in a wheelchair.'

There is a silence among the men as the pitiless choice Irish offers begins to resonate, expands and fills what space is left inside the dressing shed. The rain falls heavily once more and the beating on the roof starts again. In time the men break into smaller conversations, a layer of murmur below the drumming of the rain.

'It depends on the water,' Karl 'Charlie' Stahl says to himself. 'It depends on the wind.'

But Carleton is close enough to hear.

'What do you mean, Charlie?' Carleton asks, all eagerness, the world and its intricacies waiting to be understood and all it takes is to ask.

'If the water is flat, then it's like Billy says – hard as concrete and it won't matter how you hit, especially from our heights. But if there is a wind . . . and if the surface of the water is broken up . . . then your chances are better. Much better. Then it's just water, and there's no tension in the surface. You're a better chance of sliding into the water.'

Carleton catches on, enthralled. 'So all you have to do is break the tension, break the surface?'

Stahl watches Carleton think, watches Carleton's fervent brain turning. Says nothing just yet, lets him whir.

'So if you're falling,' Carleton says after a moment, 'if you're in mid-air, the thing to do is to throw something in front of you.'

Carleton throws an imaginary object out in front of him, acting this out.

Stahl smiles.

Carleton continues. 'Your shoe, or a coin. Even that would

do it, wouldn't it? You reach down and toss a penny from your pocket so it hits the water before you do. Hits the water, breaks it up, gets a ripple going. Is that it? Is that the trick?'

And Carleton looks across at Stahl, looks across with huge excited triumphant eyes, waiting for his response, some reward for working out a puzzle.

'That's it, isn't it, Charlie? I've got it, haven't I, Charlie? Come on, tell me.'

Stahl says nothing. He simply reaches into his pocket in answer, slow and deliberate. When his hand slides out again there is a piece of steel in it, five inches long, grey, mushroom-headed. And Carleton understands. For a long moment the rivet rests in Stahl's open palm, a key to some esoteric knowledge, as if it is imbued with power, as if it is a secret Carleton has now received.

Two

O'Hara and Stahl rise. O'Hara is up first. Always. He takes pride in it, reads in it a sign of natural authority. Or that his body will bend to his will. He is first to survey the new day, to take what bearings it might offer, to set its course. 'It's blowy, lads,' he'd say after an overnight shift in the weather, or 'Big day ahead of us,' or 'What did you get up to last night, Sullivan? Something you wouldn't want your mother to know?'

O'Hara is already dressed and has sniffed the air outside his own bedroom window when he turns the handle of Stahl's door and enters without knocking. He leans over the bed where Stahl sleeps, leans close over the other man's face to measure his breathing, to watch the movement of his eyelids, to read what dreams might be projected onto their inner screen. O'Hara senses Stahl not far from waking, and leans closer over his friend, feeling the touch of Stahl's night breath cool against his own freshly shaven cheek. O'Hara reaches further and gently pinches one of Stahl's ear lobes, a delicate pressure. It wakes him.

Stahl doesn't object, though he would never enter O'Hara's room like this. O'Hara takes his own permission, shapes relationships with men so that no consent is needed, or given. The others like it when O'Hara enters rooms in this way, joins private conversations, gives them nicknames which take hold, become currency. There are intimacies O'Hara takes that would be intrusions by others.

They do not speak. O'Hara has withdrawn to the chair by the window as Stahl props himself up on an elbow and shakes his head to rid himself of the night's residue. O'Hara gazes from the chair into the half-dark beyond the window, as Stahl dresses.

A possum screeches in the night, its mating hisses coming in through the window from the branches of the mango tree in the yard next door. O'Hara takes the glass of water from the bedside table and tosses it through the darkness towards the tree. The sound of water on leaves and branches cracks the night, the first booming shock followed by a falling clatter as drops of water cascade through the foliage to the ground. There is a fresh possum hiss, fierce, followed by a scrambling of fur and short legs through the tree, and into the next and soon it is gone, and O'Hara is smiling to himself.

Then, with the darkness thinning, and the echoes of possum-flight still hanging in the air, a murder of crows starts up. 'Black dingoes', the way they sit eternally alert on a pole or fence or rim of a forty-four gallon drum and lift their heads back to caw, their cunning, their faultless sense of danger. Stahl

Bridge

lathers to the sound of two crows plotting some intrigue in the street outside, slaps water onto his face from a basin while O'Hara and the black birds mark out their territory, runs a blade across his cheek as a third crow arrives. Stahl finishes and looks around for his towel.

'Charlie,' O'Hara whips his name at him, the first word of the day, and Stahl turns his head to see the towel flung through the air towards him. He catches it and holds it to his face in the one movement before tossing it back to O'Hara, who drapes it over the windowsill again. In the moment it takes Stahl to tie the long laces of his boots O'Hara has left the room and is waiting at the front door of the boarding house, the crows wheeling away from him through the crepuscular light.

Into the half-dark they step, the two of them, the sound of their bootfall crisp and full as they stride along the footpath down the Harcourt Street hill. For a moment these men and their boots are one. O'Hara and Stahl stretch their legs into Brunswick Street and lean into the slow hill, the day gathering strength at their backs, the bridge before them emerging, slowly, from the night.

O'Hara stands on a wooden platform of six-inch planks, the platform mounted on top of the bridge's northern shoulder. Stahl beside him, the river three hundred feet below.

O'Hara loves the height. The power, the possibilities, the close horizon. Especially the horizon. He loves this view of the edge of the world. He looks out along the river to the silvery haze of the bay, and the elongated sand islands thirty miles away. Islands which protect his town from the Pacific. Across the morning, clouds stretch themselves flat and the sun crawls up and over them. The day has begun, has shrugged off its lateness and he is there to greet it. O'Hara sucks it in – the morning, the view, the height – and rubs the back of his right hand hard against his nose till the skin between lip and nose burns with the friction of it.

He owns this country. No one, *no one*, he feels, perched on the northern shoulder of the bridge, the working day still ahead of him, owns it like him.

A single fishing trawler returns from its night's work, motors in on the dying tide, noses towards its berth. Each morning this boat and its Greek captain leave and return alone, keeping different hours from the rest of the fleet. O'Hara gathers a ball of spit from his chest, gathers it long and deep and guttural, and holds it in his mouth as the trawler nudges closer. O'Hara measures the breeze – easterly, and slight. He pauses, counts to himself, then launches his spittle into the air with a sharp whip of his head and neck, the spit tumbling over itself down towards the trawler. O'Hara leans forward to watch it, the globule shrinking with the distance, though big enough still for him to see the trawler slide safely under it before it hits the river and is gone. Lucky bastard, he thinks, and considers the correction he needs to make next time. Trial and error: the weighing of variables, experimentation and the accumulation of results, the precision of the calculation. The science of spitting.

O'Hara looks along the line of the bridge to the other, twin shoulder, a second collarbone of steel. From where they stand he and Stahl can see the perfect line of the steel chord dropping away down the sweet sloping descent of the northern cantilever span, before levelling out into the flat of the suspended span.

Bridge

But then ending. Stopping abruptly at the narrow gap between the two halves of the bridge, as if the two shoulders are waiting for a neck.

Mirror images, the two halves have been growing simultaneously towards each other from opposite banks of the river for a thousand days. There is only the smallest of spaces between them now – a single remaining section to be swung into place, a mere morning's work.

And yet now that they are so close they are told they must wait.

Ambition blows like a wind at his back, fills him, keeps him awake at night.

O'Hara's grandfather arrived from Ireland at Maryborough, a few hundred miles up north. The man arrived hungry, the stench of bad potatoes still in his nostrils as he disembarked. He, and then his son – Jack's father – Roberts both, settled into the timber country to the north, logging the bush, clearing the land and selling the wood. Hoop-pine for floorboards, cypress and silky oak for cabinets, she-oak for wharf-piles, spotted gum for planking and buggy shafts. Timber-getters and timber-cutters, and then briefly farmers with failed crops of bananas, before returning to the forests. His family cut their way south to Brisbane, that's how O'Hara sees it. Cut their own path over fifty years down to the city. But in the city, where O'Hara was raised, he took up a trade, became a boilermaker, learnt to work steel.

With steel came a new knowledge, a knowledge that belonged to the future. Where his father and grandfather had known timber, he knew steel; where they built houses, he would build bridges; where they built settlements, he would build cities. And this bridge – what an opportunity, what a prize! O'Hara claimed it, not only for himself, but for all the O'Haras. Because he understood history and the arrowhead of its trajectory. He understood that you stand on the shoulders of those who've gone before. Here he was, third generation, perched at the highest point in the city, the work of his own hands. Jack O'Hara, boilermaker to the sky.

A high-flying crow passes above O'Hara and Stahl, between them and the rising sun, full of shadow, spreading it as it goes. Stahl calls out to the bird as it passes, *ark, ark*, imitating its sound, but the crow ignores him and continues on its way. O'Hara sweeps his eyes one last time across the horizon, taking in the space more than any detail.

'Too clear,' he says to Stahl.

Stahl looks out, blue-eyed, at the low cloudbank on the eastern horizon, and the wisps of white cloud which soon will be burnt away. But it is through his hands – long-fingered and beautiful despite the work – that Stahl understands things, through his hands that objects take their shape. Now Stahl runs his right forefinger along a girder, slowly, the pad of flesh pressing against the steel. Gentle, firming, then brushing soft again as his finger rubs against the steel's surface, working the steel, finding the weight of the cloud on the steel. It is spontaneous, unthinking, but practice for later when he will take up his pencil and draw charcoal on paper, capturing the shape of cloud through his fingers.

Bridge

'There's too much light,' O'Hara says again. 'It'll get too hot, too quickly. It won't happen today.'

O'Hara speaks with authority, as if he is responsible for more than heating rivets. As if this is O'Hara's decision to make, and not the Canadian steel engineer who is probably below them somewhere already measuring the temperature in half a dozen places along the bridge. Something suddenly dawns on O'Hara.

'That's why they've got him here – Lawrence.'

'What?' says Stahl, his hand now stilled.

'That's why Lawrence's here,' O'Hara exclaims. 'So if it's a stuff-up, if they're out and the ends won't join, they'll have someone to blame! Hah!' he laughs. 'Poor bastard. The entire city will be on his back if it goes wrong.'

Three

The Canadian steel engineer, Arnott Le Roy Lawrence, sits at his desk in the site office at Kangaroo Point, in the upper floor of the northern wing of what had been the Immigration Depot before it was appropriated by the engineers and their bridge. He has been at his desk since before dawn, since before the temperatures were taken out on the bridge above, and run in here to his office for him to consider, to weigh, and to make judgment.

Light enters the room through the large dormer window which was added after they moved in, when the bridge had begun to grow and to dwarf the building and to starve them of sunlight. In front of him, on the desk, are cards. Everything cleared but these playing cards, suffused with soft light. Face up

Bridge

in front of him are jacks and queens and kings in their finery. As the engineer moves the cards they dance as at a royal pageant, pirouetting, spinning backwards, somersaulting, exchanging places. And there are the number cards, two to ten, doing the work they promise, no more, no less. Finally the ace, the changeling. She is both one, in all of her completeness, and then suddenly, as on a whim, eleven. There is something unknowable about the nature of the ace. Ragged musings enter, then leave Lawrence's mind. He has barely slept.

The temperatures taken, the engineer has begun to play cards. Playing for a solution, playing for certainty, playing for reassurance. He does this – turns cards in the hope a solution to whatever mathematical conundrum is occupying his mind will fall into place. He can play solitaire for hours. Sometimes the pattern of the game unfolds. On those occasions, rare, it is beauty itself that is revealed, and whatever calculus has been eluding him will fall out and the engineer will reach for a piece of paper and record the answer delivered by the game.

Earlier, years ago now, at the start of his journey, the engineer had written, in what seems another man's hand:

> *Under suitable weather conditions the suspended span is swung into place, and the bridge is closed. During closure operations, allowances are made for the possible variations due to temperature and wind and also for the actual movements required to match the upper and lower chord connections and to swing the suspended span free of the wedges. These movements are functions of the elastic properties of the main trusses and their values are derived from the deflections of the points concerned before and after closure.*

The Comfort of Figs

As if it is all merely science, merely mathematics. As if there is no luck. As if there is no terror.

The city was obsessed with taming the river, with building bridges. The bridge-lust was in her. It was rampant. Brisbane was not alone, but Lawrence could see she had it bad. He perceived this as soon as he arrived, puts it together, the pieces of the story he has entered, ignorant of so much.

The briefing he'd got before he set sail was different, all facts, dry but for the promise of the new. And yet all the facts were there for the reading, in the history he was given:

> *In 1925 the newly established Greater Brisbane Council appointed the Cross River Commission. It recommended a bridge at Kangaroo Point, but the proposal stalled. Other bridges satisfied the city's need for crossings. The Grey Street Bridge was opened on 30 March 1932, the bridge between Brisbane and Redcliffe on 4 October 1935, the Indooroopilly bridge on 14 February 1936.*

But this one, the big dream bridge, 'the Kangaroo Point bridge', had lingered.

Enter the dreamer, persistent beyond all reasonable boundaries, the man Lawrence would stand before, beside – ultimately behind – John Job Crew Bradfield. The man Lawrence needs to know, the man Lawrence studied as they dined together at the Criterion Hotel in the first evenings, the man he still asks people about, collecting biographical detail like his hometown squirrels hoard nuts. The man whose bold history Lawrence has pieced together.

Bridge

Dr J.J.C. Bradfield is a Brisbane-boy made good. Born in bayside Sandgate, he moved with his family to Ipswich as the thirteenth son of a brickmaker, won a scholarship to Sydney University, studied engineering and joined the New South Wales Department of Public Works.

But he is no ordinary engineer. Bradfield radiates intent. Not only was he Chief Engineer of construction for the Sydney Harbour Bridge during the long years of 1923 to 1932, but the design plans carried his name. *'Ad gloriam Bradfieldii'* a member of Parliament exalted him from the floor of the New South Wales lower house, as it passed the *Harbour Bridge Act* on 16 November 1922. Bradfield knows the need to influence politicians and, as far as Lawrence can make out, he is their darling.

So, on 1 December 1931, with the Sydney bridge joined and the first train only a few weeks from making its inaugural harbour crossing, Bradfield had written to Arthur Moore, the conservative Queensland Premier, proposing a bridge across the Brisbane River: *There is no difficulty in designing a bridge, aesthetic and satisfying all interests.* He'd repeated it to whomever would listen, a mantra of certainty, *there is no difficulty.*

But an election had intervened and it was 1933 before the new Labor premier, William Forgan-Smith, established his Bridge Board to devise a way across the river at Kangaroo Point. A Board of three: Kemp, the Main Roads Commissioner; Brigden, the Director of the Bureau of Industry; and Story, the Public Service Commissioner. These chosen three had appointed Bradfield as their consulting engineer. As if there was anyone else.

Bradfield had set to work in January 1934, and by May he'd

recommended a cantilever truss bridge for the site. Has to be a cantilever, Bradfield said, on account of the stratification of the schist, its vertical cracks. The pull or the thrust either from the anchorages of a suspension bridge, or from the skewbacks of an arch, could cause the rock mass to move. It has to be cantilevered. So the Bradfield designs were provided to the Board. Forgan-Smith had insisted on tendering for the bridge-builders, but the process achieved the desired outcome anyway. There were only two tenders, both Australian. The Brisbane tender, a joint proposal from the steel fabrication company Evans Deakin & Co and the roadway construction firm of M.R. Hornibrook, was successful. Brisbane was a fiercely parochial town even then when the tender was approved on 29 April 1935.

The clod-turning ceremony took place on 24 May 1935, when Lawrence was newly arrived. It was the twenty-fifth anniversary of the reign of the English king, George V, Lawrence's head of state as much as Bradfield's, and so the bridge acquired its working name: The Jubilee Bridge.

A shovel broke the earth. Lawrence watched Bradfield step forward from beneath the shade of a fig tree, a small bespectacled man with neat three-piece suit, moustache, bulging forehead and ambitions yet unfilled:

'The cantilever bridge with its bold towers and curved outline, sturdy shoulders, with graceful curves, will harmonise with the picturesque and rugged beauty of the Brisbane skyline.'

These are the notes from Lawrence's work-book of years before, an engineer's doodles:

Bridge

Cantilever. Cant – a corner, an angle, a corner piece, a triangular piece. Lever – a bar resting on a pivot used to raise or dislodge a heavy fixed object. A cantilever bridge to span a wide, well-trafficked, flood-prone river. There can be no mid-river piers, nothing to interrupt the flow of water. Two giant, triangular cantilever arms each projecting out across the river from main piers on either bank of the river. The cantilever arms themselves linked to the earth by anchor spans. Each arm reaching out towards the other. The steelwork of the arms extending girder by girder without stagings, the steelwork being cantilevered across the river. The cantilever arms complete, the final span of the bridge – the central span – is suspended between the cantilevers. The final pieces dropped into position, secured, held in place by the cantilever arms. Neat, perfect, permanent.

Soon after the ceremonial earth was turned their great undertaking began. And the epithets appeared: 'The largest steel cantilever bridge in Australia'. *The Home-Grown Bridge.* The Bridge made 'by Queenslanders for Queenslanders, using only Queensland materials'. Lawrence listens to this glory-making quietly.

He is surrounded, but untroubled by it. Bradfield the consulting engineer, a local. Colonel Evans the steel man, a local. M.R. Hornibrook the bridge man, a local. The tradesmen employed to construct the bridge – the boilermakers, the riveters, the pass-boys, the fitters and turners and the painters. Local men, all, or near enough.

The materials too. The concrete was mixed from the Brisbane earth: the gravel dredged from the bed of the river itself, just upstream from where the bridge will cross it, and the sand from the Pine River to the north. The clay for the cement from nearby Darra, the lime from coral dredged at Mud Island in Moreton Bay. And though the iron ore was mined at Iron Knob in South Australia, and the steel manufactured at Newcastle and at Port Kembla, the steelwork was fabricated in Brisbane.

Lawrence had set to work and the science of engineering took over. Workshops set up at sites on the southern and northern banks of the river. The steel fabrication workshop established at Rocklea six miles away – the girders and struts and beams cut there and transported to the bridge sites when needed.

To build a bridge:

Concrete towers – the piers – are erected at intervals leading up to both banks of the river. The piers are linked by steelwork, before the roadway decking is laid horizontally upon the steelwork from tower to tower until the bridge is complete. Their task in constructing this bridge was complicated by the different heights on either bank of the river, and the width to be spanned: the southern bank is at water level, the land a low finger of ground, while the northern bank is a cliff, the bridge hurtling off the escarpment into space.

So first the concrete. There were the approaches to the bridge. The southern approach rising long and gradual from the flat-tipped peninsula so the land itself is lifted higher, and then sealed into place by reinforced concrete retaining walls. From the north the streets were reconstructed and redirected, the northern approach a roadway leading towards a cliff.

Then follow the piers. Pair after pair sunk into the earth. Thick concrete towers marching two by two towards the river from

Bridge

the south. Then the anchor piers, one on either side of the river, massive and immovable, lynch-piers for the steelwork, later. Finally the two main piers sunk below the river, with the south main pier one hundred and thirty feet deep, the last thirty solid rock.

How to excavate so far under water, how to pour concrete below the waterline? Watertight airlock chambers were ordered, and the men sealed off under water, under earth – sealed in caissons, the chambers open at the bottom, the water kept out by the air pressure. But the air pressure is always dangerous, deadly for those working in the underwater chambers, so the men had rotated in one-hour shifts below the riverbed, the slow return to the surface taking one and a half hours, for fear of the bends. And the constant noise of shovelling concrete then was deafening.

These working chambers, the cylindrical caissons, had sunk day by day deeper into the earth below the riverbed. The walls of the concrete caissons are nearly ten feet thick, the cylinders thirty feet across. Eventually they become permanently embedded there, and metamorphose from excavation chambers, to the very foundations of the piers themselves. The men left and the chambers of air were filled with liquid concrete, which sets in time and place.

Upon the foundations of these caissons now, the two main piers themselves rise. Like the smaller approach piers, the main piers are two tapered rectangular shafts, though tied together below the waterline, and braced again at the top in an elegant arch.

After the concrete, the steel. 'Man's masterpiece,' Bradfield likes to say to Lawrence.

Four

Stahl rests the flat of his palm against the girder in front of him at waist-height. First on the outside where the sun hits it and then the inside where it is in shadow, feeling the difference in temperature already.

'Come on,' says O'Hara, and he motions Stahl with a nudge of his head towards the ladder.

Stahl backs towards the edge of the staging, finds the ladder's top rung with his right boot, and steps down. As Stahl disappears O'Hara bends his knees and squats for a moment, feeling the muscles along his upper thighs stretch tight and burn. He rises again, straightens, and shakes his legs out before following Stahl down the ladder.

They descend through the steelwork, picking a course

Bridge

down the webbing of girders. They drop through the sections of bridge-work they know so well, so differently. They know it physically, as their searching hands and uncertain feet and thumping hearts have learnt it. An extension of their own bodies. As if it is a part of themselves that has been growing.

They also know the steelwork as the engineers have asked them to learn it: as a pattern of letters and numbers. Like a jigsaw, with each piece of the puzzle marked. AU4 – anchor span upper chord member number four. CL5 – cantilever span lower chord member number five. SM2 – suspended span middle member number two. A neat pattern of letters and digits. Like numbered vertebrae making up a backbone. Each with a designated place, each with its fit.

They descend the steel until, nearing the lateral bracing of the bridge deck, they realise they are not alone. It is still early, the city is still rising, but making his way along the deck on the other half of the bridge is the tall figure of the engineer, Lawrence. Immaculately dressed in coat, shirt and tie, he is striding along the southern half of the bridge towards where the work has paused, his cane feeling its way in front of him towards the chasm in the centre.

On their half of the structure O'Hara and Stahl reach the decking, dropping with only the lightest of sounds from the vertical to the horizontal. O'Hara touches Stahl on the arm and they turn, moving towards the middle of the bridge, moving now towards the engineer. They step along the ten-foot timber boards laid as walkways over the deck's steel framework. They pass beneath the travelling crane, quiet on its gantry like some giant slumbering insect. The two men duck under its hanging proboscis and the length of chain suspended from its tip. As they pass the machine O'Hara reaches up and pushes the chain-links, casual, familiar. The chain sways and creaks behind them, slow and calm.

The engineer has reached the end of the southern suspended span when O'Hara and Stahl reach the limit of the northern decking.

'Morning,' O'Hara calls out across the thirty feet of space between them. His voice is clear, but the gap in the bridge is a vortex that sucks words, language, into itself.

'Good morning, gentlemen.'

'Not today, Mr Lawrence?' O'Hara enquires.

'Not today, gentlemen,' the engineer says. He is firm, final, though his decision was made only now, in this moment of speaking. By the time it reaches the two of them it is almost a whisper. *Gentlemen*. Quaint.

'Thank you, sir.'

O'Hara had intended the 'sir' to carry a light irony, a subtle pointedness in response to the engineer's 'gentlemen'. But it doesn't. Irony is not something he yet knows how to control. Not over this space. Instead his words sound perfectly polite and O'Hara feels the small failure of his communication: that the engineer will not recognise in him anything more than yes sir, no sir, three bags full sir.

Across the gap, the engineer turns his back and makes his way off the bridge.

Five

O'Hara and Stahl enter the Empire Hotel on Brunswick Street, deep in Fortitude Valley. It is breakfast time now, and there are already men inside leaning over plates with food letting off heat. The two of them locate Hodges at a table, dwarfing a plate with his shoulders. Hodges' eating is a physical thing. His shirt sleeves are already rolled above his elbows, his day's work begun with this meal. His thickly haired forearms and the muscles beneath are taut with effort. Hodges' ragged felt hat is still on his head, broad-brimmed, though pushed back so that the entirety of his blank forehead is visible. He doesn't notice O'Hara and Stahl until they are on top of him.

'You're murdering that breakfast, Billy-boy,' O'Hara greets him and takes a seat.

'Huh?'

'Take your time over it, Billy. String it out. We're not going in today.'

'What?' Hodges looks from O'Hara to Stahl and then back to O'Hara.

'Laid off until further notice,' O'Hara says.

'What!' Hodges exclaims. 'You're not serious!'

'Look at that face,' O'Hara says, nodding towards Stahl whose chin is lowered into his hands, his elbows propped on the table, acting glum, 'is that the face of a joker?'

'Noooo,' Hodges says, examining Stahl's face. His dubiousness transforms into anger. 'I don't believe it. What happened? What . . . ?'

'Just came from the site office. There's a sign on the door of the changing shed. A health and safety problem.'

'What's it say?'

'It says,' O'Hara intones like a newsreel reader: 'On Account of William Hodges' Excessive Consumption of Baked Beans for Breakfast, this Site has Become a Health Hazard.'

'Bastards,' Hodges mutters as Stahl begins to laugh. 'Bastards,' he says again and shakes his head before returning to his beans and toast.

O'Hara reaches over and slaps Hodges on the shoulder. 'Come on, Billy-boy, you've got to admit that you do get a bit ripe about mid-morning.'

'Piss off,' Hodges growls.

The waitress, a middle-aged woman with long dark hair pulled into a bun, calls out to them. 'Ready to eat boys?'

'Same as him, thanks, Betty,' O'Hara calls back, motioning to Hodges' plate and giving him a wink as he looks up.

Bridge

They've gotten to know the waitress since they've been coming here and they like her. She is older than they are, but not yet beyond them. She manages them. Is stern or teasing or efficient, depending on her mood, or theirs. She looks after them and, for what they are doing, she respects them.

'Righto then,' Betty says as she takes down the order. 'Charlie?'

'Toast and coffee,' Stahl says looking up at her and noticing the pins in her hair. She gives him a smile before making for the counter and placing their order.

Stahl turns to Hodges. 'Jack's serious. There's no work today. The conditions aren't right. It's wait and see tomorrow.'

Hodges ignores Stahl and continues to eat.

'Hi ho!' A high-pitched voice calls out from across the room. Carleton comes towards them. He lives at home, has breakfast before he leaves, but likes to join them here before the working day begins. He reaches the table and settles clumsily into the remaining chair.

'The weather's not right. It's not happening today, Carleton,' Stahl tells him.

'Don't believe a word they say,' Hodges mutters.

'We've just seen Lawrence down at the bridge,' Stahl continues. 'It's too hot a day. The bridge can't be closed. We've got the day off.'

Carleton looks across to O'Hara who gives a short nod.

'Settle in, Carleton,' O'Hara says, 'we can take our time this morning.' O'Hara pauses – 'Seconds of beans for you Billy?'

'Piss off.'

Carleton can't hold on any longer, and the question bursts from him: 'What's happening?'

137

The high-pitched enthusiasm of his greeting distorts into a childish plea. There is something here the men know. And he – young, growing, shining Carleton – is desperate to have it.

O'Hara answers, patient.

'We can't link the bridge unless the weather's just right. We're looking for a day when there is only the smallest temperature change. It's got to be warm enough in the morning, but not rising too much. So the whole bridge is the same temperature. An overcast day, that's what we're after. That would be perfect.'

Carleton looks at Stahl, at Hodges, but neither of them are listening.

'I still don't understand,' he says to O'Hara, his need to know greater than any embarrassment.

'What do you know about steel?'

Carleton looks at him blankly, the question too big before him.

'Expands with the heat, contracts with the cold,' O'Hara answers his own question for the boy.

Hodges laughs, the sound of a mule, and thumps Carleton on the shoulder:

'You'll learn about *that* when you get older,' he snorts.

O'Hara ignores him.

'On an overcast day there's less risk of one side of the bridge heating faster than the other, of the bridge itself getting out of shape.'

Carleton starts nodding.

'I've got it,' he says, his head bouncing up and down, faster and faster in growing enthusiasm.

Bridge

'Watch it, lad,' O'Hara says to him, 'you'll shake something loose if you're not careful.'

O'Hara goes out onto the street where he buys the morning edition of the *Telegraph* and brings it back for them to read, dividing it and handing pages to Stahl. They eat and read without talking, though Carleton is distracted, caught still in his thoughts, and doesn't look over O'Hara's shoulder as he usually would.

When they are done, Betty clears their plates and brings them coffee, wiping her hands on her apron by habit as she lingers at their table. She knows their routines, knows their work, follows the progress of it, even feels part of it through them. She passes on the stories they tell to her husband at night, to her girlfriends. Stories with currency, weight, authority.

'You boys should be getting off to work, shouldn't you?'

Stahl fills her in.

'Uh-huh,' she says, her head nodding slowly as she considers what Stahl has said. She feels let down, slightly annoyed. She can't help it, though she has no right. Partly it is from the disappointment, but it is also because she feels left out. 'So it's out of your control, then? You spend four years getting this far, and at the end of the day it's still Nature's say?'

None of them respond. There is more than just observation in her comments. They feel the criticism. It is personal. They don't know what to say, though she stands there still, wanting an answer of some sort.

'So, Nature's still in control,' she repeats, prodding, challenging.

'Yep,' O'Hara says, short and curt and irritated, ending the conversation. The waitress turns away shaking her head.

'No,' says Carleton when she is gone, 'I think they know exactly what they're doing.'

Carleton is the boatman. While the others work the steel a hundred feet or more above, Carleton works the river, patrolling the water under the bridge in his dinghy, collecting anything that falls from the superstructure and floats. He ties his boat up under the Howard Smith Wharf on the northern bank every evening, and every morning at eight o'clock rows out to the centre of the river where he stays for as much of the day as possible, positioning the dinghy beyond the range of falling objects. Whenever a steamer passes by he pulls anchor and returns to the bank, rowing hard to evade the ships, their wake and the obscenities hurled at him by their crews.

On the river Carleton has learnt to listen. Spending all day on the water in the middle of the river waiting for objects to fall, it is impossible to see everything. So Carleton learns to hear. Usually when something goes over a worker will call out from above, and if Carleton himself hasn't seen the thing plunge, he'll follow the pointing man's finger to the place on the river where it has landed, expanding ripple-rings marking the spot with precision.

So Carleton knows the sounds of objects hitting the river. He's learnt to discriminate between the routine noises of river life — oars entering and leaving the water, ropes thrown from boat to wharf and falling short, gulls diving for food, and pelicans taking flight — and the sounds of things falling accidentally from the bridge into the water. First Carleton learnt to filter the familiar sounds so it was only the sound of debris hitting the surface which turned his head. Then he learnt the different sounds that things make through the air in the split-second before hitting the water. That the whistle of air from a plank of wood is different from a paintbrush, or a tin, or a man's jacket or his hat. That falling objects have their own accents.

Carleton sits on the river and longs to be part of the brotherhood high on the steel above. To be accepted by the workers, one of them, and part of this great bridge. To prove himself.

But there are obstacles. He is on the water, they are in the air. He is the youngest. And – it is this he fears is fatal – his background sets him apart. Carleton is a son of the professional class, the connected class. His parents know the chief steel engineer Lawrence, personally, a relationship which led to the job. There had been a dinner party at the engineer's home, a dinner to which even the 'children' were invited, Carleton having just finished school. He paid keen attention to the engineer's reports of the bridge's progress, and the engineer had been impressed by the boy's interest, his unusual enthusiasms. Later Carleton's father enquired over a pipe of tobacco in the drawing room after the meal if there might be any work for his son. The engineer offered to see what he could do, and called the next day about the dinghy job. The perfect job for a schoolboy rower like Carleton, the engineer had joked with him his first day on the river. Later, in moments of doubt, Carleton wondered if the position had been created for him, though he was too fearful of the answer to ask.

Carleton feels the things that set him apart, but he is determined to make up for them.

And he has his stories. Though they are not stories in the true sense. More theories. What Carleton does, is unveil theories.

Great verbal maps of how the world works: intricate patterns of behaviour, of class and migration and wealth and war. Of economies and what shakes them. Of nations and what holds them together. They are the products of sleepless nights, and days floating on the river, of his whirring, fervent, dreaming, wondering mind.

'I've got this theory.'

That was how he'd start. It was always unexpected. The men would be drinking beer, throwing darts, or waiting at the racecourse for the gates to open. There'd be a pause in the talk, and Carleton would lean in towards them, catch one or two of them in the eye and say it: *I've got this theory*. Someone would groan, or laugh or slap him on the back in mock-derision. But they listen. His theories are irresistible. They hear him out. And laying down his theories he is no longer an awkward youth with an ambiguous job on the river. He is transformed. He is an entertainer, strange and unpredictable, vulnerable and powerful.

After the waitress from the Empire has left their table, turned and left them with their inadequacies, Carleton says, 'I think they know exactly what they're doing. Listen, I've got this theory.'

No one teases him today. They are off-balance, and are glad for the distraction, something to fill their uneasy silence. And if Carleton's theory offers an explanation to a doubt which is in them too, then so much the better.

'There's nothing they don't know,' Carleton continues, feeding off their interest. 'The engineers and the surveyors know. They're just giving Nature her head for a bit. But they'll reign

Bridge

her in when it's time. Like breaking in a horse.' Here Carleton turns to Hodges who comes from the land. He animates his words with gestures. 'Let them play, let them wear themselves out, wait for the right moment, then bang: the bridle's on and you've got 'em.'

'It's different,' Hodges says. 'That's just a horse, this is about building a great bloody bridge over a great bloody broad river, mate.'

'The principle's the same, but,' Carleton responds. 'They know building bridges like you know breaking horses.'

Carleton isn't sure if Hodges has ever broken in a horse but he takes a punt.

'They know every piece of this bridge,' he goes on. 'Better than any of us. We're just filling in their plans. They know to the half degree how hot the furnace needs to be before the steel can be fabricated, to the cubic inch how much cement we're going to need, to the foot how many ironbarks and how many grey gums need to be cut for the falsework. They even know exactly how many rivets are needed to hold this thing together. It's all been worked out. *Everything!* Everything's been factored in.'

Carleton quietens. They are with him. He senses it. He leans forward, across the table, closer to them all, his face flushed. They wait for him, for the next part. The heart of it, this, his theory.

'And I reckon they've factored in how many of us are going to die building this bridge.'

There's a silence.

He sweeps their faces, searching out their reactions, whether or not he has lost them, whether he has gone too far. O'Hara is expressionless, staring at him hard, waiting for him to continue. Stahl is intrigued. But Hodges. Hodges rolls his eyes, derisive.

'Bloody hell, kid. Accidents. *Accidents.* That's all they are. It happens or it doesn't. It's no one's fault, or if it is, it's whoever made the mistake. Jackson, or Myerhoffler or whoever slipped up.'

Carleton doesn't answer straight away. The two dead men have joined them. He understands that, though they died before he started. He never knew them, but Jackson and Myerhoffler have been called up by Hodges and now sit with the four of them.

Jackson died on 13 May 1939, carrying a plank of ironbark across his shoulders. A rogue gust of wind took it and twisted him around and off-balance and off the main deck and then long seconds later onto the ground below. Myerhoffler was hit by a section of steelwork being craned into place the previous July, his temple taking a clean blow from the swinging frame, his body crumpling.

O'Hara and Stahl wish Hodges hadn't spoken the names of the dead men, hadn't violated their memory by using them for what is, after all, just an argument. Hodges shouldn't have called them up. No one says anything for a long time.

'I'm not saying that they *caused* the deaths, but.' Carleton begins again. 'I'm not saying any of the engineers actually killed Jackson and Myerhoffler. I'm not saying that at all, Billy. What I'm saying is that they know how many there'll be. It's like the rivets. They may not know which rivet goes where, but they know exactly how many they need. It's the same thing. You heard Irish the other day. He's seen men die around the world. The Golden Gate in San Fran, and the Sydney Harbour Bridge before here. He's seen men die. It's always been the same. The

Bridge

Pyramids, the Great Wall of China, Westminster Cathedral, Big Ben, the Empire State –'

He is getting excited, looks like he is ready to list every great building or monument he knows. But O'Hara interrupts him with a piercing look, pinning him:

'How do they work it out then, in this theory of yours?'

Carleton calms himself with a couple of slow breaths. 'I don't know that. But it's just a calculation, that's all it is. There'll be a formula. Based on what they know from other bridges, from other building sites. Based on how long construction takes, what type of job it is, how much height work there is. Those types of things. It's factored in. They'll know.'

'Rubbish,' Hodges snarls, glaring at Carleton.

'No, it's not.' Determined. 'And you know what? It's probably even in the tender. It'll be in the plans – the number of lives they expect to lose.'

Carleton hasn't thought about this before. This wasn't part of the theory he'd been developing on the water, waiting for men to fall. It just rushed out, this need for corroboration. Rushed out under the pressure of O'Hara's question, and the heat of Hodges' disdain.

'Rubbish,' Hodges says again, but this time it is a mutter which trails away and swallows itself at the prospect the boy's theory could be proved.

'I bet you it's in the plans,' Carleton repeats, 'that there's a number in there.'

It is quiet. Nothing happens. There is a long lull. Like waiting for the wake of a small boat to reach the banks of a wide river. In time the men rise from the table and leave the hotel, the prospect of death accompanying them, opaque and ambiguous.

Six

Men die on bridges. It is what happens. Men die that a bridge is born. They all understand it, each of them who leaves his home in the morning to mount the steel. Men will die. Enough precautions cannot be taken. Or sometimes, the most superstitious of them believe, it is in spite of the precautions. *Do not test the Lord your God.* Some of them will die. Some among them will be selected. They know this, are ready for it, or at least accept it. What they do not know is who. The certainty and the uncertainty draw them closer, and into a larger destiny, rarefied.

But Carleton does not understand. He does not understand, as he lists the engineering feats of his schoolboy history lessons – the Pyramids, the Empire State Building, the Hoover

Bridge

Dam, the Sydney Harbour Bridge — that O'Hara and Stahl and Hodges *long* to be part of that history. They all know the toll but they have no need to speak of it. The sixteen who died for the Sydney Harbour Bridge. The eleven on the Golden Gate. That Brooklyn Bridge claimed twenty-seven. That Hoover Dam, ruthlessly pursued by its engineers gluttonous for construction bonuses, took one hundred and twelve lives. That thousands perished pushing blocks of Egyptian granite into pyramids. That New York, which sought to span earth and sky rather than merely the banks of a river, was unrelenting in the human tithe paid to it. Some of the men on the bridge could give these statistics if they were pressed, like cricket scores. But the figures are ephemeral, almost inconsequential. Pale and mean beside the achievements themselves. Beside the great events of the age.

The thought is intoxicating: that history might one day add *this* bridge to that group! That provincial Brisbane with its four hundred thousand citizens and its fat lazy river, has given them a chance at glory.

Carleton understands none of this as he rows his boat about on the river below them, busy with *saving* things, with *preventing* things.

No, it is not the dying that disturbs them, but that the engineers might already know the exact numbers. That the game is rigged. That the forces of fate can be documented in advance, history calculated according to some formula. It is this that feels like an abuse of trust. A blasphemy.

Seven

It is nearly three-thirty in the afternoon. O'Hara and Stahl rest on the grass in a park at the northern end of the bridge.

O'Hara balances a pyramid of small stones on his elbow, which he has raised parallel to his eyes. The pebbles are sedimentary gravel dredged from the floor of the river, destined for concrete mix if he hadn't scooped this handful from the pile at the foot of the north pier. O'Hara balances the pebbles on his cocked elbow and then, when perfectly still, whips his arm forward and catches them mid-air. The stones thud into his palm. He increases their number by one with each successful catch. Eight, then nine, then ten, until there are too many to fit in the mitt of his hand as he scoops them out of the air. When eventually he drops some and the stones clatter to the ground,

Bridge

he begins the game again. Increasing the numbers one by one till he misses once more. O'Hara passes the time. He balances, whips, catches. Balances, whips catches. Testing himself.

Beside him Stahl is sketching. A pad rests on his knees and he is intent on whatever river scene has caught his attention below them. His head rises from the pad to take something more in, or to check or correct what he has seen, and then he lowers his eyes once more and his hand with the charcoal resumes its work on the paper.

Something distracts O'Hara from his game. In the mid-distance the engineer Lawrence appears, accompanied by a girl. The engineer and the girl walk up the slope towards the park and the steelwork. Her presence softens the tall man in the suit. Her skin is white where she has pulled the sleeve of her school coat up her forearm. The hem of her skirt sways with her gait. She follows the engineer with a deliberate stride until together they stop at the escarpment on Bowen Terrace, their faces to the river and the bridge.

O'Hara knows the girl is Lawrence's daughter. They all do. They have seen her visit the engineer at the site over the years, sometimes by herself, sometimes with a younger sister. Coming over from her school at the close of day to meet the engineer and walk with him down to the ferry terminal at Customs House, going home together across the river. Over the years she has grown up before the men, almost without them being aware.

The engineer's daughter lingers beside her father as he stands like a statue looking out over his work. She knows better than to touch his elbow, or break the quiet. She too looks across the river, trying to follow whatever course her father's steady gaze is taking. She sees river, and streets and roads and steelwork rising and boats like toys moving under the half-built steel bridge. She shrinks as she sees nothing more than this at the end of his gaze, knows she cannot penetrate his contemplation, though she feels the growing weight of duty upon her father.

On the sketch pad in Stahl's lap the girl and her father have begun to take shape in charcoal.

O'Hara turns to him. 'Charlie, why don't we ...'

They get up and make for the two figures standing on the escarpment. The engineer and the girl have not moved for some minutes. They look like twin pillars on the cliff. O'Hara and Stahl slow down as they approach the man and his daughter, not ready to be seen.

They watch the girl in her uniform standing still with her back to them in the hard light. A brimmed school hat is pulled down on her head, a ribbon of neck between hat and coat and her straight shoulders. A slight breeze moves across the ground, whispering off the cliff before disappearing into the fall. The breeze shushes itself against the girl's back, pressing her coat and skirt firm against her legs. O'Hara and Stahl see the outline of her calves beneath the skirt for the first time.

O'Hara wills her to turn around, and in time she does. The engineer first, but then, in what seems a synchronised movement, she is turning too. The wind slips under her coat-flap as she shifts, and blows the lapel open as if in slow-motion. With her left forearm she presses the lapel back to her breast

Bridge

and they watch her hands and fingers as she buttons the jacket. Then she is at her father's shoulder again, stepping away from the cliff, walking, brisk, in their direction. Their paths must now cross. O'Hara's heart quickens and his thinking grows suddenly tangled by imagined conversations with the engineer, and the shape of the girl walking at the engineer's side. Before he has settled on something to say, the father and daughter are onto them and O'Hara knows he must speak, but there is nothing and instead it is the engineer's voice he hears.

'Perhaps tomorrow will be our day, Mr O'Hara, Mr Stahl. Let us hope tomorrow will be our day.'

Stahl and O'Hara nod as the engineer and his daughter pass by, and as they follow the departing figures both young men's eyes fix on the girl, and find her looking over her shoulder back at them too.

Eight

It seems to Evelyn Lawrence that her life is fixed on the bridge. She is seventeen. She has been in Brisbane four years. Four years since she completed the long journey from Montreal: the train across Canada to Vancouver, the ship across the Pacific to Sydney, the final leg by steamer from Sydney to Brisbane, the bay and the river narrowing as they neared Petrie Bight where she disembarked. She and her father arriving ahead of her mother and sister. Being the elder daughter, she was the one chosen to accompany her father on the voyage to Australia, the one who would help him settle in and prepare a house for the rest of the family. They began with a rented house in the odd-sounding suburb of Coorparoo, then when the others arrived, a grander home at Kangaroo Point,

Bridge

closer to her father's work, more suitable for entertaining in the evenings.

Evelyn has watched the bridge grow day by day from her school perched on the high bank of the river. Each lunchtime she comes out onto the terrace, a viewing point protected within the walls of the old school. She observes the men and machines moving about on either side of the river and on the steelwork between. When she first began to watch, all she saw was movement. Human bodies arriving or leaving or waiting. Random movement of shapes that were not people, not men to her, but merely figures – scaled-down versions of the dolls she played with as a child. She saw nothing that was not moving, not a blur.

In her watching it was always the figure of her father she sought, high up on the bridge deck in front of her. He was easily distinguishable up there on the bridge. Tall and lean and carrying his light maple-wood cane. It was not until one of her new classmates asked, that she realised her father didn't actually need the cane. Had no limp.

He'd been to war, she knew. She had seen the citation for his Military Cross: *For conspicuous gallantry and devotion to duty while repairing a track. He succeeded in maintaining practically uninterrupted communications though the track was broken in nine places and the shelling was very heavy*. Her tall strong father was once a Captain in a war, though as far as she knew, he'd come back unscathed.

In the days when she first arrived at the school, if she did not find him out there on the bridge at lunchtime when she looked, she would return to class with panic stirring in her stomach. In those early days she retreated into herself, was even further away from her classmates than usual.

★

At first she was a thing of interest to the other girls, a thing to be wondered at and talked about. She was tall like her father, and her skin was pale. When she first arrived she wore hats they saw in magazines like *The New Yorker*, which they read in the drawing rooms of the wealthier parents. With the school years between Montreal and Brisbane out of kilter, she was six months older than most of them, six months more mature. Or six months more sophisticated, something her classmates felt but could never admit. Her accented way of saying things, and the sure rhythm of her speaking, added to her allure.

As did the distance she kept from them. At first it was a polite distance, or a homesickness, or so they thought as they competed with each other for her attention. But as each of her would-be best-friend suitors fell away, as she failed to share gossip about the bridge, as the distance she claimed from them remained, she was allowed her place apart. Allowed her ritual of going out onto the school terrace alone each lunchtime to stare at the bridge.

She would usually catch sight of him. An erect figure with a long stride, appearing and disappearing behind fretwork. Or a man in a suit standing motionless before a group of attentive workers.

As the early months passed she began to lose the sheer physicality of her disappointment if she could not pick him out among the other men on the bridge. Finally, when it was a year, and then a second year, and she continued to grow and to settle, each day's lunchtime searching for him had become habit rather than need.

Bridge

Increasingly she saw shape and detail in what had once only been movement. The crane standing further along the gantry, its head pointing north or south or east or west depending on the wind. Motor lorries parked where they hadn't been the previous day. New girders added. A growth in the scaffolding, extra trusses. Fewer – or greater – numbers of men on the scaffolding. Men other than her father.

Yet time passed too slowly, the bridge marking her days girder by girder, her life measured in the gradual years of the bridge's growth. In the face of her father's unfaltering attention to the lengthening steel span, there are moments when she feels captive to it. Some days, standing on the terrace, the bridge arcing vastly across her vision, she resists it, tips her head and loses herself in the wide sky above.

Nine

Time passes slowly. They enter a second day of waiting, their instructions clear: when the conditions are right, we will send a taxi to pick you up. Early. Don't come in until then.

Many of them go in anyway. To see it, to be near it. After working on it for so long, it is impossible to stay away now. The bridge is a magnet.

Beside the bridge is the school, a citadel or a prison. Irish likens it to Alcatraz. And he tells the men about the jail on the island in the harbour at 'Frisco, which they looked down on as they built the Golden Gate. Here, he says, it is the jail that looks across at you from the top of the escarpment.

Bridge

It reminds Stahl of other things. Of family legends. The scenes his father described of his blood country, the country his father had left. Medieval Rhineland castles. Castle upon castle perched on outcrops of high land looking over the trade-route which was the river Rhine. He knows them by name, like stops on a train line. Schloss Rheinfels, Schloss Schonburg, Gutenfels, Pfalzgrafstein, Stahlbeck, Reichenstein, Rheinstein. The country of his father's youth, river country which his father left for the ports in the north and, later, the long passage to Australia. One day you will see them for yourself, his father tells him, time and again, shaping Stahl's river-memory.

From family legend comes also myth. At a bend in the river, a bend like Petrie Bight though broader and wider in its sweep, sits the Lorelei. It's the sacred bend of the fable of the mermaid and her seductions. On the banks of the Rhine a young mermaid sings, her beautiful voice drawing lonely sailors to their doom on rocks submerged in the river.

Stahl sometimes looks across the airy chasm, at the school, and feels the pull of mermaids.

The afternoon lesson bell rings. Girls leap up and stand by their desks, waiting for permission to leave. Only when there is absolute silence, only when they are all utterly still, their final prayer said, does the nun nod. The girls swirl out of the room, and past Sister who stands like an iron sentinel beside the door. Girls disgorge from classrooms into the courtyard. Those who are not boarders make for the convent gates. There is this daily excitement, and relief, though it is muted by the nuns stationed on balconies, in doorways, behind windows. God *might* be watching, but the nuns definitely are.

Evelyn and her sister Meg walk down the steep driveway towards the arched wrought-iron gate and the public street outside. They are part of a stream. At the street, the current of students parts and the schoolgirls swing either left towards the city or right into the Valley. Evelyn and Meg turn towards the Valley, following the school's high convict-built perimeter wall, as it runs towards the Fortitude Valley shops before turning, a sandstone curve, back up the hill towards the cliff-top and the bridge-site where they will meet their father.

Stahl sketches. He draws the lines of the school building with its turrets, and its austere rows of windows, losing himself in the building's perfect angles and perspectives.

Then he hears the school bell in the distance, chiming the end of classes.

'Come on,' O'Hara says, rising.

Across the road from the school is the vacant block of land set aside for the largest 'new' Cathedral in all of Christendom. Its foundations have been marked out, a below-ground crypt completed, and a fine low sandstone wall teases at the ambitious Cathedral planned for the site. But construction has paused. The Cathedral's completion must now wait until the Archbishop's funds are replenished, following his unsuccessful speculation on the discovery of vast and profitable oilfields at Roma on the Downs country to the west. Roma, Rome, the

Holy See. There were good portents in the name, but the venture was a failure.

Still this remains the Catholic end of town, land where the Catholic businesses took root. And O'Hara is at ease here, feels it is his part of town more than it is Stahl's. Not that he's ever asked – it barely matters. He's just assumed Stahl is Lutheran, like the other Germans he knows. And that therefore O'Hara has some title to this part of the city – no matter how vague – that Stahl does not.

It was not always like this. The first whites in Fortitude Valley were passengers from the *Fortitude*, free men and women, Scots mainly, lured to Australia by a puritan pastor and his promise of land. Pastor Lang was not just an advocate of migration, he was an advocate of *Presbyterian* migration, the only hope for a morally debauched colony, brimming as it was with Catholics of convict stock. The promise, however, went sour. There were no land grants. The two hundred and fifty-three from the *Fortitude* were cast ashore at Moreton Bay in 1849 to settle in the shallow valley to the north of the colony, the valley running down from the river cliffs, and from the hills named for Bowen, a governor.

The Catholics came later, at the turn of the century, when the river rose up and they were forced to flee their south-side homes and businesses. The floods arrived in 1893, and again in 1897, wiping out their South Brisbane shops. Always in exile, always seeking refuge, this time from the river, the Catholic businesses moved into the Valley. Retail stores with names like T.C. Beirne, and Barry & Roberts.

So the Valley is the Catholic business district, but it is the Protestants who run the City. In the early years of the 1930s, when all the talk was of a second bridge across the river, it was the City business lobby that won out. The Grey Street Bridge was erected from South Brisbane to the city centre near Roma Street, a boon to City trade. This new bridge, however, the expansive one where Evelyn's father strides, will serve the Irish Catholic businesses rather than the Protestants, by directing more traffic and more custom their way. From the south side into the Valley, bypassing the City, the bridge offers Catholic prosperity.

Nevertheless, from the girls' convent school, fortress-like behind its high walls on the hill between the Valley and the City, at eye-level with the bridge, the nuns look down upon the Valley and its commerce in some faintly reproving way. This generation of girls, Evelyn's brood, remains unprotected by a great cathedral beside their school grounds.

Evelyn and her sister skirt the Valley, and walk down to the cross-river ferry terminal near Customs House, also sandstone, and copper-domed. A ferry is docking as they reach the jetty. A small group of girls boards the boat for the Holman Street terminal, their school shoes clattering up the plank before dropping into the boat itself, Evelyn and her sister among them.

'My feet hurt,' Meg says as she sits on a wooden bench in the hollow of the ferry.

'Take your shoes off for a minute then,' Evelyn says and Meg bends over to undo her laces and free her feet. There is the noise of the narrow gangway being drawn, and the gate closed. The engine sound deepens and the ferry pulls away from the jetty and into the stream.

Evelyn leaves Meg and makes her way to the front of the

Bridge

ferry where she can feel the wind against her face, and watches the other bank approach. Then she closes her eyes.

'Hello.'

The male voice startles her. She catches her breath and turns. A thrill follows the moment of panic.

'Hello,' she replies. It's the two men from yesterday, closer now. Perhaps only a little older than her, but men, from a world beyond uniforms and bells. The one who had spoken – taller and darker, more muscular across his shoulders – smiles at her, broad and confident. The other man is the more handsome: sandy haired, blue eyes, skin soft despite the workman's tan. He stands half a step back, almost behind his friend. He is smiling too, but to Evelyn, in this shortest of first moments, his eyes rest a little more gently.

'School over?' O'Hara asks.

'Just the homework now,' she says. She laughs out over the railing, but feels disappointed too. That he asked about school, that she replied with homework.

'So you can't escape, hey?' O'Hara grins. 'They won't let you go.'

'It's not too bad.' She feels light-headed. The breeze off the river rustles the locks of hair around her temples, loosens her uniform.

'When do you get to have some fun?' O'Hara asks.

She looks out over the water at the approaching riverbank. 'What's it like?' she says abruptly, turning the conversation.

'What?'

'Working on the bridge.'

'From the top you get the best view in town, for a start,' O'Hara says.

'You can see for miles,' Stahl joins in. 'The mouth of the river and the Bay. The range on the New South Wales border, out to Ipswich, up to the Glass House Mountains.'

'It sounds magical.'

'Yes.' Stahl smiles at her.

'You're lucky,' and for a moment she wishes she could join them, high on the steelwork of the bridge, all giddy excitement and danger.

'And that's just for starters,' O'Hara says. 'From up there, you're so high you can see people moving around below you.'

Evelyn raises her eyebrows, inviting him to continue.

'People doing things. Women in their backyards. Kids in the street.' O'Hara pauses and winks. 'Girls going to school.'

'Well you *are* lucky, then,' she says, hoping she sounds calm, fearing it is too forward, or worse, pathetic.

'Girls catching ferries,' he continues, 'girls talking to handsome men ...'

They all laugh.

The ferry bumps against the Holman Street jetty and the pilot puts the boat into slow reverse, manoeuvring it alongside the wharf. The deckhand tightens the rope which he has looped over the iron cleat, pulling the ferry firm against the timber landing.

Evelyn returns to the bench where Meg has put her shoes back on and is retying her laces. O'Hara and Stahl remain on the front deck. Evelyn wonders if they will get off here too, or did they just come for the ferry ride? The passenger gate slides across and people pass through it onto the gangway, the hollow sound of footsteps on timber suspended over air. Meg stands. Evelyn picks up her own satchel and leads the way to the gate, glancing at O'Hara and Stahl as she passes through.

Bridge

'I hope you enjoyed your day off,' she says, and smiles.

They laugh.

Evelyn is walking down the gangway, stepping onto the jetty, leaving the two men on the ferry, wondering if this is all over now.

'Come for a swim!' O'Hara calls out finally, almost too late.

A shiver runs down the back of her neck.

'Where?' she says, turning half around, not quite facing the two of them leaning over the ferry railing above her.

'The Mowbray Park Baths. Been there before?'

'No.' She must be blushing. The deckhand is watching as he unhitches the rope and prepares the ferry to depart.

'You can almost . . .' O'Hara turns to look downriver, to see if the pool is visible from here. But it is not. 'Right beside the ferry terminal at Mowbray Park. Take a ferry. Or you could walk.'

'Thanks,' she says, and she begins to move away.

'Tonight!' O'Hara calls out.

Ten

A rectangular mesh of wire and wooden palings hangs off big timber pylons sunk into the riverbed, cordoning off a fragment of the river as a swimming pool. Electric lights hang on poles over the pool and the bathing sheds, casting overlapping circles of light.

At eight o'clock Mowbray Park Baths are full of summer swimmers. Young children with their parents. Older children with their friends, adults after work. O'Hara and Stahl have been here for an hour already, swimming and resting and watching and waiting.

The girl and her younger sister arrive. O'Hara and Stahl get out of the water to greet them.

'You made it.'

'We've just finished supper.'

O'Hara wonders if the two girls had difficulty getting away.

'The water's lovely,' he says.

'Come on, then,' says the young girl. 'Let's swim.'

'This is my sister Meg.'

'Hello, Meg,' says Stahl. He is about to introduce himself, to bow even, with some low sweep of his arm, but she is impatient:

'Where can we get changed?'

O'Hara and Stahl answer together, pointing in awkward overlap to the changing sheds.

In the pool they swim. Evelyn's long, languid strokes. Meg swimming out to the fence, touching it, and returning. Laughing, tapping Evelyn lightly on the head, and swimming out again to the perimeter fence with the swiftest of strokes. O'Hara and Stahl treading water, then disappearing below it in duck dives and reappearing in a different spot and Evelyn feigning not to notice. The pool is full of bodies. They lose one another for a time. Meg turns at the outer fence, tiring. She hangs off the perimeter railing catching her breath, and looks for her sister through the swirl of bodies. Evelyn is talking with one of the men near the stairs, the taller one. Bodies splash next to Meg and when the splashing subsides she looks across the pool to the stairs and sees that Evelyn has gone, swimming away, while the man is still there, watching Evelyn's path through the water. Meg waits for her sister to stop so she can wave and catch her attention. A ripple of breeze moves across the water. Suddenly a hand tugs at her ankle below the water and she squeals, kicking the hand away. Stahl bursts from the water in front of her and together they laugh. Evelyn reaches them, pausing to rest on the fence. Floats on her back, her hands reaching behind her head to hold the top rail of the fence, her legs breaking the surface of the water in regular kicks, the water splashing up and out and over them.

Across the river to the north-east a jagged flash of lightning momentarily links earth and sky. Clouds blunt the moon and stars. Swimmers turn in the direction of the strike and count. One, two, three, and get to ten before the thunder begins its roll towards them in the pool. Ten seconds, ten miles. They read summer storms like mariners once read stars, know there is no danger yet, return to their play.

The storm builds, growing out of a strange quarter, for Brisbane, for summer. The flashes in the sky get closer, the rain still distant. Gradually swimmers get out of the water, one by one or in clusters, and walk or skip or hurry to where their towels hang over a railing.

'Come on,' Meg calls finally, 'let's get out! It's getting close.'

She is looking at the lightning and feels the pull of the other bodies leaving the water. A tide of people getting out, the ebb of their bodies. She looks at her sister and then at O'Hara and at Stahl. None say anything, though she knows they have heard. She calls again, this time with the irritation of being ignored.

'Come on, everyone. Time to go.'

Again the other three do not respond and Meg fixes her older sister with a stare.

'Evie, are you coming?'

In silent reply Evelyn curves her body up and away from Meg in a clean dive and disappears below the surface. Meg huffs, turns, and strokes to the shallows where she finds the porphyry stone steps in the pool wall with her feet and climbs out. She grabs her towel from a fence and dries down with the other swimmers who have also left the water to watch the oncoming storm. When she is done, she sits on the stone retaining wall and drapes the towel over her shoulders, pulling down hard on both ends with her hands, feeling the tension of the material across her shoulders. Meg sits and, sulking, waits for her sister and the boys to get out too.

Evelyn is diving. Staying under for long seconds before bursting into the air for just long enough to take her breath. And then she is diving again into the dark of the water. She is momentarily lost to O'Hara and Stahl. Dive after dive she goes under while, above, the storm closes. The boys take short backward strokes, their eyes constantly searching for Evelyn's appearing then disappearing body. They dive too, imitating Evelyn, taking her lead, but their dives are edgy and shallow.

The lightning strikes close. The time between thunder claps shortens. The air thickens. A gust of breeze passes over the surface of the water. O'Hara and Stahl both know the childhood rules for electrical storms: don't stand under trees, and don't stay in the water. Trees and water: both conductors of earthward bolts of light and power.

The sky is illuminated again with another strike across the river. There is pool and river and red-iron roofing of the houses on the opposite bank brought momentarily into blinding relief, and then there is nothing. A giddy nothing, and for the smallest moment afterwards the world around the three swimmers is perfectly black. Their eyes refocus. Slowly the small electrical lights hanging over the pool once more throw their inconsequential light. And just as the swimmers' eyes have grown accustomed to the lantern-lit view of the world, it is taken from them again by a great flash of power.

Each flash gives up the cloud banks that fill the sky. Dark muscular clouds which roll across the heavens.

O'Hara and Stahl stop their diving. Stop their nervous movement and just tread water, trying to stay calm. A lightning bolt strikes the earth somewhere close on the opposite bank of the river, and so lights everything that they see the shape of Evelyn's body under the surface of the water near them. Then she emerges, her head and long hair with water streaming off. She does not gasp for breath but calmly exhales, and breathes in, controlled.

A small playful smile appears on her face as she fixes O'Hara, then Stahl with her gaze. They are the only three left in the pool. She is utterly unhurried. Another strike of lightning illuminates the sky and they tread water, their three small bodies facing each other, marking a triangle on the river. She looks at them, serene. O'Hara and Stahl, treading water before the approaching storm, are held in place by her unspoken challenge. Elemental like the storm. Neither of the boys quite understands the nature of the test, or how it was issued. But it is there, powerful and real. The boys tread their water before the girl, as the storm rushes on.

From what seems like the furthest distance, Meg screams at them to get out, get out.

The storm front's messenger breeze is now a wind which chops the water surface, makes their treading more difficult. A gust of wind rushes across the water, and in its trail big drops of rain begin to thump against the river. The rising wind is everywhere and begins to hollow out a space in O'Hara's mind.

Bridge

Suddenly he hears the urgency of Meg's screaming, and the feel of the raindrops hard on his scalp, and the charging of each of the beads of river-water on his neck and shoulders with static electricity.

And then, another clap of thunder, this time beside his very ear, inside his ear and O'Hara breaks. A reflex turn of his head to look first one way, then the other, searching out – what? But looking outwards now. The thread between the three of them severed. O'Hara turns to the bank and, with strong urgent kicks, is soon at the wall and pulling himself out as the sky is lit again with a sustained series of flashes, O'Hara's flesh a harsh white.

Stahl and Evelyn are only a few strokes behind O'Hara, and they scramble over each other to get out of the water. Meg is there shoving towels at them.

'Idiots! Come on, it's going to bucket down.'

They shelter beside the wall of the changing shed, their four bodies leaning in a row against the weatherboard. The lightning illuminates the driving rain, single and double-headed strikes which crack earthward. The storm has lifted Evelyn. Another lightning strike and she is hooting with laughter and the electricity that is fizzing just beyond their shelter. Her delight is infectious, Meg giggling now too at the stupidity of them all getting caught out. Stahl just laughing, strong.

But O'Hara has gone quiet, has withdrawn, has pulled away from the others. He looks out into the teeming rain. The narrow shelter under the roof's overhang is too small, and O'Hara feels constricted between the rain and the wall and the other three.

Eleven

Saturday, 28 October 1939. Dawn. There is a banging at the entrance to O'Hara's sleep. Bolts hammered into a dream, cracking it open. The knocking shifts to the front door at the end of the hallway as O'Hara opens his eyes. A boarder in another room curses. There is a brief pause in the banging before it starts again, a fistful of the sharpest knocks. O'Hara tosses the sheet and is out of bed, turning the handle of his bedroom door, and padding along the worn hall runner to the end of the corridor. He opens the door onto a man with a beret and a thick moustache.

'O'Hara, Stahl?'

The arrival of the taxi driver is no surprise, but O'Hara is irritated that he has overslept, is not awake to greet the driver.

Bridge

'Be with you in a minute.'

'That's all you've got, mate.'

O'Hara turns, and hurries back down the corridor towards his room, Stahl's head emerging now from his own doorway.

'We're on,' he says.

O'Hara pulls on the clothes that lie draped over the chair in the corner of his room. In less than a minute he is ready and draws the door of his room closed behind him. Stahl has already emerged from his, and is turning a key in the lock. The two of them move quietly down the corridor towards the front door, behind them the sound of other boarders snoring in fits, heaving stale air around their rooms, through the moulded slats of ventilation screens, and into the hall. The taxi driver has returned to his car and the front door of the boarding house is ajar. The doorway is full of a muted light. The two men walk towards it. Their departing footsteps beat a discordant rhythm against the snoring at the back of the house.

O'Hara and Stahl are the first two in the taxi. The driver consults a piece of paper with a long list of typed names, five of which are circled in pencil. He pulls away from the curb in front of the boarding house and makes for a second New Farm address. Then a third. Soon five of them are in the taxi, and then the driver is dropping them off at the bridge-site. Other taxis are arriving and depositing their men.

It is grey and overcast. Low clouds muzzle an early, dull, sun.

The dressing shed spills over with expectancy as the men change into their work gear. The engineer Lawrence gathers them together outside and gives them instructions, a half-time speech from a football coach. Irish mutters as they break and move in different directions along the bridge. There is no need for the instructions. They have been ready for a long time, understood the task and prepared themselves. Soon enough they are moving into position, each aware of what they must do.

To close a bridge: a dull sky, a derrick, the final trusses, the wedges, some men, their bolts and their rivets.

The wedge-operating crews take their places. The eight wedges have been in position for weeks, four at either end of the central suspended span, which is still in two halves, almost brushing, indecently close. *The wedge mechanisms:* eight of them, each as big as a man. Each wedge is forged steel, six feet long – two feet at its widest, tapering down to twelve inches at the thin edge. The wedges have been built into the steelwork, constructed into the superstructure between the end of the cantilever span and the beginning of the suspended span.

A man stands before a wedge, feet planted, shoulders set, hands gripping the rim of the hand-wheel. Now! He heaves, and shoulders the mechanism into movement. The hand-wheel turns the worm-wheel turns the operating screw, the wedge being at the end of the screw. In fractions of inches the eight wedges ease out, and the two halves of the bridge temporarily shorten. The crane lowers the last chords into place, into the newly expanded space. Delicate, precise. Each wedge eases out a little more until the suspended span and the holes of the members of each chord are perfectly aligned. Then in! The bolts driven home. The top chords first. Then the chord splices, the laterals. Then the bottom chords. Pins are driven

Bridge

into the holes – and the suspended span is one. With the last of the pins driven home, the jigsaw is complete. The wedges are withdrawn.

And the river is bridged.

O'Hara folds his arms across his chest and leans back against an upright. Observes people rimming the cliff-tops around them, gathering on the riverbank below. Even from here he can see the smiles, the flutter of pointing hands.

'How's that, mate?' he says.

'Not bad, Jack,' Stahl replies. 'Not bad at all.'

The men laugh and whoop and toss hats all along the bridge. One of the derrick cranes honks its horn like a crowing rooster: *cock-a-doodle-doo*. The second crane joins in, finds the meter of the first, and they are soon hooting in unison *cock-a-doodle-doo, cock-a-doodle-doo*. The hooting swallows the men. Two giant mechanical insects leading them in a round of celebration. Tugs start up on the river below, cars pick up the tune, and the air resounds with the mechanical crowing of scores of counterfeit roosters.

On the water Carleton beats out the same tune on the outside of his wooden-hulled dinghy. *Bang a bang da-bang, bang a bang da-bang.*

From the school on the hill, the girls hear the rising cacophony through their classroom windows and guess. The nun at the head of Evelyn's classroom relents and the girls stream out of the room to the viewing terrace where they look wide-eyed across at the bridge now linked. *At last*, Evelyn thinks, *at last*. She sees her father standing on the decking, hands folded behind his back. She sees her father and smiles for him and his achievement. Though today it is not only him she is seeking out.

Twelve

By the time they are off the bridge, it is after midday and the brewery at the top of the cliff has set up a five-gallon keg inside the changing shed. O'Hara works the tap. He pulls beers, and jokes as he thrusts glasses into his workmates' hands. All the room is before him, the men and their success. O'Hara watches the engineer Lawrence move among them, speaking with one, then another, like a prince at a royal reception.

'Come round this side and take over for a while,' O'Hara says to Carleton, who is lingering near the keg, observing the atmosphere from a distance. Carleton beams. O'Hara pours a last beer. As he hands over the tap to Carleton he roughs him on the shoulder: 'Most important job in the house. Don't muck it up.'

O'Hara approaches the engineer.

'Congratulations, Mr Lawrence.'

'Not at all, Mr O'Hara,' he says, and accepts the beer O'Hara offers. 'This is your work. It is I who should applaud you. So well done, Mr O'Hara. You've done well. We've all done well.'

The two men raise their glasses, take long draughts.

'It went off without a hitch in the end, didn't it?' O'Hara says.

'That it did.'

'According to plan?'

'Quite.'

'Did you expect any problems?'

'One never knows. One plans as well as one can, Mr O'Hara, and the rest is left in the hands of fate.'

The voices of other men bubble inside the shed, boiling out through the doorway, spilling around outside. Someone hoots, another man is slapping people hard on the back.

'What will you do now, Mr Lawrence?'

'There is still work to be done here, Mr O'Hara. After that? Who knows. I expect that the war will keep us busy. But until then,' and Lawrence is extracting himself now, 'there should be work enough here to keep us.'

Bradfield and the politicians arrive for the following morning's front page. Forgan-Smith, the Premier, attempts a speech. He has barely begun when Hodges at the back of the room starts up a chorus of 'Roll Out the Barrel' and the others join him, loud and insistent, till Forgan-Smith gives up and joins the song.

★

Bridge

Out on the decking the roadway workers employed by Hornibrook are still toiling, following the steelwork, laying bitumen behind. The steel men pour ale into billy-cans, disguising the beer and walking the cans out onto the decking, where their mates slough the warming beer down their throats and onto their chins, across the fronts of their chests and onto the hot tar.

The keg empties and the steel men head into the Valley.

The school day finishes and Evelyn is anxious to leave, has been for hours. To get closer. To learn. She collects Meg. They leave the school gates and skirt along the high sandstone wall as they do every day. But today is charged with moment, and Evelyn is impatient in a way which is new to her, finds herself breaking into a run. From ahead, around the curve, comes the sound of voices. Whooping voices competing with each other, then breaking into laughter. Evelyn slows on the footpath, and halts as the towering wall begins its arc up the block. The voices grow, like a wave rolling towards her. She leans forward, her feet still, craning her head around the sweeping curve of the wall, as if it might somehow shield her. About forty men are striding out together along the footpath, coming down the hill from the cliff and the bridge. She catches herself. She takes Meg's hand and waits for the men to reach the intersection and then to pass in front of her on their way to wherever it is they are going.

Behind her other girls are backing up, and though she hears them asking what is happening, she is too excited, too anxious to answer. Soon the men are at the intersection, and all of the girls hush. Evelyn stands at the line of the wall. The men must pass directly in front of her. The laughter of the men pauses briefly when they notice the girls. One of them shouts something. The first of the passing workers bows low in exaggerated greeting, and then each of the men as he passes is laughing and bowing or doffing his hat at the group of stricken schoolgirls blushing on the street corner. Evelyn feels vaguely like a princess.

She recognises most of them as they pass by in a blur. She recognises the men as shapes she has seen from the school at lunchtime, or from her after-school visits to the work-site to collect her father. But the close-grouped smell of them, and their togetherness, and the confidence of it, is strange to her. Also strange, and unsettling, to be looking for one in particular among them.

The wave of men finally delivers Stahl. He sees her too, and slows. Pulls himself from the stream of workers, and stands before her. Then he has her hand in his and is lifting it to his lips and she is standing paralysed, her body belonging to someone else. She feels the touch of his lips on the back of her hand, and his eyes not leaving hers.

Then he too is gone, swept away, and Evelyn is left with the humming voices of her schoolmates behind her wondering aloud what has just happened.

She is unsure what she has witnessed, what she has been part of. A man has kissed her hand. In mock chivalry — she knows that — but it was *her* hand all the same. There has been too much passing by. Evelyn is tired of it. The river traffic passing by on the water below the school, the bridge itself passing by her consciousness as it grows too slowly towards completion, her father moving silently and at a distance through the years of her life. Evelyn can't stand the passing by any longer.

'Go on home without me, Meg.'

She doesn't need to keep them in sight. She knows where they are by the migrating din of their voices. She descends into the Valley after them. She doesn't know what she is doing. Knows only that something is happening. Trusts it. She rounds a corner and sees the tail of bridge-workers going into the Empire Hotel. A tram passes, its rumble refracting into mere sound, undistinguishable. She has stopped thinking. She draws closer, and soon is passing across the hotel doorway, neck turned, peering in, seeing the swirl of men's bodies filling the pub out, unable to see Stahl among them in the quickness of her glance. Evelyn turns around and passes before the hotel again, pausing longer this time at the doorway. Stopping. Among the men inside she sees O'Hara. Sees him talking, sees his hands moving, sees him place his glass of beer on a railing so both hands are free, gesturing. He reaches for his glass again and raises it to his lips, taking this as an opportunity to scan the room. And then it is her that he sees through the doorway.

Evelyn pulls herself out of sight, emitting a startled cry, then stifling it as quickly again with her hands. She feels suddenly exposed. She lets out another muffled sound and shakes her head. She should go. She fears hearing O'Hara's voice calling to her. She starts to move. Then a voice, though not O'Hara's.

'Wait up.'

She keeps walking.

'Hey, wait up a bit.'

It is Stahl.

Evelyn almost doesn't stop. When she does she mumbles

The Comfort of Figs

something, her eyes not settling. Her head lowered still, conscious of so much.

'Hello,' says Stahl. He is smiling.

She slows now. Breathes. Lifts her head.

'Hello.'

'We joined the bridge today.'

'Yes ... congratulations.'

A short pause.

'I enjoyed the swim,' he says, excited, proud, brave.

She smiles, nods.

'So did I.'

'Let's do it again.'

'I'd like to.'

Stahl leans across and kisses her again, this time on the cheek.

'I'd better go,' she says.

'Let me walk with you.'

They walk together back up the hill, and down to the ferry terminal, and she is getting on and he wants to touch her hand but doesn't.

The engineer Lawrence watches his daughter's ferry pull away from the bank of the Brisbane River and observes the riveter Karl Stahl standing by the terminal railing long after the ferry has gone.

Stahl visits. Evenings of waiting in the riverside park opposite Evelyn's home, leaning on the trunk of a low-branched fig tree, the city at his back across the river. A sliver of moon, or none at all. He is always in shadow. On the other side of the street is her house, tall and erect and grand and alluring. During the day, or lit up, the house is crisp white, trimmed with emerald green. The front stairs rise through a thicket of azalea bushes to a landing, then rise again to the wide verandah which wraps around three sides of the house. Evelyn has described to him the territory beyond the verandah, beyond what he can see from the road. She has pointed out the master bedroom, and in the wing of children's bedrooms which one is hers. She has described the drawing room with fireplace where the engineer and his friends smoke pipes after evening meals, a piano room, a lounge room. From outside where he waits Stahl sees a chandelier hanging from a ceiling. 'Venetian,' she had said to him. 'Murano glass my parents brought back from a trip to Italy.' The mention of Europe is a small thrill to him, an enticement.

Stahl watches for movement. A body passing across a light or a window. Someone rising from an armchair in the reading room, a lamp muted as sheet music or a closing piano lid passes across its beams. The front door opening, light flooding out. The engineer and his wife at the doorway, and guests leaving.

Then Evelyn in her bedroom. She draws a curtain open and knows he will be waiting in the street. She draws a curtain and is haloed in the light of the room. Stahl watches her silhouette appear, watches her arms as they signal. It is safe. It is not. I can come. I cannot.

Tonight she comes. The light goes out in her room. Stahl moves away from the tree and the house. He stays in shadow, moving through the narrow park till he reaches the hospital grounds. He crosses a patch of lawn and descends a flight of rock-hewn steps to a viewing terrace and a bench facing the river. The evening murmurs. He looks for the moon once more. He waits again, so long, and feels himself tremor.

Evelyn leaves her house, carefully opening and then closing the door which leads from the breakfast room into the backyard. She finds the gate in the dark and raises the catch, careful not to make a sound. At the foot of the gate is a stone which she nudges into place with her foot, leaving the gate ajar. She walks down the long easement, tall timber fences on either side overgrown with vines. The easement opens onto the street. She turns to her right and is on Main Street, which she follows before rounding the block and making for their meeting place. Stahl, seated on the bench, rises as she approaches. She takes his hands.

Lawrence looks for Stahl. He comes out of his site office and walks onto the superstructure. He holds his cane mid-length as he walks along the temporary decking, tapping it against his leg. Men greet him as he passes.

'Careful there, Mr Lawrence,' someone says as he steps over a gap between two planks.

Lawrence nods in acknowledgment. He feigns interest in the progress of some task, watches as Stahl and O'Hara and Hodges work, punching rivets. The team breaks for lunch and Lawrence calls.

'May I have a moment, Mr Stahl?'

Stahl and O'Hara and Hodges glance at each other, before Stahl separates from the other two.

'Tell me about yourself, Mr Stahl.'

'Sir?'

'Who are you?'

'I'm sorry, sir?'

Stahl is nervous. He is working for this man. He is seeing his daughter.

'Your life, Mr Stahl, your life.'

'My life?'

'Your background. Your name. Where do you come from, Mr Stahl?'

'My father worked in the shipyards in Germany before coming out.'

'Where exactly was that, Mr Stahl?'

'Hamburg.'

Lawrence nods. The great port city, active again now in the build-up to war, the German rearmament. He adds this, despite himself, as evidence against the boy.

'But you were born in Australia?'

'Yes.'

Stahl feels he is being reduced.

'Have you ever been there?'

'I know it. From stories. My father's stories.'

'And where is your father now, Mr Stahl?'

Stahl is reluctant to give the engineer any more, doesn't know where he is leading, what he will do with this information.

'Here.'

'In Brisbane?'

'Yes.'

'He works, Mr Stahl?'

'In the shipyards still.'

'With Evans Deakin then?'

'Yes.'

'So that's how you came to work here?'
'Yes. Through my father.'
'You live with your family, then, Mr Stahl?'
Stahl hesitates, this intrusion too great, this belittling too much.
'Does this interrogation have a purpose, sir?'
The reversal unsettles the engineer, and he stumbles.
'Well I . . .'
It is Stahl who breaks away.
'Thank you, Mr Lawrence.'

Lawrence rides Stahl's team: rides them hard as they cook and punch their rivets. The art of riveting: too cool and the rivets won't fit, too hot and they scale and have to be replaced. And the inspectors are ruthless, mean men who get pleasure in rejecting rivets each evening, marking the scaled ones with chalk. Lawrence pulls an inspector aside, gives the man his head, pointing out Stahl and O'Hara and Hodge, then sets him loose. That evening the rivet inspector takes his chalk to their work, tracing vicious circles around rivet heads, scaled or clean.

Lawrence comes to his daughter in the evening after supper. He knocks on her bedroom door and enters. She is lying on her bed, not yet out of her school uniform. She is on her side, her elbow propping her head as she reads from a book.
'What are you reading, dear?'
It is unusual that he enters like this.
'Emily Brontë, Father.'

Bridge

But Lawrence is not listening.

'He seems nice, Evelyn.'

She goes cold. She does not know where to look. The words of her novel lose shape.

'What do you mean, Father?'

'Charlie Stahl.'

'I don't –'

'I've seen you with him, Evelyn.'

She swallows. Cannot meet his eyes. She waits for what he knows.

'He seems nice, Evelyn, but listen to me. You are too young. You do not understand these men. I do not want you to see him again. You must not see him again.'

Evelyn is silent.

'You understand?' he demands.

She looks up at her father's face for a moment. To let him know that she has heard him. Nothing more. She lowers her eyes again, returns to herself, barely hears his footsteps as he leaves the room. She is seventeen. He cannot hold her.

The long minutes pass. Evelyn places her book near the bedside lamp, then turns the light off. She listens to the sounds of the house. Quiet from Meg, already asleep in her room across the hall. Her mother rustling away to bed. The door of her father's study opening, then closing, and the sound of his footsteps moving down the house. There is the flicking of light switches, and the glow that seeps in from under her bedroom door dulls a little more after each flick. Her father enters their bedroom and she hears a murmur. A pipe shudders as water is released in their bathroom. A shower, drawers, the murmuring once more, a final light switched off, then darkness and silence. How long is enough? This is the most difficult thing. Evelyn lies in bed and counts. She does not trust herself to know otherwise. She counts in her head. One and two and three and... Till she gets to sixty. She extends a finger of her closed hand. One minute. She starts her count again, collecting minutes in her hands. When she was younger she did this to fall asleep. Half an hour passes without sound. Evelyn slides out of bed, goes to her bedroom window, opens the curtains.

Moonlight floods her room.

She sits on the end of her bed and peels off her stockings, rolling them into a tight ball. She slides open a drawer of her silky-oak dresser and places her stockings neatly inside. In front of the dresser and its scallop-shaped mirror she unhitches her school uniform, the skirt and tunic. She straightens her long back and looks at herself in the mirror, gazing at her reflection in the moonlight. The still head, the long neck, her shoulders and the hollows below her collarbones. Her breasts fill out her singlet, and then the singlet falls away to her stomach where it gathers again. Evelyn leans forward and tilts the mirror downwards on its frame to examine the rest of herself. Her waist, her slim hips. She touches one of her hip-bones, cups her palm around it. The angled mirror lengthens her legs.

Evelyn opens a wardrobe and lifts out a dress with a delicate floral pattern. Small red roses are luminescent in the evening light. She steps into the dress and pulls it up over one shoulder then the other, loose-fitting. She does up the line of buttons one by one, pressing them against her chest so she feels their hard knots against her body through the material. When she is

Bridge

finished she bends under the dresser, collects her shoes in one hand and tiptoes barefoot out of the room.

At the park Evelyn folds into Stahl's arms, swiftly, deeply. After a time he takes her hand and they walk. She leans in close and Stahl puts his arm around her, leading her.

They come to a small timber boatshed. Stahl reaches for the bolt on the shed door and slides it back. He swings open the doors. It is dark inside. Stahl enters first and finds the kerosene lamp which hangs from a nail driven into a post. He takes matches from his pocket, strikes one, and lights the lamp, adjusting the wick with the turn-wheel. The inside of the shed is aglow now, and Evelyn sees rowing boats held in their cradles above the ground. From a box Stahl takes out a blanket. He spreads it on the floor, and places the kerosene lamp next to it.

'Close the door,' he whispers.

She enters, lingers just inside the doorway. Stahl sits down on the blanket and reaches behind his back, reaches under his vest. He takes out a soft leather, rolled pouch, creased where it has been tucked under his belt behind his back. He unties the bootlace that loops around the pouch. The leather falls open and Evelyn sees sheets of paper protected within it. She comes over and sits beside him, and he shows her his sketches. There's the river, the bridge in construction, her school, two figures standing on the escarpment looking out over the river. She reaches for this sketch, pointing to the figures with her index finger, almost touching the girl with her shoulder half-turned against her father.

'Is that . . . ?' she says, not finishing.

'Yes,' he says. Then he turns to the next sketch.

Evelyn gasps. She sees herself, in pencil. Drawn from memory, but transformed, the schoolgirl gone. The dress has the cut of her uniform, but not the pleats, none of the square edges. They are all brushed out of the image, erased so it is a casual dress she has been sketched into. The school hat tilted back on her head has become a dress hat, her long hair wild and tousled beneath it as she stands in the wind above the river on the cliff.

Stahl turns the drawing over, and takes a pencil from his pocket. *For Evelyn*, he writes and hands it to her. She accepts this gift, weighing it in her hands before putting it down on the other side of the lantern, and reaching then with her hand for his cheek. Evelyn touches Stahl, her fingertips brushing his face, exploring it in the lamplight, finding his lips. She shivers. Stahl leans forward and catches her forefinger between his teeth, laughing as he does this, playful. She goes to pull away but he holds her finger tight in his teeth before releasing it. She laughs, giddy. Stahl places a hand on her shoulder, pressing her to the ground. Evelyn's body gives, so that she is lying on the blanket, on her side, her head propped by an elbow, looking at him.

Stahl reaches forward with his pencil, and she smells his body close, the new scent. He rests the side of the pencil on her upper arm. The wood is cool against her bare skin. Slowly, deliberately, he rolls it along her arm, turning it lightly along her skin with the fingers and the palms of both his hands, as if it is a rolling pin. Evelyn feels the ribbed edges of the pencil on her skin. She feels the cool pressure moving down the length of her arm, massaging her. She feels it reach her wrist, pass over, roll across the back of her hand. Her fingers stretch open, an involuntary reflex and Stahl rolls the pencil over the backs of her fingers and onto her hip where the palm of her hand rests. She closes her eyes and is aware of Stahl's body shifting, and the feel of the pencil turning across her hip and then beginning to run down the outside of her thigh. Evelyn lets out a cry. She pivots her body towards his, grasps his hands and reaches for his lips.

Thirteen

The sixth of December 1939. The day has risen long and slow, the sunlight muted by bushfire smoke rising off one of the sand islands in the bay, the sun's heat vehement still. They are riveting on the sway-frame, the crossways bracing that strengthens the road swingers and takes the sway out of them. There is a lull on the bridge since its linking, an ennui that has settled on them and threatens their mood, challenging any part of themselves they do not understand. There is a heat below things, indirect, brooding. The men casting around, casting out into the chasm.

'How's that girlfriend of yours going?' Hodges says.

'Keep your eye on the dolly,' Stahl returns.

Hodges lifts the dolly against the rivet, his body on one side

Bridge

of the sway-frame, O'Hara and Stahl on the other. O'Hara shoulders the rivet machine up to the frame, Stahl leaning on O'Hara's elbow, adding his force, the two of them joined for the moment. Stahl's strength is needed to help O'Hara with the weight of the rivet machine.

'Playing with fire, Charlie, playing with fire,' Hodges continues, a sing-song lilt to the taunt. Hodges hums the bars of a tune, while holding the dolly firm against the rivet.

Stahl ignores him, but Hodges won't let go.

'The boss's daughter, Charlie. How could you? The boss's very own. Playing with fire, Charlie.'

Ordinarily O'Hara would pull this up, would tell Hodges to keep his mind on his work. But O'Hara wants something too, wants to hear about Evelyn. Stahl has said nothing to him. Not as they've worked. Not at the boarding house before Stahl slips quietly away in the evenings after dinner, not in the mornings when O'Hara wakes him, sleepier than usual. O'Hara lets Hodges run.

'Charlie-boy.'

Hodges wants Stahl to look at him, teases him to look up.

'Hey! Charlie-boy,' he says again, shorter, with punch.

Stahl lifts his eyes, a wearied look. And now that he has him, Hodges raises his right forearm so it is vertical, clenches his fist, and slaps the palm of his left hand against his bicep, grinning.

'She's a good girl, is she, Charlie,' he taunts, 'the boss's daughter?'

'You're a prick, Hodges,' Stahl replies, eyeing him evenly. 'How your wife puts up with you.'

'My wife?' Hodges grins. '*You're* not thinking of marriage are you, Charlie-boy? You haven't done anything to start thinking like that have you, Charlie?'

Hodges cannot imagine greater entertainment than this. He turns off the air compressor. He shifts the dolly to the next rivet, swinging it from rivet to rivet, a simple movement, honed to precision. He's done it a thousand times, ten thousand. But this morning the weight of it catches and the dolly slips off the face of the sway-frame, drops, and bangs against his knee, the end of the dolly hot from riveting. Hodges groans.

'You hurt yourself, Billy?' O'Hara asks.

'Damn,' Hodges mutters, 'another piece of skin off.'

O'Hara waits for Hodges, lets the rivet machine fall, not wanting to spend too much of himself, the weight of the machine swinging like a slow pendulum between his outspread legs.

The dolly rests on the planking beside Hodges, a mirage of heat swelling the air around it. He bends down to roll his left trouser leg and look at his knee. He quietens, and drops to his haunches on the staging. Hodges is squatting, O'Hara and Stahl watching him. And as they watch he is turning pale, and his eyes are fluttering – and he is leaning backwards, teetering, falling.

There is nothing behind him. No planks, no railings, and he is falling backwards, his arms thrusting into the air.

O'Hara lurches forward and grabs him by the ankle, the entire weight of Hodges' body there. The terrible weight. And his grip poor, precarious, impossible. Hodges' boot coming away in O'Hara's stranded hand, and Hodges toppling, his feet scuffing against the staging plank before disappearing over the side.

Stahl cries out.

Carleton hears – the steel bridge, grey against the grey morning sky, Hodges falling serenely through the grey air, the water

Bridge

darker but grey still, the blood draining from Carleton's face leaving him dizzy. He hears, head snaps up, watches the fall.

Hodges makes no sound. Not as he leaves the bridge, not as he passes through space to the river below. Is he man still, or in his falling is he just body? The falling shape is stillness itself, turning the slowest of turns, his curved, muscled shoulders tight against his dark shirt. Carleton close enough to see the vein in the left side of Hodges' neck bulge and then disappear. A split second. He sees the man close his eyes just before he hits. Or rather sees one of them – his left eye – slowly close, as if deliberately. That night Carleton will dream that the falling man was winking at him. Will dream the man turning his head and meeting his watching gaze, will dream him nodding his head and winking his big left eye at him. But now, in the elongated moment before impact, the boatman sees a vein bulge and recede, and an eye close.

And then there is impact.

Time crumples with the body. He is back in the urgent, pitiless present, the thud of body on water reaching him in waves of echoing sound. He thrusts his oars into the water and rows hard for the place where Hodges entered the river. And, as the panic begins to fill him, Carleton sees Hodges' hat, like an unexpected encore, following the body, the air catching in the bowl of the hat, and then the worn felt sliding over on itself, upside down, and falling like a heavy fig leaf onto the dark grey water. Carleton makes for the hat.

Fourteen

'Give it to me again,' O'Hara demands.

'They have to know. They can't *but* know,' Carleton replies.

The funeral is over, the wake has begun, the coroner's inquest is still days away. O'Hara and Stahl and Carleton have broken away from the other men who crowd the cottage in Woolloongabba where Hodges' widow lives. There are more than a hundred of them here, filling the living spaces and spilling out into the yard at the back. The brotherhood of the bridge.

'More.' O'Hara is terse, unforgiving. 'Give me more.' An echo of Hodges' scepticism comes to him, the need to be faithful to him, to his doubt.

'They're engineers. They plan these things. They know.'

Bridge

'How, for fuck's sake, Carleton, how? I was there, Carleton. Don't forget that. He was fucking beside me. He overbalanced. He just fucking overbalanced. How can fucking Lawrence or fucking Bradfield or any other fucking one of them know that come six December nineteen thirty fucking nine, William Leslie Hodges, husband and father of two young kids, is going to fall. Tell me fucking that, Carleton. Tell me fucking that.'

O'Hara is almost spent.

'Let me read you something.'

'What?'

'A rhyme.'

O'Hara glares at Carleton, incredulous, incensed.

'Don't play with me, boy. Don't fucking play with me.'

Carleton burrs up.

'I may not have known him like you, but I was the first one there. Don't forget that, Jack. I was there too. I didn't want him to die either.'

Carleton's chest is heaving, his face red with speaking to O'Hara like this.

'Come on, boys.' It is Stahl. 'We're here for Billy. Let's not forget that. Let's just take a deep breath or two.'

O'Hara tips back his glass, pouring the beer down his throat in one. Makes for the kitchen where the drinks are. He returns with three glasses: pots of beer for Stahl and himself, a ginger beer for Carleton. To hurt him, to take control again.

'Alright, Carleton, you've got a poem?' he says. 'One of yours?'

'Not a poem . . . a rhyme.' He is still exhausted from running himself out as far as he had.

'I don't care what you call it. Tell us about it.'

'I'll read it.'

Carleton reaches into the back pocket of his trousers for the folded piece of paper. He takes a steadying breath:

'The drudge may fret and tinker
Or labour with dusty blows,
But back of him stands the thinker,
The clear-eyed man who Knows;
For into each pipe and tabor,
Each piece and part of the whole,
Must go the Brains of Labour,
Which gives the work a soul!'

'Where did you get this?' O'Hara interrupts.

'Ask Charlie.'

'Charlie?'

'Evie gave it to me,' Stahl says calmly. 'It was something her father showed her a week or two back.'

'Lawrence wrote it?'

'No. But Lawrence liked it. They're going to use it at the bridge's opening ceremony.'

O'Hara rubs his eyes with his hands, shaking his head to himself.

'And how come you've got it Carleton?'

Stahl answers for him, shrugging his shoulders as he does: 'His bridge theory ... I thought he might appreciate it.'

O'Hara takes it in, then says to Carleton.

'Keep reading then.'

'Back of the motors humming,
Back of the belts that sing,
Back of the hammers drumming,
Back of the cranes that swing,

There is the eye which scans them,
Watching through stress and strain,
There is the Mind which plans them –
Back of the brawn, the Brain!'

Carleton looks up when he's finished. Looks for O'Hara's response which, when it comes, is reluctant, indirect, incomplete.

'A fine recitation,' O'Hara says, his jaw tense, his fury yet uncooled. 'You could make yourself really useful and get us another couple of beers.'

Carleton takes their glasses and moves away, wounded.

'Not too hard, Jack. He doesn't mean any harm.'

O'Hara plays with the throat of his shirt near the top button. He pulls the collar away from his skin, stretching his neck left and right, as if to free himself from the shirt.

'What do you reckon, Charlie?' he says. 'Does Lawrence really think that?'

'What?'

'The poem – *back of the brawn the brain.*'

'Probably.'

'And what do *you* think, then, Charlie? Do they know the exact numbers already? Billy was the third. Do they already have a total for the bridge? Four? Five? Six? Ten? Are they on target? Fuck.'

Stahl lets him go.

'A man doesn't want to believe it, does he?' O'Hara mumbles.

Without the comfort of a glass O'Hara fidgets. He looks down at his hands. Something catches. O'Hara lifts his hands, palms upturned, and inspects them in the afternoon light.

Sinewy, calloused, scarred. He holds them in front of him. Tenderly, as if they are broken. Or not his. He looks at his hands and sees Hodges' boot – scuffed brown leather and worn sole, the sole so thin it is cracked right through. He sees the nails in the sole. He could count them. For long moments Hodges' boot lies resting in O'Hara's hands.

The afternoon light begins to fade.

Stahl looks around. Hodges' wife sits in the living room of their cottage, sunken into a worn couch, tired but taking visitors still. There'll be a compensation claim, but a lifetime still lies ahead of her. One of her boys, three or four, nuzzles at her side, her arm around him drawing the child close. Bradfield and Lawrence and some of the others have gone now, having paid their respects. Stahl looks around, sees his workmates in suits, though they are more relaxed here at the wake than they were at the funeral. They will all return to work tomorrow, return to their allotted tasks on the bridge. To their jobs and their height money.

From the corner of his eye Stahl sees Irish approaching, empty glass in hand, making his way towards the bar and a top-up. He nods as he reaches them, serious, respectful. He is about to pass them when Stahl catches him, blunt.

'Irish, tell us, is it possible the engineers can calculate the number of deaths on a job?'

Irish answers without breaking stride:

'On your New York skyscrapers, boys, the formula was a life for every floor.'

He continues on his way, leaves them to his broad-suited back and the echo of his words.

'The oracle has spoken,' O'Hara says bitterly.

They lapse into silence again, too many possibilities competing with each other now.

'What do I think, Jack?' Stahl says. 'I think it is possible they know.'

'Alright,' O'Hara says, 'let's find out.'

Fifteen

Night comes. It is lowered upon the earth. The moon has whittled to a sliver, to almost nothing. Carleton unhitches his boat from its mooring under the Howard Smith Wharf, and pushes off into the water, alone. He works the oars, pulling the boat across the dark water towards the Kangaroo Point side of the river, where he was told to wait.

With the night, the bats. They come in chorus, charting their course along the river from day roost to night feeding grounds, their numbers spreading a path across the firmament, their blackness darker than the night. The Milky Way and all the stars smothered by the swathe of black.

Carleton watches the bats move upriver. They take their bearings from the watercourse itself as they make their way

Bridge

through the night. The bats sweep through the sky as the river curves across the earth. Carleton watches them reach the metalwork of the bridge, sees them still confused by this new obstacle across the sky. Watches them prop and stop and turn and rise, buffeting against freshly displaced air which carries now the smells of steel and man where those smells had never before been. Carleton senses their agitation. All is moving darkness, and above him devil-shriek.

In the boat Carleton rows, caught between confidence and fear. There is the strength, the power that comes with O'Hara taking him seriously. He thinks, *Jack's listened to me, he's really listened*. But the pleasure of this thought won't settle in him for long. The moment O'Hara's approval begins to warm him, an unexpected, formidable anxiety takes hold. More than the bats and their agitation. It is the anxiety that his theory has taken tangible form, is being acted on, so everything has changed. As if the sealed container that held his theories – like a glass jar he might present to them for show – has cracked, and his theory has now escaped, moving in the world, shaping it. It frightens him, this unknown.

Carleton draws in to the south side of the river, pulls into the bank just back from the point, and waits.

O'Hara and Stahl have alighted from the ferry. Their boots hard, first against the gangway, then the concrete, then the bitumen. Hard and committed to their purpose. Stahl leads – this is his territory, at night. He is changed, O'Hara thinks. There is sureness in him.

Stahl leads him through the park, to Evelyn's house, perched high on the street. In the shadows opposite, Stahl whispers, points out what he knows. O'Hara listens, following the line of Stahl's gesturing finger, squinting, intent. But he needs more. He breaks a twig off a bush, hands it to Stahl.

'Sketch it for me.'

The two drop to their haunches, the house still in sight. Stahl scratches a diagram in the dirt. A crude floor plan, incomplete, half Chinese whisper. He draws a window, names a room, points up beyond the sweeping verandah to the house inside it, just as Evelyn's described it to him.

O'Hara crosses the road and smoothly takes the steps up onto the verandah. The living room window is open, as they were promised. O'Hara props the sash wide enough to slide his body through. He is tall, but he is agile. Inside he crouches low on the carpeted floor. He waits while his eyes grow accustomed to the dimness, until he can see objects. With the diagram in mind, he moves from the living room into the dining room. Past a long table with a candelabra set in its centre. He runs his hand along its edge and feels its cool, smooth, polished surface, some foreign timber neither his father nor grandfather would ever have cut. Under a low arch and into the sitting room. There is a fireplace, cold for months. In a further wall of the sitting room is a doorway. O'Hara approaches it. He turns the handle. It is locked, precisely as they were told it would be. O'Hara takes a step back and sees the coffee table. On it the small box. He reaches out and feels its sandpaper-rough surface. He wonders what it is made of. The lid of the box is smoother, inlaid with shell, or ivory or bone. He cannot tell in the dark, his fingers inexpert. He levers off the lid, removes the key, replaces the box.

Bridge

This door opens into a small room which is the study. O'Hara closes the door behind him and takes out the candle he has brought. He strikes a match and holds it to the wick till it catches. The room flickers around him. There is a desk, cabinets, oak-panelled bookcases on three sides. He places the candle and its holder on the blotter and lowers himself into the desk chair. He tries the drawers first. There are piles of letters which he does not read. Papers he does not want. He knows this much at least about the object of his search.

He goes over to a cabinet in the corner of the room. It is tall, with three deep drawers, more strange wood. He slides the first drawer open. In it is a fresh, leather-bound album with embossed writing on the front cover, the words themselves indistinct in the candlelight. The leather is tender, calm. He turns the pages of the album and they fall randomly, perfectly, to what he is looking for. His nostrils flare with the discovery.

O'Hara moves through the leaves of the album, folio after folio, page after page of diagrams, the bridge emerging from the half-dark. The bridge in diagram. The sketches unfolding beyond the size of the pages, long maps of the bridge concertinaed into this album. This must be what the bridge would look like from the school. In the candlelight O'Hara recognises the spans, the piers, the outline of the bridge entire. The bridge reduced to diagrams on leaves of soft paper. And beside each diagram, notes. Directions, though it is too dark to read them. He rests the album on the table and returns to the cabinet. There are more maps, diaries, bridge notebooks. So many. O'Hara piles them on the table. When he is satisfied there is nothing more he closes the cabinet drawers, lifts the pile of papers under his left arm and clamps them to his side. He dampens the thumb and forefinger of his spare hand with his tongue and reaches for the candle, squeezing the life out of it. There is the brief hiss of the flame being extinguished, and then a waft of smoke. Beguiling. O'Hara pockets the candle and leaves the room. He closes the door, relocks it, and returns the key to its tiny box.

O'Hara retraces his steps through the house to the window. He slides back through and lowers it after him. The outside air is cooler on his face, almost sharp. O'Hara moves down the verandah, treading as softly as he can. He reaches the top of the stairs and sees the dim shape of Stahl waiting under the tree across the road. With his left arm holding the papers against his chest, he reaches out to the railing with his right arm. He takes the stairs, guiding himself down in the dark.

As he reaches the final steps, the sound of a single car engine separates itself from the night. Car lights stretch out along the street. O'Hara drops to his haunches, his heart quickening. He sees Stahl illuminated faintly in the beams of the headlights, before disappearing around the trunk, sliding into the safety of its lee. O'Hara looks around. Thoughts enter his head, but he cannot weigh them. *Back up the stairs. Down the street. Run. Hide.* Between the stairs and the house there is an overgrowth of thick bushes. O'Hara keeps low and crawls in, deep as he can, acting on instinct alone.

The car and the headlights and Stahl lose shape behind the layers of azalea branches and leaves and flowers. O'Hara feels sweat forming – on his brow, under his arms. A bead rolls off his forehead, takes a path between his eyes, drops from his nose, seems to *slap* against the ground at his feet, louder even than the blood pumping in his heart.

The car turns up the driveway of the house, the headlights

sweeping across the azalea bushes and the stairs. It stops in front of the garage and Lawrence gets out and swings the garage door up on its hinge, returns to the car and drives it forward under the house till it disappears from O'Hara's view. The engine cuts out and the sound of O'Hara's heart is suddenly too loud again. There are voices.

Evelyn and Meg are out of the car, moving ahead of the others, away from the vehicle and their parents, up the stairs. Meg is leaning into Evelyn, whispering in her ear as they pass the place where O'Hara is hiding. The girls are almost running up the stairs.

Then Lawrence is speaking to his wife. They are close. O'Hara sees the woman's shoe as she places it on the first step. Her ankle and the hem of her dress. Then the tip of Lawrence's cane and the soles of Lawrence's own black shoes hit the wooden steps hard and he is on the stairs, passing.

O'Hara joins Stahl down the street.
  'Close.'
  'Oath.'
  'Let's go.'
They move on, legs and hearts pacing fast, talk superfluous.

In the house Lawrence notices a faint tinge of smoke. He pauses to take it in. Not cigar, not pipe. Not his. The lights are now on. He closes his eyes to shut them out, sniffing hard. He thinks he finds a trail, follows it. In the study it is strongest. Still present. He hits the light switch. No one. Nothing. He scans the bookshelves, the surfaces. Undisturbed. His gaze falls to his desk chair. A little close to the desk, tucked too tight. He pulls it out and thinks perhaps there is a depression in the cushion. He places his palm on the seat, warm. He begins to open drawers. His desk, his cabinet – a cabinet drawer empty. He does not understand. The plans, the manuals, his notebooks, gone. He calls out:

'Evelyn, Evelyn!'

Minutes later he is calling the police.

Their route back is different from the one they took across, the night's last ferry now departed. They make their way instead to the river beach where Carleton will be waiting as arranged. They give themselves some distance from the engineer's house before talking. Stahl knows where there is lamplight.

'What did you find?'

O'Hara pats his hand on the collection of papers under his arm.

'It's all here.'

'What?'

'Plans and diaries.'

'You've *taken* them?' Stahl says, amazed, seeing the bundle under O'Hara's arm for the first time.

'Here.'

'The tender?'

'I got everything that was there.'

Stahl can't believe it.

'But you were just going to read them. You were going to read them *in the house*. You –'

'It was too dark,' O'Hara cuts across him. 'There were too many papers. And anyway –'

'You shouldn't have, Jack.'

'. . . if we didn't have the papers, we wouldn't have any proof.'

Stahl's mind is racing, trying to think. They reach the park. Others have also sought its seclusion, couples in the night. Lamplights ring the park's circumference, but in the centre, deep, it is dark. O'Hara and Stahl approach one of the lights, squat at its base, enter the circle of its radiance.

'Got a smoke?' O'Hara says.

Stahl reaches for the inside pocket of his vest, removes a tin of tobacco and hands it roughly to O'Hara, who places the thick bundle of papers and folders and albums on the grass. Stahl reaches across to pick one up but O'Hara pushes his hand away.

'First things first, Charlie.'

'I want to know what Evie's risked, Jack.'

'Relax for a bit, will you.'

'You shouldn't have taken them.'

O'Hara rests the tobacco tin on his thigh and rolls a cigarette with his fingers, seals it with his tongue, hands it to Stahl. He rolls another for himself, and takes the matches from his pocket. His fingers brush against the candle and the small pool of wax which has run and now hardened in the bottom of his pocket. O'Hara peels the wax from the cloth of his pocket, rolls it into a warm ball with his fingers and flicks it out into the night. He lights his cigarette and tosses the matches to Stahl, a slow loop. In the lamplight the arcing box casts its thin trajectory of shadow on the grass.

They draw back on their cigarettes. Above them a flying fox sweeps low and plunges into the branches of a palm tree close by. It shrieks, shifts its weight and settles to feed.

A siren sounds somewhere. O'Hara and Stahl look up. A long, mechanical howl, not far away. They meet each other's eyes.

'Can't be,' says O'Hara.

They listen as the siren cuts out, and its echo dies in the night. They both pull hard and long and deep on their cigarettes.

'Evie *does* know, doesn't she?'

'Not that we'd take them. Not that we'd *steal* them. *Christ*, Jack.'

Stahl's words sharp, hard, reverberating. O'Hara shifts.

'Sorry, Charlie.' Then, an afterthought, 'Don't worry. We'll take them back later. I'll make it up to her.'

They are silent a while, pulling on their smokes.

'The boss's daughter, as Billy put it.' O'Hara whistles. 'You've got some pull over her, Charlie. Some pull.'

Stahl says nothing. He looks up into the lamplight. Insects flitter around its glowing, moths and flying ants bunting against the lamp. He looks past the insects into the light itself, directly into it, and holds till his eyes begin to blur and to water.

'The boss's daughter,' O'Hara says again.

'She's had enough of that.'

'Of what?'

'Being Lawrence's daughter.'

'Ahhh,' O'Hara says, drawing it out. His smile long. 'Are you that serious about her, Charlie?'

A car engine approaches. O'Hara and Stahl drop their cigarettes and stamp them into the ground, rising as they do. O'Hara has the bundle under his arm again, and without speaking the two of them retreat deeper into the park. They pull in behind a fig tree planted in the middle of the space, and take shelter behind its thick trunk. They watch as the engine becomes a car and recognise the shape of a slow-moving police vehicle. They sink further behind the fig's girth, become invisible between the fig's tentacled buttress roots. The car skirts the perimeter of the park which is bounded on three sides by street. O'Hara and Stahl are aware of a torchlight probing the park from the car's window. A couple who had been embracing on a darkened bench rise, turn their backs to the intrusive beam and hustle away, no longer touching. The police car finishes its inspection and moves on, increasing its speed as it moves away.

'Let's go,' Stahl says.

They make for the riverbank where Carleton will be waiting, half a dozen short blocks away. Leaving the park, they take a narrow street. They stride along the footpath for a time, hugging the fence-line of the houses, where trees sometimes hang over the path and the street, interrupting the glow of the streetlamps. Then they turn into another road, smaller and narrower. It is dark, electric streetlamps not yet having reached this far. Here Stahl notices that the houses are all dark, and he realises how late it must be. He tries to read his wristwatch but it is too dim and he rolls his shirt sleeve back over its face. The two men pull out into the centre of the street, confident, side by side. To their right, running parallel, the southern approach to the bridge begins to slope upwards to the steelwork. In front of them at the end of the street, the work-site, the riverbank and Carleton.

They quicken their pace, begin to jog, so close now. They

reach the perimeter fence which encloses the work-site. The gates will be locked. O'Hara hands the bundle of documents to Stahl, finds a fence post, feels with his boot for a toe-hold, then swings himself up and over the fence in one fluid movement. Graceful. On the other side O'Hara kneels and prises the bottom of the chain-mail fence off the ground, enough room for Stahl to push the documents under. O'Hara takes them, stands, secures them again under his arms.

Suddenly a car turns into the street which runs along the fence-line. Stahl swivels to meet it and the headlights catch him. The sound of the car engine lifts, and the vehicle increases its speed. The siren blares.

'Come on, Charlie.'

Stahl does not move, the car a hundred yards away.

'Come *on*, Charlie, move!'

Something in Stahl shifts. Some primitive instinct takes over. Stahl bursts into movement. Not over the fence to join O'Hara, but along its outside. Running, pounding, his head down, arms driving. Ahead of him is the bridge's concrete approach-ramp, the solid shape of a massive sandstone pier looming, his goal.

O'Hara stifles a cry. He looks for Stahl, now broken away, leaving him. He watches Stahl's shape distort through the fencing then disappear into the resonance of bootfall pounding on earth. The sound of his friend's running is swamped by car engine and siren. O'Hara flattens himself to the ground as the police car approaches, still picking up speed. The car rushes past, the sole object of its interest now Stahl.

O'Hara picks himself from the ground. He lingers, confused. He leans forward into the fence, pressing his right cheek against the wire in an attempt to glimpse Stahl and the police car pursuing him. The angles are wrong, and there is nothing to see. O'Hara clamps the documents tight under his arm, and scales the fence once more to look for Stahl. At its top he hovers, the weight of his body on his free hand, the wire of the fence cutting sharp impressions into his palm. O'Hara balances on the top of the fence like a gymnast on a high bar, and with the extra height sees Stahl reach the foot of the approach pier. He watches as Stahl leaps over a fence blocking off a set of stairs running up the outside of the pier, and sees Stahl zig-zagging upwards to the decking of the bridge.

Smart, O'Hara thinks, as he drops back to the ground. The bridge is Stahl's home territory. Even in the dark he'll know every step, could cross it with his eyes shut.

Alone now, O'Hara picks his way through the work-site, past the gravel-rinsing plant on his left. Piles of fabricated steel bracing, lorries parked overnight, toolsheds, the men's changing shed. He breaks out through the sheds and before him finally is the river, the bridge, and Stahl clambering up onto the superstructure somewhere to his right.

Running the last yards, O'Hara reaches the small jetty. Carleton has drawn his rowboat tight beside the wharf, the boat partly hidden beneath the timberwork.

'Where's Charlie?' Carleton whispers.

'It's fine,' O'Hara says, urgent. 'Let's go.'

'The siren just then?'

'I said it's fine, let's go.'

O'Hara drops into the boat, his feet thunking against the hollow timbers. The boat sways, then takes his weight as he settles onto one of the benches, hugging the bundle of documents close against his chest.

The tide is running out now, not long turned. Carleton looks at O'Hara, sees him whispered and frantic, somehow altered in his excitement. Something has gone terribly, horribly, wrong.

'Jack, we can't leave Charlie.'

'Go! Now! Now!' O'Hara snaps.

His uncertainty growing, Carleton pushes off from the jetty with his left hand, then uses an oar as a pole to thrust them further from the bank. He sets out across the river, rowing diagonally against the slow tide.

'Jack,' Carleton asks again when they are free from the bank, the boat pulling strong across the dark water, 'what's happened to Charlie?'

'Shh,' O'Hara hisses, knife-edged, silencing him.

Carleton rows, reaching forward with the oars, dropping the steady blades into the water, then pulling till the oar handles are nudging against his ribcage as his chest heaves with his breathing. Head bowed, he rows, unable to look at O'Hara, gut-sick with uncertainty, the thought rising in him, shocking, unfaceable, that perhaps – perhaps, Stahl has been abandoned.

The boat moves into centre-stream. O'Hara is facing Carleton, but his eyes are on the bridge, his neck craned so he is looking up, intent, at the southern span. O'Hara whispers again:

'Stop for a moment. Carleton, stop rowing. Listen.'

Carleton pauses, lifts the oars from the water. There is the noise of the city pulsing across the river, the breathing of the two men, and drops of water falling off the oar blades and slapping against the surface of the river. O'Hara holds his breath, silencing that sound at least. Carleton too is listening hard. This

Bridge

skill of his, developed, of listening. Something else emerges from the night. A hollow, regular thumping reverberates in the distance above them. Footfall on planking.

The boat is drifting now on the current, the slow tide pulling it downriver, the bridge floating closer. Even on a moonless night the bridge casts its image onto the dark river. The tide draws the small rowboat directly beneath the bridge. O'Hara has never seen it from this angle, fresh, new. He sees the southern approach span, and the underbelly of the timber decking which has followed the superstructure at a distance as the steel was cantilevered, piece by piece across the river. O'Hara sees the line where the decking peters out and gives way to the steelwork of the newly linked centre span. Stars emerge, flickering through the steel girders.

O'Hara and Carleton listen to Stahl on the bridge above them. The sound of his running, sure and regular, a distant drumming in the night. The rowboat drifts. The breeze shifts and a mullet leaps from the river. An eddy sucks against itself on the water surface, and a dark cloud begins to muscle its way across the sky. The beat of Stahl's running becomes distorted, swollen – oddly magnified. O'Hara and Carleton listen and realise that the change is the sound of another set of boots, stumbling, or perhaps it's two, hitting against the decking further back. Stahl is being chased.

The tremolo of Stahl's running stops where the decking itself stops, near the middle. O'Hara and Carleton look up again. They see a shape now, Stahl, moving onto the bare steelwork. Reaching out with his feet along a beam, step by step. The drifting boat emerges from beneath the bridge. Stahl above them, treading the chords, the sound of his pursuers a muted backing for Stahl's high-wire performance. No one would chase him across there.

A foot mapping out the dimensions of a girder in the dark. A boot-sole tapping forward in increments. Then Carleton senses the movement before O'Hara. A boot overreaching, catching on space. A hand pushing against air for balance and finding nothing. Carleton looks up.

Stahl is detaching from the bridge, coming off it like a flake, peeling. Awkward, rough, twisting against himself, his arms momentarily flaying. Then Stahl's body rights itself. The work of a stage dancer, of physics defied. His body slows. It half-turns through the long soundless space between steel and water.

It's the grace of the fall, the impossible dark beauty of it. There is bridge and river and diving body and watchers. All else space and silence.

STORY

One

The air swells with the morning's light and its growing warmth. Robbie steps outside into the bright air rising, out onto the balcony, the reason he has come.

He breathes and feels the air at his flaring nostrils. Out here on the balcony his father is not just behind him inside, is not just in another room, another light, but is further away, deeper behind him, in another place entirely. He calms his breathing and closes his eyes. A gust of wind on his face and in his hair. It draws him outside himself, separates him. He's high on the edge of the balcony facing down to the river below. He thinks of Freya, strong. As she was before. Freya at the Centenary Park pool, Freya standing at the end of the diving board, high above the water, Victoria Park around her, arms outstretched, a moment before launching into space. Powerful. Robbie opens his eyes and blinks for the light.

He rests his forearms on the balcony railing and looks out across the river to the park he'd been in the day before, a kilometre away by a crow's reckoning – too far for him to see anything with the naked eye. So he raises his mother's binoculars, turns the adjusting wheel, and from the blur emerges a single, clear picture – the bridge. So strong at full magnification that he can make out a line of rivet-heads which appear like stitching in the seam of a steel girder.

Robbie follows the decking of the bridge until the roadway reaches the north bank of the river, and then swings the binoculars off the bridge and onto the cliff-face – a sheer sixty-metre-high concave wall of schist and tuff rock, quarried naked by years of scraping. Robbie shifts his view to the right and finds the park. The bench is empty, though red and gold beer cans which had not been there yesterday now lie strewn beneath it, and the bin on the footpath behind the bench is also overflowing. A strange curiosity has gripped him, but there is no one there now, nothing to be seen.

'It's lovely you've come to visit,' Lily says, stepping around to face him, looking into his eyes, questioning him.

'I thought we could have breakfast together.'

'What a lovely idea.'

She continues to look at him in silence for long moments, this characteristic half-stare of hers which used to discomfort Robbie's childhood friends when they came to visit. They could never work the stare out, never knew if it was inquisitorial or merely vague, but it was enough for them to avoid visiting Robbie at his home. Now, like then, it is in her own time that Lily turns away and busies herself in the kitchen with bowls and cutlery and boxes of cereal and juice.

Robbie lifts the binoculars again, shifts his view from the bench, along the park, beyond the sliver of grass, over the fence and along the ledge of ground between the retaining wall which props up Bowen Terrace, and the cliff-edge itself. A flange of concrete juts out from the roadway there, a footpath where walkers and joggers are already journeying in and out of the city. But underneath it, beneath the concrete rind, Robbie finds what he'd guessed might be there. Still, he is shocked.

Though the morning light has not yet pried open the deep shadows, Robbie sees bodies on the narrow ledge of earth above the cliff. They are motionless: sleeping, or lying steady against the coming day, shrouded in blankets. Around them are pieces of flattened cardboard and blotches of white which he guesses are plastic supermarket bags. Robbie keeps the binoculars trained on the sleepers for long minutes. He's appalled, and intrigued, looking for movement among the sleepers lying at awkward, disordered angles to each other. Then he looks harder, searching for the boy body by body – but can't make him out, not with any certainty. The sizes of the bodies are warped by the angles of their repose, the shadow and the distance. But he's satisfied, he *has* found something, after all. The visit has been worth it.

Freya stands in the cool of the laundry beneath the house, the washing machine set on a small slab of concrete, two old wash tubs beside it, their colour faded to grey. A naked light bulb hangs from a beam above her head, throwing a clean harsh light.

Spider webs shimmer above her, wafting in the currents of air her body creates in this still space.

She faces the washing machine. It is as white as a hospital ward. Resting on its lid are the clothes that have lain there since New Year's Day, the clothes she wore when she was assaulted.

Her clothes only. Robbie's had been thrown away by the hospital. They'd been too messed up: his bloodied jeans, his stinking underwear. His shirt sliced open by surgical scissors in triage so he could be lifted out of it without pain, the cotton material no longer a shirt — returned to being a piece of cloth cut from a sewing pattern. Robbie's clothes had been destroyed — *incinerated*, she guesses — while hers had been returned to her in a closed white plastic bag. Seemingly undamaged.

Freya reaches for the pile and recoils at the first touch, the smell of fear still in them, the memory of the night visceral. She lifts her shirt, holds it up to the light bulb and finds the tiny entry hole in the front. She brings the material to her eye, and through the hole sees the glowing bulb of light suspended from above. Just a pin-hole, smaller than she'd imagined. Not big enough even for a finger, but large enough for violation. She shudders.

Freya takes her jeans, almost fresh. She finds a piece of paper in the back pocket. She unfolds it and sees her own handwriting, neat given the circumstances, on the pages of a medical note pad. She reads what she'd recorded of the doctor's advice: the names of viruses, odds of contraction, recommended post-exposure procedures. These facts have been repeated to her since then, but this paper is the first tangible sign of what may happen to her. She reads the name of the prescription drug printed on the bottom of the paper: *zidouvidene*. The word odd on the page, then strange to her ear as she says it aloud. Not Latin, the language of medicine, but exotic, like something Persian. She attempts the word again but her tongue cannot hold it. Just one more thing she cannot hold.

His mother pauses at the doorway to the balcony, breakfast tray in hand. She looks at Robbie inspecting the bridge. She remembers the peregrine falcons and the nest they had built the previous year at the top of one of the bridge's two shoulders. For months they'd been there and she would bring the binoculars out to look for signs of chicks. She puts the tray down on the patio table.

'What is it, love? What do you see?' she asks, leaning over his shoulder.

'Nothing, Lily,' he replies, and sits down with her.

When he has gone Lily raises the binoculars to her own eyes and runs them along the bridge. It is the family story itself which she sees there – constructed piece by piece, year by year, telling by retelling. She sighs, lowers the binoculars, and fits their plastic caps over the lenses.

He's returning, she thinks to herself, he's coming home.

Two

Each morning now, Robbie visits his mother. Each morning after leaving Freya, and after dropping a strangler fig into the crook of a camphor laurel, he makes his way to the apartment.

It's always the same: he enters the apartment and walks down the hallway, glancing at the door to his father's bedroom. And every time he is relieved to see it closed, as his mother promised it would be. His mother is a woman who keeps promises. Every morning he collects the binoculars from the kitchen bench, and makes his way straight to the balcony.

For a week Robbie keeps watch on the group of bodies across the river from the apartment. He comes to recognise the seven people who live there on the cliff-top, sheltered by the road's overhang. Some mornings he sees them stir and rise, other days he watches only their rest. Sometimes he sees them pick their way along the cliff-top towards the bridge, to the place where they take their pisses and their craps. Other times he watches them slug water, or the dregs of beer from bottles which seem to glow, as if light itself has been trapped inside them. Once he saw two of the men grapple at each other with their hands in argument, an altercation in slowest motion. And some mornings he sees the shape of the boy sitting upright, blanket round his shoulders, his young back leaning against the wall like a weary sentinel torn between rest and duty.

After a week of visits, it is almost an afterthought. Robbie raises the glasses one last time, his coffee now just a hardening stain on his cup as he is about to farewell his mother. The morning is hazy from the summer's exhaust fumes trapped close to the city, suffocating it. The sun is blurred in the sky, throbbing with heat behind the haze.

Through the binoculars Robbie sees one of the men making his slow way across the cliff-face, loosening his belt as he shuffles into waking. He squats, and Robbie is a moment from dropping his glasses and leaving the small lean figure to his privacy – when the man overbalances and falls on his backside. He moves to stand, but his foot slips and the man hits the ground again hard, tumbling awkwardly, without control, towards the cliff, a jerking character in a silent film. Robbie watches, frozen, as the man slides feet-first off the edge of the precipice and disappears into the cliff-face foliage below.

Robbie's heart lunges against his ribcage and he jerks the

binoculars back to the shelter where no one is moving. His blood pounds faster as he wills one of them to rise, wills one of them to hear the man's screaming. Surely he is screaming. Surely someone in the camp must hear. But there is nothing and the still bodies remain still. The schoolyard ditty comes to him – *and if one green bottle should accidentally fall, there'll be six green bottles, standing on the wall*.

It's as if he's gone deaf. He waits. He begins to doubt what he has seen. He drops the binoculars to his lap, then raises them to his eyes once more. The same silent stillness. His brain plays the scene again. And again. The seconds tick by until his waiting becomes macabre. Finally a horror wells in him so strong he spins out of his balcony chair and runs through the apartment to the door, his mother calling after him.

Seven minutes in his car from the apartment across the Story Bridge to the park on Bowen Terrace. The man's falling has over-filled him. He brakes fiercely when he gets to the park and rushes across the road. The grass is dewy when his foot first makes contact and he slips, then catches himself without falling. He runs across the park and is soon catapulting over the guard-fence at the end and landing on the rough ground on the other side.

'Hey!' Robbie yells. '*Hey*, get up! *Get up!*'

Rather than wait Robbie leaps over the sleeping bodies, and the crunching sound of his boots on the ground is as urgent as his yelling. He slows down as the ledge narrows, and stops at the place where the man fell. The ground is flat by the base of the retaining wall, then curves away towards the cliff before arcing sharply and disappearing over the edge. There is nothing to see. Nothing at all of the man. The absoluteness shocks him.

He tries to think. To listen. He concentrates, but the blood is beating loud in his ears, and for long moments he cannot hear anything over it. Slowly it begins to settle, and Robbie leans forward, straining to pick up any sounds from below.

'What the hell you think you're doing?'

His attention is torn from the cliff's edge to the voice. He sees the boy, wide-eyed, the imprint of the day not yet on him. Behind the boy, a large shirtless man, his tight-swollen, thickly haired gut, his rough voice, and his challenge.

'*Shh!*' Robbie brings a finger to his lips to quieten the man, to calm him.

'I said what the hell you doing?' the man yells. 'Bloody turning up like that, I'll give you bloody what-for.'

'Shut up, will you!' Robbie shouts back at him. 'Someone's gone over.'

But his words make no impression, so he points his finger over the edge and shouts it again: '*Your friend's gone over.*'

The big man begins to blink. His brow contorts in dumb confusion, as his gaze follows Robbie's finger and then comes back, blank.

'A man,' Robbie says. 'He's gone.'

The boy understands suddenly. He yanks his boots off and tosses them behind him towards the base of the retaining wall. They thud against it and settle as he lowers himself onto his hands and knees and crawls towards the precipice. Robbie watches the soles of the boy's feet, dirty with the build-up of sweat and grime. The boy's toes feel out the ground as he inches forward. Without speaking, Robbie kneels behind him and grasps his ankles, ready to clamp them tight if he begins to slide. The boy accepts Robbie's contact.

Inch by inch the boy squirms forward, his child's chest flat against the ledge as the earth curves away. Closer to the edge until Robbie feels the boy's body straining against itself. His head is over the lip now, and Robbie is holding him, taking his weight, as if holding scales in balance. Robbie feels he has all of the boy's weight in his hands, that he is in contest with gravity itself, that he can't be responsible for this. And just when he must say something, must begin to haul the boy back onto the ledge, the boy cries out.

'Pop, Pop, I can see you.'

The boy's yelling ripples back through his whole body, and Robbie feels the vibrations of the child's voice in his hands.

'Pop, are you alright?'

Robbie stops breathing, his hands locked in place around the boy's ankles, waiting for a response. But there is none. Or nothing he can hear.

'Pop, are you alright?' the boy cries again, and this time his voice is trembling, faltering.

Robbie feels the boy's body loosen in his hands, feels gravity begin to claim him. Robbie checks the boy's fragile surrender, jams his elbows into the hard ground, then hauls. Though small, the boy is like a weight of concrete, and Robbie has to drag him back in fits, in disconnected, exhausting jerks. And when he has him back on the ledge, the boy is sobbing in great chafing gulps of cliff-air and tears. Robbie lifts him up and sets him down by the wall.

A crow caws somewhere above them before taking to the air with heavy wing-beats. And then, coming in on the echo of the crow's wing-thumps, from what seems like the very air itself, there is a moan. A sound that on another morning might have been lost in the rumble of cross-bridge traffic.

Three

The ambos tend his wounds at the cliff-top, the old man refusing to go to hospital. Their latex-gloved examination reveals no fractures, nothing punctured. Just grazes on his arms and legs where he'd lain wedged between the cliff-face and the trunk of a sinewy rock-fig, the tree having seeded and grown large in a cleft, just over the ledge.

'Hardly a scratch,' the old man says, 'they're just souvenirs.'

'We're dressing them anyway.'

The man is even older than Robbie might have guessed, and much smaller, though not yet frail. Despite the age there is a vitality in him. In his wiry hair. In his shoulders, unstooped. He sits up, and swings his legs off the fold-up stretcher. One of the ambos stands close to the old man, hands on hips in navy shorts. The second waits to the side, arms folded across his starched white shirt as if he has entirely lost interest in this one, this difficult patient.

'Don't worry,' the old man says. 'I'm fine. There's nothing broken, nothing bruised. A short roll off a ledge. People go on rides at the Ekka more dangerous than that.'

The boy paces behind the ambulance officers, never taking his eyes off the old man. The boy is the only one who remained. The others had fled as soon as they could, slipping away in the early confusion ahead of the siren. Only the boy stayed with the old man, hovering behind the ambos and the police, never straying far.

They give the old man fresh bandages and antiseptic powder and wish him some sort of luck before packing and leaving. The police take their statements, cold notebook accounts, and leave too. One of them farewells Robbie as he goes, but not, Robbie realises, the old man, not the boy.

'You right, mate? You need a lift anywhere?'

'I'm fine. I've got a car. Thanks.'

Robbie is left with the boy and the old man, and suddenly he is awkward. The only sound is the bridge and its traffic. He is shaken himself, but it occurs to him that he is standing in the middle of their home, uninvited. How very much a stranger he is here.

'I might sit for a bit,' he says anyway, his words so tentative they become a request.

'Okay.'

It is the boy who answers.

Black plastic milk-crates are positioned upside-down near the concrete wall, in a rough semi-circle. Robbie selects one and lowers himself onto it, feeling the chequered pattern of the plastic moulding sink into his buttocks. The old man and the boy do the same, taking a cautious lead from him.

It is mid-morning now, and rising hot. Behind his head the concrete wing generates its own dusty pulsating heat. Robbie becomes aware of the smells which the heat draws out of everything around him, as if this sense has been suspended until now. The trees and the bushes in front give off dank odours: sweating leaf litter and ancient, decaying foodscraps curdling in the heat at the base of low bushes. His nostrils pick up other, discrete smells, acrid and human. There is stale beer, vinegarised bladders of wine, and rotting food trodden into the earth. A trail of ants pulls at breadcrumbs on the ground in front of him, and he is grateful, in his awkwardness, that he has somewhere to direct his eyes.

'Thanks,' the boy says to break the silence.

'Nothing,' Robbie replies.

Robbie feels calmer. After a time he looks across at them. For the first time he notices that the boy is dressed in the same jeans, top and boots he was in when Robbie saw him a week ago. The old man is white-bearded, white-haired, a stripe of grey surviving at the back of his head. He wears a brown coat buttoned at the front, the four large leather-plaited buttons like badges on his chest. The coat is large and neat, and under it Robbie sees a grey cotton shirt, stained and fraying at the wrists. The man's trousers are patterned by grass stains, but otherwise seem fairly new. Robbie examines the man's ankles. Where he expected to see swollen joints he sees instead ankle-bones like pins protruding under papery skin, and the man's scuffed brown shoes cutting a line around his ankles, as if ring-barking him. Close-up like this, Robbie wonders if the two are long-term homeless, or more recent arrivals.

'It looks dangerous,' Robbie says, 'sleeping so near to a cliff.'

Neither responds.

'If you rolled in your sleep . . . ?' Robbie gazes over the cliff.

'It's alright,' the boy says without looking at him.

'But isn't there somewhere else you can . . . go?'

'Got something in mind?' the boy snaps, their recent closeness now swept away. 'How about your place then – got a key for us?'

The boy's eyes are fixed on the ground for a second or two, before rising to Robbie's face and smiling, a tired smile which takes an eternity to unfold. As if it is the boy feeling sorry for him. 'Just joking.'

'So . . . I'm Robbie.'

'Yeah, I know.'

'Aaah, the wallet. Of course. You remembered . . . What's your name?'

'*Jesus*, mate.' The boy shakes his head with irritation, winces as if Robbie's intrusion hurts.

'Good to meet you, Jesus,' Robbie tries again, thrusting his hand in the boy's direction. The boy looks at him. Robbie is not sure whether it is doubt or disdain in the boy's eyes, but the boy takes his hand anyway, a single, quick shake.

'And your friend?'

Robbie doesn't address the old bloke directly. He has been silent, disengaged.

The boy does not answer. Protective, Robbie thinks.

'How did you come to live here under the bridge?' Robbie asks, trying again differently – looking first at the boy, then the man, hopeful, though no longer expecting a response. But the reply to this comes fast.

'He built it!' the boy says, flinging the words at Robbie like a hand of cards slapped upon a table. 'He built the bridge, so he's got a right to live here.'

Robbie's ears ring, as if he's been clapped hard across the side of the head — the way his father administered flashes of unexpected discipline, with a *clip across the ear*.

When he feels he has control of his speech Robbie says slowly, 'What do you mean?'

'He *built* it!' This time the boy's voice contorts into a high-pitched half-screech.

'But what do you *mean*, he built it?' Robbie says, the muscles in the pit of his stomach tightening. He looks now at the older man, examining his face for anything that might explain the boy's words, but it is blank and motionless: his thin pursed lips and narrow chin, the sharp angle of his nose, all still. The white eyebrows are steady above watery unblinking eyes, but Robbie imagines he sees the man's chest rise with a slow intake of breath, a small gesture of pride.

'Just that,' the boy says. 'When he was young he built the bridge, so he's got as much right to it as anyone.'

Robbie hears this as an article of faith from the mouth of an innocent. For a long time Robbie says nothing, the old man quiet as rock, the loyal boy confused by the growing silence. Robbie's own story is spinning hotly within the confines of his brain, hitting against bony casing.

In the end he says only, 'It's a beautiful bridge,' looking at the old man.

'And isn't it,' the old man speaks, a gentle cadence to his voice.

'A beautiful bridge. Nineteen thirty-five to nineteen forty,' Robbie continues, seeking to draw him to reminisce or to embroider, not sure how long he can hold this feint.

'A beautiful bridge,' the man nods, 'a work of art.'

'Designed to demonstrate the artistry and poetry of the science of engineering, so as to express simplicity, beauty and service,' Robbie says; the words his father had made him learn by rote as a child have come back to him for the first time in twenty years. And it surprises him he has the self-control to deliver the hated formula so calmly now.

'The artistry of engineering,' the man repeats. 'Yes, the artistry of bridge-building. We did a great thing.'

He sighs, and Robbie thinks there's a movement on the watery film of the old eyes, a rippling before the man blinks.

Is all this just the delusion of a destitute old beggar? How long has the man lived like this? Robbie wonders. What toll has it taken, on his body, his mind? He might be seventy, he might be eighty. But how many years does living rough add? Robbie does the reckoning. Sixty years since the bridge was completed in 1940. That puts the old man at ten to twenty years old when the bridge was completed.

'You're a bit young to have worked on the bridge, aren't you, mate?' Robbie tests.

The old man responds by throwing back his head and laughing, laughing till his heaving chest trips into a cough and he has to press both his papery hands against his breast to calm the shaking.

'Well then, son, tell us about some of the great enterprises *you've* been working on. Tell us about *your* grand achievements.' The old man grins as his cough subsides, still chuckling to himself. 'It's alright, son,' he says to Robbie, 'I know what you're doing. You're not the first.'

The old man turns to the boy.

'Jimmy,' he says, 'bring over the pictures.'

The boy rises and walks to where one of the mattresses is laid out flush against the concrete retaining wall. He reaches into the space between mattress and wall, and takes out a cardboard cylinder smudged with dirt, the red postal symbol still visible through the grime. The boy hands the cylinder to the man, who pries the plastic cap off one end, then wipes his hands against the breasts of his shirt to clean them. It does no good, so he has the boy pour water from a plastic bottle over his hands as he rubs them together, wiping them this time on the inside lining of his coat. Then he takes up the cylinder again and taps the end of it against his thigh until a tight wad of paper slides out. He unrolls the large sheets of cardboard paper with his thin hands, and Robbie sees then they are paintings. Or rather, reproductions, dirty prints. When they are flattened out he spreads them on the mattress, weighting their corners with small stones.

The old man starts through his collection of prints, Robbie watching, intrigued. He peels away a Tom Roberts bushland setting, an Arthur Streeton painting of the Hawkesbury River valley, more Sydney Harbour Streetons. Vision after vision of the country. Sidney Nolan's myth-making is there: Ned Kelly, and Burke and Wills, and Mrs Fraser's Convict. Lame attempts, Robbie thinks, though more alive now with the dirt and muck and grime on them from the old man's hands.

When the national heroes are all peeled away, they come to what appear to be smudged charcoal sketches of the Story Bridge and its surrounds. The old man flicks through half a dozen of these drawings till he finds one which he turns for Robbie to see, swivelling it around. A young man posing at the end of a jetty, leaning against a railing, the bridge in the background. It could have been the old man in his youth. But it could have been anyone.

'So you worked on the bridge,' Robbie says.

The old man smiles to himself.

'What was it like?'

'We were making history,' the old man sighs nostalgically.

'Do you remember much about it?'

'Everything.'

'Memory like an elephant,' the boy breaks in. A phrase he's heard.

'And like an elephant I've come home to die,' the old man says, stretching his legs and smiling again now, his watery eyes shimmering with some breeze of the mind Robbie cannot see.

There is a rustle, and a bearded dragon darts across the hard earth in front of them, scooping a piece of gristle from the ground. The lizard stops and lifts its head to the three of them, then scurries away under a bush with its prize.

'Do you remember a bloke by the name of Jack O'Hara?' Robbie asks. He doesn't know why he does this. Doesn't know whether he is trying to trap the old bloke, or whether there is a part of him that believes. Perhaps both.

'*What?*' the old man's reply like a gunshot.

Robbie is stunned by the force of the word, and immediately regrets the question.

'What did you say?' the old man snaps again.

'Nothing really . . . Jack O'Hara . . . a bloke who worked on the bridge, as well – I was wondering if you remembered him, that's all.'

The old man is leaning forward, leaning closer to Robbie, sharpened.

235

The Comfort of Figs

'Why?'

'I was just asking. Thought you might know him, that's all.' Robbie feels pathetic in his retreat.

'Who are you?'

The challenge is harder, commanding. Robbie meets the old eyes, the fierceness of them – everything about the old man suddenly funnelled into his eyes.

Robbie resists. He breathes. He does not succumb. He begins to gather himself. For long, long seconds he says nothing, taking the old man's gaze, staying with him.

'Who are you?' the old man demands again, but now his breathing begins to shallow, a crack opening in his voice.

'Who are you?' the old man pants.

'Whoa, mate, it's okay,' Robbie says. Only now he wonders what it is that is so important to the old man, who's nearly weeping before him through gulps of breath.

It is the boy who answers at last, who puts a small hand on the shaking shoulders of the man.

'Robert O'Hara, Pop.' Gently, firmly. Frightened too. 'Remember the wallet? His name's Robert O'Hara.'

At the boy's young voice the panting stops. The man's eyes flicker and fade. He slumps in his seat, withdraws into himself and is gone.

Four

The day lengthens, and still Robbie has not returned. Freya waits. She is not sure why. She tries to rest. Sometimes her eyes are open, sometimes she sleeps.

From time to time she gets out of bed. Each rising the start of a journey. To switch the ceiling fan on or, later, when the heat has ebbed, to turn it off again. A trip to the backyard at the height of the day, where she fills a watering can and walks it to the herb garden, pouring water over the dill and the parsley and the basil before abandoning the aluminium can on a stone.

So he's staying out all day, she thinks, finally.

★

His day has swollen, beyond the point of any containment, beyond thinking of Freya. Already he has secreted a fig sapling in the branches of a camphor laurel, and breakfasted with his mother on the balcony of her apartment. Already he has seen, way across the river, an old man from a make-shift squatters' camp fall from a cliff-face. And already a man, rescued, has whispered to him *I know about your father*, and has then snapped shut, leaving Robbie to stumble back from the cliff's edge, the world suddenly gone out of focus.

So he turns from the old man, and the cliff and the bridge, and drives to the council depot. 'I'm ready,' he says to them, 'I'm ready to start again.' And he knows he is. That he is strong enough, surging; ready enough to return to the council and its public, transparent plantings.

Robbie thinks of the old man at the cliff. He marks out a garden bed and thinks. He drags a pick along the ground, tearing the grass, opening the earth in a shallow, ragged line, and thinks of the man he left near the bridge that morning.

He is making a bed around a sandpaper fig. The soil is hard, compacted. Breaking it with a mattock, he adds water to soften the ground first. Then he lifts the mattock above his head and brings it down in its arc, his back bent, his shoulders rolling to their work. His arms swing past the brim of his hat, past his ears, past the line of his jaw, and this breeze of his own making cools the perspiration on his cheeks for the briefest of moments.

He works in the fig tree's shade as the day moves, migrating with its shadow. As he labours, he thinks: a trace of the past. This man knew my father.

Robbie digs holes a foot and a half deep. He mixes fertiliser and soil, and cradles shrubs, low-growing lilly-pillies, into the holes. He presses the soft soil mix around the roots of each shrub and stands back to ensure it is straight. As a tree bends so shall it grow. Robbie wheels barrow-loads of bark chip from the truck. He tips the bark in piles onto the ground, like so many anthills. He leans the barrow against the side of the truck and takes a shovel, thrusting it into the mounds of bark again and again, spreading the bark across the ground. He thinks about the old man recoiling from his father, even after all these years. One by one he razes each pile till all around is bark chip, the unmoved sandpaper fig surrounded by a rust-red sea of bark.

Five

Late afternoon light smirls through the window, catching her shape under the sheet. Freya is shrivelling: she is balled up, her thighs against her chest, her hands grasping her legs firmly below the knees. Freya has come to know her legs these last weeks: the ridges of bone at the top of the shins, the long sinewy straps of muscle running their length, the light downy leg-hair under her fingers, the pale feet hanging weak from her ankles.

Freya is collapsing into herself. She doesn't understand it, the low-creeping anxiety that has found and enveloped her since she was stabbed, the way she is responding to it. The fear, too, of her own reaction. The fear of fear itself, is that what it is? What trauma does to you, and the changes wrought by each passing day. And the aloneness of it.

The strength of her need for Robbie, and today, today especially, her disappointment.

Finally there are the footsteps she has been waiting for. Slow and firm. Footsteps she wants to understand. She listens to each distinct footfall on the front timber stairs, hears the different resonance each step makes when hit, the different character of each. Their tones rise, like dull piano scales. Then there's the key in the door, the handle turning, the tongue of the door retracting into itself, sliding against the door jamb and then clicking into space as the door swings open. There is more air, more light in the room than Freya feels she can bear.

'Robbie,' she says.

He closes the door carefully, comes from the hall into the bedroom, following her voice.

'Frey.'

He sits beside her on the bed and strokes her hair, half expecting to see traces of silver, like glowing phosphorus on a midnight beach, come away on his palm. Freya smells him as he leans into her, his hand, the sweat dried into his shirt and his shorts, grass seeds clinging to his leg-hair, his socks.

'What have you been doing?' she asks, her voice hoarse from under-use.

'Huh?'

'The smell of you . . . where have you been?'

He presses her forehead with his thumb, finding creases, rubbing them out. He takes her hand, presses a piece of bark chip into her open palm, and folds her fingers over it. She brings it to her nose.

'Pine bark,' Freya guesses, though there is none of the joy which used to fill her when they played this before. So he's gone back to work, she realises, without telling me, she thinks.

'You're a genius,' he smiles.

But the game is inconsequential to her. She is elsewhere, and his smile fails to reach her, falls short, flattens somewhere in the space between them.

'How are you?' he asks.

'I went in to the clinic. For a check-up.'

Robbie's body tenses, and he withdraws his hand from her brow.

'You should have told me. I would have come.' And then the next thought, 'What did they say?'

'Nothing.'

The room darkens. An overhanging jacaranda branch moves against the corrugated-iron roof, stirred by a laggard breeze, scratching the tin, muzzling the golden afternoon light.

'Still the same. They won't know for six months,' she says, as if by rote. 'Blood tests at three months, and again at six.'

'It'll be okay. Come on,' Robbie says, 'let's eat.'

He positions an armchair just off the kitchen and sits her down, facing him while he prepares the meal. He pours her a glass of red wine from an open bottle.

'I don't know if I can,' she says. 'I can't remember what they said about alcohol.'

'It'll be fine,' Robbie says.

He pours himself another, and raises it towards her. Freya's smile is slow, a thing of habit. She raises her glass in response to him, half a room away.

'Yes. *Salud.*'

But she remains only half-present, her eyes fixed on the swirling waves of wine settling in her glass, like a red sea calming after a storm.

The frying pan begins to spit and sizzle with oil and garlic.

'I met a bloke today who worked with my father on the bridge, back in the nineteen-thirties.'

'Really,' Freya replies, the word indeterminate, a question if anything at all, her voice flat, her conversation run dry. She sways the wine back and forth in the bowl of her glass, and even this takes effort.

'Are you up to talking?'

'Sure,' she says, 'just tired. You met a guy who worked with your father . . .'

The phone rings. Robbie answers it. It is Bec.

'Tell her I'll call back,' Freya says.

A little later Robbie asks, 'Did you swim today?'

'No.'

'You need to swim.'

'Yes.'

He leaves the kitchen bench, comes to her, squats and takes her head in his hands. He brings her eyes to his, his face to hers.

'You need to swim,' he whispers. Close, gentle, urgent.

She smiles. She nods her head. She wants to cry.

Something is missing. Freya doesn't know what. The chill that has settled in her arms feels like a withdrawal, an absence. At night she returns to the scene of the stabbing in her sleep. She opens her mouth to scream and the screeching sound of a flying fox emerges. At night Freya beats her arms against her torso, her arms dream-wings with which she would escape. But from what? When she wakes this is never clear.

'I was going to tell you about a bloke I met today,' Robbie says.

'Someone who worked with your father . . .'

'Yes. So I found this old fella, camping on the cliff-top under the bridge with a group of homeless people. Including the boy.'

'What boy?'

'The boy who found my wallet, Frey,' he says, going back to fill a gap he hadn't realised was still there — and suddenly seeing a vast space open between them.

Freya stares into the wall, her gaze lost before it reaches the vertical timber and the tongue-and-groove joints.

'You went back,' she says eventually.

'Yes.'

'Why didn't you take me with you?'

He looks at her, the thing sitting heavy in his stomach, chilling him — guilt. Just how much of himself he's kept from her. Take her with him where? Planting figs in the morning? To his mother's? To the park? How many other places are there she could rightly ask about?

'You should have taken me, Robbie. *You've* already got back what *you* lost. You should have taken me . . . You shouldn't have left me.'

Freya rises from the table. She drops the bark chip on the hoop-pine surface and turns for the bedroom. Robbie follows her down the hall, a few paces behind. He starts again, a tumble of desperate details. To talk the weight in his gut away, to try and dissolve it. He tells her of cliffs and rivers and falls and rescues – of how he hadn't *meant* to go without her. Not really.

In the bedroom Freya peels back the sheets, gets into bed, lies down, turns from him. Robbie sits in the hardbacked chair in the corner of the room facing the bed, and in the half-light continues. A boyish enthusiasm begins to grow out of the story.

'So the old man tells me he worked on the bridge when it was built. Then he starts to reminisce, and as he's talking I'm trying to work out if what he's saying is true or if it's all just fantasy. He's talking about the bridge . . . and so I ask him if he knows my father.'

Robbie leans forward in the chair, towards Freya, confident he can pull her round with this story, that he can heal whatever hurt he is responsible for, and bring her in.

'Then everything changes, Frey. Like flicking a light switch. Suddenly he's suspicious. He starts asking me, "Who are you? What do you want? What do you want to know for?" And he's angry . . . or he's scared . . . or he's agitated . . . and I just don't know why. Everything was fine till I mentioned my father's name – but get this, Frey – the name set something off in him. The more I think about it . . .'

Robbie fades out. He catches himself – his breath after the rush of words, and thoughts. He speaks more slowly, across Freya's back, over her turned shoulder, still undaunted by her silence.

'This is what I think. The old bloke *did* work on the bridge. He *did* know my father, and for some reason he's scared of him.'

In the darkness of the bed Freya wants Robbie to comfort her, to tell her he loves her, to cradle her and soothe her. She wants him to lie beside her. She wants his arms and the room to envelop her. She wants to say, 'I don't want to die.'

Instead she turns her face to him and says, 'Do you hate your father that much?'

Six

Robbie doesn't hate his father, but he has no fear of the truth, is prepared to name things for what they are. This is what he says to himself. What he will prove to her.

So – he returns to the cliff-top shelter, alone.

There is a haze in the air where bushfire smoke from the hills to the west has drifted across the city overnight. Robbie parks his car near the escarpment. He pauses for a moment behind the steering wheel before getting out. He has thought this through. He will say to the old man: *I don't want to cause you any trouble, I just need to know: What sort of man was my father?* Or he will say: *It looks like my father is a burden to both of us.* Or he'll start the conversation with: *I know my father is a bastard – I need to find out why.*

Robbie crosses the grassy slope of the park and sees from a distance the cardboard and mattresses under the shade of the concrete overhang. But he senses already a different quality to the stillness. By the time he reaches the fence, and vaults over it, he realises the encampment has been deserted. He walks through the vestiges of the small cliff-top colony. The mattresses and the milk-crates remain because they are too difficult to carry, cardboard because it can be found anywhere. Robbie crouches as he looks around. Everything else gone: the plastic shopping bags stuffed with clothes, the suitcase he'd seen belonging to one of them, the cans of food, the cardboard tube of pictures. Nothing else left.

Robbie rises to his feet. He walks back through the old camp to the park and his car and his day of planting trees, which stretches strangely long now before him. An aperture on the past has closed on him.

There is much curling. She curled, she remembers, into a ball on New Year's Eve. She spent long minutes, she knows, lying on the footpath beside the river under the overpass, flying foxes screeching overhead and feeding in the night trees, curled into herself. She knows she screamed and that she doubled over. That she was punctured, and that she doubled over as if to prevent a part of herself leaking out of the hole. And that she lay on the cold concrete footpath for those long minutes *trying to close the wound off*, trying to shut off the route by which a part of herself might escape from her body.

She feels the trajectory of her life curling over. As if the straight line it had taken to this point has suddenly veered off course, or rather has faltered and swayed, has wilted under the weight of the stabbing, and is now curling backwards. She thought she would be strong enough to carry it. She forces herself to think objectively. It was merely an assault, a mere robbery. These are daily occurrences, mundane, un-newsworthy, so common they are almost rites of passage. It is not war. It is not as if she has been raped, she tells herself, or a victim of a lifetime of domestic violence. Freya had thought she would be strong enough to carry this. She is terrified to learn she isn't.

She uncurls and rises from the bed. She leaves the house and takes the short walk to the corner store at the end of the street. Freya returns the smile of the shopkeeper as he puts her bread, milk and newspaper into a plastic bag. She can't bring herself to tell him not to worry, that he should save the bag, that she can carry her things easily herself, that plastic bags are *not good for the environment*. The things she has said to him a hundred futile times before. The opaque blue bag hangs from the end of her arm as she walks back up the street, a crude approximation of the sky above.

She crawls back into bed with a cup of tea and the paper and reads by lamplight in the darkened room. She sees the headline *Homeless Man In Cliff Plunge,* accompanied by a black-and-white photo of the Story Bridge. She reads the article and sees Robbie's name, *a passer-by*. There is a second piece on the plight of the city's homeless, and another photo, a close-up of the under-bridge squat.

She thinks, despite herself (knows she shouldn't, knows she should be above it, should be better than this): by what philosophy is my fate – me, woman, activist, lover – a lesser thing than the fate of an old drunk who lost his footing on a cliff? She curses it, her fate. The thought passes. She feels worse for having let it in.

Seven

As Robbie plants his daily *Ficus macrophylla*, laying the stranglers in the crooks of exotics, the old man returns to him, again and again.

In the mornings when he breakfasts with his mother on her balcony, he still trains the binoculars across the river to the bridge, in case the old man reappears. But the encampment remains deserted, so Robbie scans the length of the riverbank opposite for signs of other camps, new makeshift shelters.

And during the day as he drives around the city, with the tray of his ute filled with saplings or grasses or shrubs, Robbie searches the streets and the parks for people sleeping out. It becomes instinctive. He sees a shape on a park bench as he drives by and he doubles back for a closer inspection, getting out of the car if necessary, to walk over and peer into a sleeping, unshaven face.

Soon Robbie no longer returns home straight after work. It becomes a quest. For an hour each day he explores the city as it darkens, seeking out the old man. He starts by the river, searching parks near the bridge. As the grass loses the colour of the day and park benches and curtain figs and children's play equipment solidify into night, there is movement in sound. He follows it. He interrupts people in groups sitting on the ground, flashing his torch into their faces. He is yelled at, is taken for police or for security, and retreats. He learns to wait before approaching groups. Learns to ignore the schoolchildren experimenting with drink, and the street kids sniffing paint, their mouths and noses stained white and chrome like drunken circus clowns. He learns to cast his torch beam at chest height and see people's faces in the halo of the light's rays.

After he has exhausted the parks he moves through the streets. New Farm, the Valley, the business district, West End, Spring Hill. He probes the backstreets. He walks down alleys and delivery driveways. He opens the lid of an industrial bin when he hears a scraping inside and a manged cat leaps out. He is drawn to places which offer shelter from the rain and from the wind: doorways with wide awnings, overpasses, underground carparks, unfinished building sites, bus shelters, ferry terminals. As if the city was built to house people like this.

He discovers other semi-permanent camps like the one on the escarpment. A quilt of tarpaulins tied to a chain-mail fence and stretched over a collection of mattresses. The first floor of a disused building in the city, boarded up but accessed by fire stairs at the rear. A railway station where the station-master leaves the toilets unlocked at night on condition the sleepers have gone before the first commuter train passes through in the morning.

He talks to people. *I'm looking for an old man.* Or he tells them what he knows about him. *An old bloke: he likes art, carries paintings around with him, worked on the Story Bridge when it was being built. Do you know him?* He remembers the boy's name, shows them the photos Freya took at the park bench, thinking that the boy might lead him to the man. He says: *I'm looking for a kid named Jimmy.*

'Is that your son?' someone asks him.

He meets people like himself. Searchers. A father looking for a daughter. A mother for a son. A sister looking for a brother with schizophrenia who refuses to stay with her, who prefers the street. People fuelled by loss.

Robbie comes home late these days. It is seven or eight o'clock at night before he gets in, sometimes later. Freya tells him she has eaten already, or that she is not hungry. He makes himself toast and sits in the chair at the end of their bed.

He no longer brings her things. He says instead, 'Let me describe the city to you.'

He says, 'I met Jesus Christ today.' Or, 'Tonight I watched a streetwalker shoot heroin between her toes.' One night he says to Freya, propped up in the bed, 'Today I spoke with a man who is searching for his wife. He threw her out of the house one night, because she was cheating on him. Now he thinks he was mistaken. He's tried her friends, her family, everyone she used to know, but she's disappeared. The man is insane with guilt, overcome with it, lost in it. Now he's searching for her on the streets. He said he's been looking for two weeks and he's already forgotten what she looks like. He takes a photo of her with him. It is for himself, he said – so he'll recognise her when he finds her.'

The phone rings. The house is hollow with its echo. Robbie answers it in the dark.

'Robbie?'

'Hi, Bec.'

'How's Freya?'

'She's looking after herself.'

'She needs to get out, Robbie.'

There is a quality in Bec's voice, in her concern, that stills him, challenges him and makes him doubt himself.

'Got any ideas?'

'There's something happening that we thought might get her going.'

'I'll put her on.'

Robbie takes the phone into the bedroom, lit only by the bedside lamp. The curtains hang heavily across the window, blocking out the streetlamps and the play of car headlights. He hands her the phone before she has a chance to ask who it is.

'Hello?'

'Freya. How are you?'

She recognises Bec's voice from a part of her brain she hasn't entered for a long time.

'Fine, Bec, how about you?'

'Good, Freya, yes good. Have you heard the latest on the Normanby figs?'

'The Normanby figs?'

'Rumour is they're going to be cut down. That Council's miscalculated, and now they've got to take them out to widen the road. Do you believe it? After all the promises, they're going to chop them down after all. Mongrels.'

Freya makes a sound, barely audible, a murmur her friend cannot interpret.

'We've got to do something. We've got to hold them to their word.'

The phone line fills with echo.

'We've got to do something, Freya,' Bec says again.

'Yes.' Freya's voice is flat, distant.

'A demo. On the site.'

'Sounds like a good idea.'

'Are you in?'

A pause.

'I don't think so, Bec. I don't think so.'

'Come on, Freya,' Bec says. 'Fire up. This is important. This is something we can do. You've got to help out. "We don't just live in the world, we make it." Remember saying that? Well, there's making to do. We need you.'

'I don't think so, Bec. I –'

'And it'll help, Freya. Getting out, doing things... you know... it helps when you're feeling low.'

'Thanks, but I just don't have it in me.'

Freya is about to hand the phone to Robbie, then brings it back to her mouth.

'Bec...?'

'Yes?'

'I – I don't know if I should be here . . . Is this where I should be? Bec?'

'Get out. Get out of the house. It'll do you a world –'

'No – I mean – this *country*.'

'What are you talking about, Freya?'

'If . . . if . . . if *you* were dying, Bec, you'd want to make sure you were in the right place, wouldn't you?'

'Oh, Freya,' Bec says, her voice low, catching, 'oh, no. That's . . . that's just crazy thinking. You're not dying. You're going to be fine. You are. You'll see. Come on, come out with us. Come out. Join us.'

There is silence between them, Freya with nothing more. Bec unsure if she should keep talking, if she has words which might overpower her friend's thoughts, might force them to retreat.

'Thanks,' Freya says, eventually, 'but I'm just too tired. Good luck.'

Robbie takes the phone.

'Still there?'

'She's in a bad way, isn't she, Robbie.'

Eight

'Come,' he says to Freya the next afternoon.

'Where?' She's lying inert on the bed, as if grown into the sheets.

'Trust me.'

He pulls back the blanket, and sees her thinness for the first time, the weight she has lost. He helps her out, his arm around her waist. She puts on her jeans, her shoes, and follows him out of the house, hand in hand, and into the car.

'Now,' he says, 'put this on.'

It is one of her cotton scarves, a red paisley pattern. He reaches across her.

'What are you doing?'

'Trust me.'

She relents, and he drapes the scarf over her eyes, tying it in a knot at the back of her head.

'A surprise trip,' he says, 'a mystery.'

He talks to her in the car, constantly, a stream of words, a week's worth compressed into a single twenty-minute trip. Gradually she shifts, allows his enthusiasm to infect her a little. She tries to guess, but she can't. She doesn't know the city well enough, doesn't nearly know the contours of its skin intimately enough. She can't work out where he is taking her, and she can't intuit it.

When eventually the car stops, he says, 'Not yet,' but as he slams his door shut and walks around behind the car to her side, she secretly lifts the blindfold, the briefest of glances, and sees where it is he has brought her. She doesn't understand.

He opens the passenger door and leads her out, checking that the scarf is still tight around her eyes.

'Hold my hand.'

She steps from the car onto a footpath, and they walk along concrete for a few paces before turning off onto grass. The traffic noise recedes, muffled by distance and by trees. She hears a bird call, and another one answer, willy-wagtails.

'Careful here,' Robbie says as he leads her down a gentle slope. She allows it, but she is quiet now, and responds to none of Robbie's chatter. She realises he is nervous too.

Finally he stops, and when he does she guesses, though she keeps it to herself. Robbie leans over her, their bodies touching, his neck close to her face, both his arms enveloping her as he unties the scarf at the back of her head. It comes free, Robbie pulls it away, and she opens her eyes.

They are in Victoria Park – she knew this – and as she

suspected, they're at the fig he'd first brought her to, so long ago, its small-leaved canopy dappling the sunlight above them. Softening it after the blindfold. She sees the light-grey trunk of the fig flecked with dark nodes. She sees too the break in its skin, the gaping hole — what she had mistaken for a knot before she had realised it was altogether a different texture, a different colour — a different tree entirely being hugged tight by the fig. She sees the vertically grooved bark of the silky oak in the fig's embrace.

A strangler fig, she has learnt since that first time here, starts its life as an epiphyte, germinating high above the soil, from seeds deposited by birds in the branches of a host tree. Over time its roots grow down towards the soil and the fig ceases being an epiphyte and takes on an independent life with roots in the earth. As the fig matures, it slowly encircles the host tree, eventually strangling it.

'Always figs,' she whispers.

He touches her lightly on the lips, then withdraws, waiting for her response, her signal.

'Am I going to be okay?' she asks, lifting her eyes to him.

He kisses her then, on the forehead.

'I'm scared, Robbie,' she says.

He pulls her close, his arms enfolding her.

'It'll be okay,' he says, 'everything will be okay.'

Nine

I've come home to die. After weeks of searching in parks and streets and boarding houses, Robbie remembers what the old man had said to him: that he'd built the bridge and was coming home to die.

Robbie slaps his thigh with his hand. '*Yes.*' He hisses it to himself. 'Of course!'

'What's the problem?'

He is working with a crew of men, all of them sweating, planting tussocks of native grasses beside roadways, roundabouts and median strips since morning, softening this landscape of traffic. In Robbie's judgment it's a vain attempt to subdue the violence of it all.

'Damn! I just remembered something. Sorry,' Robbie says,

'there's something I've just got to check, something I've forgotten – I won't be long. I need the ute. Can you give me an hour?'

The Story Bridge. *Home*. Robbie knows the old man is no longer under the New Farm end of the bridge – he's scoured it bare – but perhaps he's settled under the bridge on the southern bank of the river.

Robbie drives to the peninsula at Kangaroo Point, unable to believe he hasn't thought of this before. He leaves the ute where the road ends and walks out across the grass to the river's edge. From the point he surveys the landscape. In front of him the land drops away to a thin strip of mangroves and then to the narrow beach where sand has built up over time. Beyond the beach is the brown river slugging by. Above, humming with traffic, is the bridge. Robbie pivots, his back now to the river. The broad underbelly of the bridge stretches above, retreating from the river to where the deck merges into the approach-way, which sets itself down, far ahead, on solid ground.

Robbie begins to walk. He follows the cantilevered line of the bridge, keeping it above him. Walking, he looks for any sliver of space where a man might sleep.

He traverses the park, skirting the bridge's massive piers, then crosses the road to a clutch of derelict old workers' cottages directly beneath the bridge, frail and pallid from lack of sun. In the bridge's deep shadow he knocks on the front doors of each. He asks after the old man, and gets shakes of the head. He goes cottage by futile cottage. Where there are backyards he pauses at the fence-line and peers inside, looking for sleeping holes. A massive weeping fig leans over the street, its long limbs cascading downwards in gentle arcs. The footpath is buckled where subterranean roots have stretched and grown, and Robbie catches the toe of his boot on a sinew of fig root which has broken through. He continues, reaches Yungaba House, once an immigration depot for migrants, then a refuge for the destitute during the depression of the 1890s. Later, he knows, the building became the site office for the bridge engineers. Now it is government offices. He peers through the locked gates of the property, sees nothing, moves on.

Past the ethnic radio station and the Italian restaurant with its lunchtime diners, he comes to the Story Bridge Hotel, a hundred years old, three-storeyed with wrap-around balconies and wrought-iron railings, painted white these days. Once called the Kangaroo Point Hotel, it changed its name after the bridge was opened, as if somehow it would prosper by mere association with the engineering achievement.

He enters the public bar, scanning faces. He asks the bartender if an old man drinks here. The bartender gestures with a sweep of his hand at his midday patrons.

'Take your pick.'

Robbie tries again.

'An old homeless bloke . . . worked on the bridge when it was built.'

'Old Man River?' the bartender says.

'Who?' Robbie asks.

'Is it Old Man River you're after?'

'Well . . . maybe. So high?' Robbie gestures at chest level. 'He likes his art. He was with a boy when I last saw him.'

'Don't know about the kid, but it sounds like it's Old Man River you want. I can tell you where to find him.'

Robbie follows the bartender's instructions. He steps outside onto the footpath and sees the concrete pier the bartender told him to look out for, sees the stairs zig-zagging up the side of it. He walks away from the graceful old pub, passes a long low-roofed shed called 'The Den' – where a blackboard lists bikie nights, poetry readings, cockroach racing – and reaches the pier. His first step reverberates up the iron staircase and he feels the vibration of the railing in the palm of his hand. He follows the bartender's directions, climbs the stairs till he is about half-way up, and then does what the bartender told him to. He looks down. What he sees is the flat roof of The Den. On the roof is a junk heap sheltered from the rain by the bridge above. There are long uncoiled lengths of ships' rope, removed from the discipline of the ship's deck and roughly intertwined now like writhing earthworms. There are forty-four-gallon drums, a doorless fridge with beer stickers on its side. Airconditioning ducts – long silver-lined concertina-tubes glittering in the sun. There are piles of old timber doors and casement windows, the glass still in the frames. There are bone-coloured metal lockers, rolls of carpet, upturned Brentwood chairs with punctured wicker seats, sheets of corrugated iron, orange witches' hats discarded or stolen from roadwork sites, PVC pipes, an old red telephone box with peaked roof and shards of glass jagging across panels at shin-height. And among the debris is a double-seater couch with a blanket folded neatly across its arm, and Robbie knows he is close now.

So he sits on a landing of the staircase and waits. People pass: joggers, walkers, a man with his bike lifted to his shoulder.

The stairs echo with footfall on iron, dull, contemplative. From above his head comes the regular sound of car tyres hitting the expansion joints in the bridge. He thinks of his mother, then plays a game to distract himself: he closes his eyes and guesses the type of vehicle passing above him by the time that elapses between the front and back tyres hitting the joint – the interval fractionally longer for trucks, shorter for motorbikes. This passes time. When eventually he opens his eyes he sees pigeons sheltering among the girders. There is a burst of wing-flutter as two of the birds compete for the same girder space. After the frenzy the pigeons settle to cooing beside each other on the beam, a handful of soft feathers floating through the air to the ground.

The cast of the bridge's shadow changes. It moves east along the ground and the rooftops of the houses below. The sun reaches in under the bridge as the afternoon lapses, its rays falling on the foot of the concrete stanchion and beginning to rise up both it and the stairs bracketed to the side of the pier.

And then the old man arrives.

It is his head Robbie sees first, as it appears over the edge of the roof, followed by the shoulders and then his chest, the old man rising in segments above the roof-line. He wrestles himself up the last rungs of what Robbie guesses must be a ladder propped against the far side of the building. Then he swings a plastic bag onto the roof and wrenches his body up after it, pulling himself to his feet. Robbie wonders if the boy will follow, but the bearing of the old man soon shows he is alone. He carries his plastic bag of goods across to the couch, and drops it on the cushions before sitting down and taking a slice of bread from inside the bag. He chews the bread with slow, deliberate rotations of his jaws. A pigeon stirs from its perch above Robbie

The Comfort of Figs

and glides through the air, landing with a flutter of its wings on the rooftop near the man. He doesn't seem to see the bird, or perhaps he ignores it. He finishes the bread, and rolls a cigarette, lights it and lies back on the sofa, face to the exposed ribs of the bridge high above.

Robbie waits again.

After the cigarette the old man remains lying on the couch in the lowering sun. He is so still Robbie can't tell if he is asleep or just resting. It is only when the daylight turns from white to gold that he sits up. He rolls another cigarette, lights it, and then rolls another half-dozen. He puts the cigarette tin in a jacket pocket and rises, gripping the padded arm of the sofa to steady his legs. He gathers himself, straightens fully and shuffles across the roof to the ladder, where he disappears from Robbie's view.

Robbie leaps down the stairs, breaking into a run when he reaches the ground, taking the footpath round the back of the hotel till he turns a corner, blind, and sees the man emerge from a delivery driveway behind the pub. Slow and shuffling, the old fellow walks beside the pub, shadowed by its wide awning, until he reaches a glass side door. He leans on one hip and swings a leg up onto the first step, then disappears inside the hotel.

Through the pub's big plate-glass window, Robbie watches the old man approach the bar, exchange words with the bartender and look around the room, then shrug his shoulders and take the beer offered him. He doesn't join the regulars on their stools at the bar, instead taking a table near the main doors, facing them as they swing open with each new drinker.

Robbie enters the pub through the side door, and skirts around the bar. He leans against a poker machine, out of view of the bartender, and settles to observe the old man again, like a birdwatcher in a hide. He wonders about the limp, whether it is from the fall, or merely age come to claim him. The man looks cleaner than when Robbie met him at the cliff-top. The jacket is the same, but somehow he is fresher, his shirt and trousers newer. Robbie wonders if the pub looks after him.

Minutes pass. Eventually Robbie makes his way to the bar.
'You miss him, did you?' the bartender says.
'Yeah.'
'That's him.'
The bartender nods rather than points.
'What does he have?' Robbie asks.

Robbie orders two. He steadies himself, then crosses to the table by the door, the bartender's gaze hard against his back. Robbie pulls out a chair, his head bowed, and he is already seated before the old man looks up.

Robbie is peering into rheumy eyes, their natural slate colour bleary with opaque film. When the old man blinks, water runs from the corners of his eyes.

'Remember me? I'm Jack O'Hara's son. But there's nothing I can do about it. Please . . . have a beer.'

Robbie pushes the glass across the table. He tries smiling, tries to make the man before him feel at ease, but Robbie is nervous, and his smile contorts into something else. The old man begins to draw his breath in fits just as he had last time they met. He raises his right hand too quickly to his face, knocking the glass of beer — the pot topples, falls and smashes on the pub's wide floorboards.

The sound of breaking glass mutes the talk in the room. Every head turns. The quiet deepens. Robbie wishes, desperately, that he had some control over this. He watches the beer as it pools on the surface of the table, forms a rivulet, then runs off the edge like a waterfall in miniature.

The bartender calls out, 'Hey, River, you alright over there?'

The old man is startled. By Robbie, by the faces looking at him, by the bartender calling out so loudly across the room.

'It's not like you to get clumsy with a beer, River. I'll pull you another one.'

The old bloke remains still, as if paralysed. Robbie fetches a cloth from the bartender, who gives it to him cautiously, almost reluctantly. Robbie wipes the table down, then kneels on the floor to collect the shards of glass that have fallen around their feet.

The bartender brings across the replacement beer, placing it in front of the old man. In his other hand he carries a dustpan and brush.

'I'll finish it off,' he says, as if he is responsible not just for the broken glass, but the old man too. Robbie drops pieces of glass into the dustpan and stands awkwardly beside the table, uncertain whether he should sit, watching instead the bartender on his haunches as he brushes at the floor.

'All done,' the bartender says and stands. 'Look after that one, now,' he says kindly, pointing at the beer before returning behind the bar. 'Look after it as if it's your last.'

The sound of conversation in the pub resumes to its normal mid-week pitch and Robbie tries again.

'I don't want to cause you trouble. I just want to find out about my father, that's all. I don't know anything about him, and when you said you worked on the bridge – well, I thought you might be able to help me.'

The old man looks at the floor. His head is bent and still. Robbie runs on.

'He didn't say much to me about the bridge when I was a kid.' This is not a lie. 'And now he can't speak, so it's too late for him to tell me about the bridge. Even if he wanted to.'

The old man raises his head and looks Robbie in the eyes, a question.

'He's had a stroke,' Robbie says in answer. 'He's paralysed. He's lost his speech.'

'Jack O'Hara?' the old man says.

'Born nineteen-twenty, took a trade as a boilermaker, drove rivets on the Story Bridge, went to war, became an engineer, returned, married my mother Lily, had a son, worked on construction projects overseas for years, retired, had a stroke, is living in an apartment in Brisbane overlooking the bridge and the river and is cared for twenty-four hours a day by his wife. My mother.'

'I heard he married – Lily,' the old man says.

'Did you know my mother?'

'Everyone knew about her . . . Lily.'

The old man lifts his hands from his lap to the table, and rests them there. The yellow fingernails are hardened and thick.

'What is your mother like?' the old man says. 'Describe her for me.'

'She's younger than my father. She . . .'

Robbie halts, emptied out by the old man looking at him so hard, the eyes boring into him, as if he has some entitlement to inspect him this close.

'There's your father in you,' the old man says eventually.

'You think so?' But Robbie doesn't want an answer. He

listens to the sounds of the pub for a while – the murmur of talk, race-callers on television screens, chairs scraping against floorboards – before coming back.

'Please,' Robbie says, 'tell me about my father.'

'He's really had a stroke, has he?'

'Yes.'

The old man looks at the pot of beer in front of him, untouched. Its head has collapsed and there is a trace of foam like a high-water mark below the rim of the glass.

'I haven't spoken to your father for sixty years.'

'Since the bridge?'

'Since then.'

'Why's that?'

'Life moves on.'

'My father used to talk about "The Brotherhood of the Bridge".'

'I was never part of that.'

'He was proud of it – a Brisbane bridge made by Brisbane boys.'

'He was a proud bastard.'

'You didn't get on with my father then?'

'We had a falling-out'

'Serious?'

'What falling-out isn't?'

'What happened?'

'Aaah, son, you ask too many questions.'

'But that was a long time ago.'

'Exactly.'

The man lifts his beer. Robbie follows.

★

It is dark when he leaves the pub, and Robbie curses himself as he starts the walk back to the ute.

'Damn,' he says and grimaces. 'Damn, damn, damn, damn, damn.'

He drives home and, inside the house, strides down the corridor to the kitchen and the phone. He rings his crew leader. He's still not sure what he'll say even as he's dialling, only that he can't say he's been at the pub all afternoon.

The man is beside himself.

'What the hell, O'Hara. What the hell. Give me a story, mate, and make it bloody good. We were sitting out there on our arses for bloody ages. We ended up giving the depot a call to get someone to come out and pick us up. And don't they want to bloody well know what's happened to you!'

'Sorry, mate, sorry,' Robbie says, falling into another language. 'It was an absolute emergency. Freya, mate. She had a doctor's appointment. I just had to be there, and afterwards – well, you know how it is. I just had to be there. The time just totally got away from me. Sorry. I know I left you all in the lurch, mate. I'm really sorry.'

'Shit, mate. A doctor's appointment? I wish you'd told us.'

'I know, I know, I just forgot.'

'Shit.'

The man relents, and his voice changes. 'So how is she, mate? Things alright?'

'She'll get there.'

'Alright, Rob, alright. You're right for tomorrow, are you?'

'Yeah.'

'Alright . . . well . . . I hope she's on the mend.'

'Thanks, mate. Thanks for understanding. See you tomorrow.'

Robbie puts the phone down and rubs the palm of his hand across his forehead and down to his jaw where he feels the roughness of stubble coming through. He thinks, that was close. Then he turns and sees Freya standing in the doorway.

Ten

You need to swim, this the thing Robbie keeps saying to her. But does she? What does she need? Bed rest? Sleep? A mother's care? Negative test results? In the meantime, a demonstration to save a tree? Before, it wasn't just a tree, but the whole damn road she'd wanted to stop.

Freya rises from her bed to make yet another cup of tea. Her mail is accumulating on the kitchen bench, opened and incuriously read these last weeks. Or is it months? Things she must get to. Bills, newsletters, postcards from friends. The letters from the university: handwritten notes from lecturers whose calls she hasn't returned, worried she's not been at class, followed then by the formal notices warning her of the pending cancellation of her enrolment. None of it yet having touched her.

The Comfort of Figs

She takes the tea onto the front steps and watches the odd little mickey-birds playing in the grevillea below, sucking nectar from the coloured blossoms before making their flitting way off again. When she is finished, listless, she reaches into the low branch of a eucalyptus tree, for a leaf which she crushes in her hand for the scent which is still foreign to her. Will it always be strange, this place? Will it always remain exotic? She smears the traces of eucalyptus oil and its fragrance on the inside of her wrists and returns inside.

What *does* she need?

She goes to the kitchen table, and the large wood-turned fruit bowl at the centre. In it are the daily offerings Robbie presented to her over so many months. She sinks her hand into the bowl, swirling through this collection of his gifts, feeling the different textures of a dried silky oak leaf, macadamia nuts like polished marbles, birds' feathers still soft, sharp pieces of rock and tiny seeds and bark both rough and smooth. Of dried and shrivelled Moreton Bay figs, dimpled like testicles. She immerses her hand in the bowl of naturama, until her hand disappears from view, swallowed by the exotica of his country.

She assesses her life. I am twenty-seven. I feel ancient. I may be dying. I am in a foreign land. I am too tired to love. I am surrounded. I need to swim.

Freya enters the street. She walks, strides with her arms swinging in long arcs. She feels the blood pumping inside her chest, her heart an organ apart. Her feet slap against the footpath hard, her hands clench into fists and her arms are driving now,

Story

everything about her body fierce in its rhythm. She pushes on through the streets, this body of hers issuing some challenge to fate with each step.

She walks until she feels the skin at the top of her chest begin to warm. There is a dizziness filling her head, a dizziness she enjoys. A giddy power. A clawing back, a retrieval.

She walks harder, following streets down hills and then up new ones. Along ridge-lines, as if she is tramping the uncovered vertebrae of the country, the beasts lying buried beneath it. She crosses small parks and strides past corner stores, and through streets which slowly thicken with people. The city is nearer, and curving around its office towers are glimpses of the brown river ahead. Her eyes follow the line of the river looking for the Story Bridge, Robbie's bridge, the uneasy monolith which shadows his city.

South to north, Freya crosses the river by the low Grey Street Bridge, and walks until she hears herself panting, hears her breath start to labour. The giddiness in her head becomes a thumping: of blood and the echo of her heaving lungs. At the top of the Normanby Fiveways hill she slows, the river at her back, the boulevard of distressed figs before her. She is suddenly tired and, weakened from inactivity, she falters. Freya feels her skin prickle as if her blood is about to burst through. As she rests against a low brick fence under the freckled shade of a poinciana, her head bowed and sweat dripping off her face, she thinks: Is this a sign, is my blood now bad?

She walks along the ridge, in snatches. She counts each hundred paces then pauses to catch her breath. The skin at the top of her chest is aflame. Beside a school building a grey tap rises from a garden bed and she kneels before the running water, splashing it onto her neck and her chest, dousing her burning skin till schoolchildren watch from first floor windows.

She reaches the park: long, thin, precarious Victoria Park. She takes off her shoes and finds the grass hard and hot against the soles of her feet. Barefoot, she continues through the park, walking against its slopes as though she's mapping a line of contour for Robbie. She passes beneath the fig trees, over-large, their shade too deep after the midday sun's brightness. Her eyes swirl, and can't adjust to the changed light. The world blurs, and she stumbles out of the dangerous shade, propelled from it towards the high fence of the swimming pool ahead.

At the pool's entrance Freya brushes past people queuing to enter. She pushes through the turnstiles, banging the aluminium tubes with her hips. The pool is before her, glittering. Behind her the voice of an indignant attendant trails until it disappears in her ragged wake. Freya reaches the water's edge, the tiles under her toes cool where the pool water laps over them with each passing swimmer.

She does not pause. There is nothing in all the world that needs be weighed in this moment. Freya reaches the water and steps off the tiled lip of the pool deck, dropping into space. Her feet, her ankles, her jean-clad legs – all of her sliding into the water-cool dimensions. Her hands meet the surface of the water as her torso enters. They slap against it, and release, as if some trigger-nerve has been struck, the shoes clutched in her fingers on the walk through the parkland. Freya sinks into the water. Sinks through blue till she is resting on the silent floor of the pool, her blouse billowing under her arms, her eyes blinking with sweat-salt and pool-chemicals, the elongated shapes

Story

of swimmers passing overhead muting the Brisbane sun, the helixed shapes of her own two shoes floating above her like dark angels. All is passing strange, and the water alone is her friend.

Eleven

Robbie goes to the pub again the next afternoon after work, and the one after that, and the next again, his days circumscribed by breakfast with his mother, and the conversations with the old man at dusk; by the figs he plants at dawn, and Freya by night.

He buys the old man a beer, sits with him, and they talk. He learns that the pub feeds him, showers him, lets him squat on the roof under the bridge. The bar staff have grown fond of him, of his eccentricities and his insularities. One of the girls brings fruit for him, another biscuits. A duty manager runs an electrical lead from the hotel up the outside of the building to the roof where he sleeps, and sets up a small fan for the hot nights when mosquitoes come off the dead water in swarms.

Story

A barman tells a journalist friend about him and one day, too late to do anything about it, he is interviewed for a piece in the local paper, gives a false name, disappears for a couple of days till he is satisfied the interest has died. He returns, and the barman apologises. The Story Bridge Hotel nourishes the old man, protects him.

'What did you do after the bridge?'

'I took a job on the cross-river ferries. Ferried people from Customs House to Holman Street. From Sydney Street to Mowbray Park.'

Robbie laughs:

'Old Man River?'

'I once counted the number of times I've crossed the river. Can't remember any more but the figure'd make you dizzy.'

'So you built the bridge, then end up ferrying people across the river. You work for years building a link that people can drive across, and then you toss it in.'

'Yes,' the old man says quietly.

'Ironic, isn't it?'

'I am old, son. Irony is like a toenail fungus, the way it grows on you when you get to my age.'

Robbie gets closer, teasing information from the old man, angling always towards his father.

'What about others? Did my father get on with people?'

'Get on with people? Son, he was a god. We worshipped your father.'

'Did he have friends?'

'Plenty.'

'What was he like?'

'What was he like? What was he like?' the old man ponders the question. 'I'm unreliable. Ask your mother.'

Breakfast in the apartment by the river. He enters, greets his mother with a kiss, receives one.

Lily sees, and waits for him to speak. In the bedroom is her husband, propped in his bed like a mute sideline spectator. She longs for things to take shape. So she can grip them, can shake them, can cast them out if that is what is needed.

Robbie longs to ask, but finds himself not yet ready, his father's name too great a weight to lift from inside him, too opaque a form.

When he rises to go –

'How is Freya?' Lily asks, for he rarely mentions her now.

'Fine.'

Freya dreams again of the stabbing: the riverside path, the freeway above, night all around. Fear and fever, and sharp things glinting with violence. Then the dream metamorphoses and Freya becomes the flying fox, screeching, screeching, screeching and soon she is awake.

Robbie gets a fresh tea towel from the kitchen, dampens it with cold water, and brings it in to her. He dabs her forehead, cools the back of her neck.

'It won't go away,' she says to him.

'It will,' he says, rocking her through the hours before dawn.

★

Story

She is not in bed when she hears the knock at the door, but is sitting on the back deck in the overcast mid-morning. There have been so few knocks at the door lately. At the second set of raps Freya rises from her chair, set to look over the gully, into the branches of the fig and the umbrella trees and the other plants competing out there for space.

'Good morning.'

'Morning.'

The two women look at each other from either side of the threshold.

'I thought you could do with a good cup of tea,' and Lily reaches into her leather handbag for a decorated tin which she offers Freya.

'Thanks.'

Freya looks at the tin but doesn't take it. Nor does she reject it.

'Come on, let me make you a cuppa,' Lily says and she bustles inside, past Freya who moves to make way, and down the corridor towards the natural light at the back of the house, towards the kitchen.

Lily talks as she moves. She is expert at this. She talks as she sums up the room, takes in the kettle, the stove, the cupboards where she will find the cups and mugs. Knows, as she talks, precisely where Freya is: standing at the boundary of the kitchen, not yet having yielded it to Lily. Knows the art of the question, how to fill the smallest of them with immediacy, with urgency. How to say *where do you keep your matches, dear?* in order to take control, or at least to signal her intentions. How to follow Freya's silence with some harmless observation — about gas and *the evenness of the heat* — even as she opens the pantry and scans its shelves for matches. Knows too, how much consent can be taken from silence.

She lights the stove, fills the kettle, names aloud the tea-leaves she has seen in the pantry, the different types of tea, their various medicinal qualities. And as she does this, she feels Freya give to her, senses the exact moment, a mere turn of Freya's shoulders which she catches from the corner of her eye. All this being for Freya's good, she thinks, because people want you to take control, they want to give themselves over. Especially when they are lost. Then, when it has happened and Freya has yielded, Lily knows to slow, to shift into gentleness, and to hand something back.

'Where shall we sit, dear?'

Freya leads her onto the deck where, seated, Lily asks, 'So how are you coping?'

Coping. A misjudgment. A word which sparks resentment in Freya. That she could be used like this. Only now does she flare.

'You mean Robbie, don't you? You mean, "How's Robbie coping?"'

Lily wonders if Freya knows about Robbie's morning visits to her, their breakfasts together. But suddenly she questions herself as well.

'I suppose I might,' she says slowly, uncertainly.

The two women look out over the railing. The trees in the gully are dulled by an opaque light from the low-clouded sky. There is a mass of vegetation, dark and indistinct. Lily's eyes search for something to settle upon, a point of reference, something from which she might start to build the conversation again.

Story

'Is that a Moreton Bay fig?' she asks.

'Yes. Robbie's fig.'

'Robbie's fig...' Lily slowly repeats the words. She says it again, but this time a query, 'Robbie's fig?'

'He calls it the most truthful of all the trees,' Freya says.

'I'm sorry?'

Freya gets up, walks back inside to the kitchen. This morning she plucked three fig leaves from the tree, and placed them, standing upright, in a glass on the windowsill. Some gesture to Robbie, unclear even to her, especially now. She takes one from the glass and out onto the deck, and sits again in her cane chair.

Between the women is a small, low, circular table, the grain of its wood hidden by a coat of paint which Robbie has talked about stripping. Freya places the leaf on the white table, and demonstrates the thing which Robbie had once shown her, turning the leaf over, pointing out its two sides, one glossy, one darkened, unhidden equals.

'The most truthful of trees.'

'Freya, dear,' Lily replies, quietly, evenly, 'you're ever so mistaken. It's nothing of the sort. The fig is riddled with secrets. It was made to hide things. It was made by God for that very purpose, its leaves so big you could even hide behind them yourself if you had to.'

She looks at Freya, says to her, slowly, mouthing each word, giving each the same weight, as if each is precious, and none can be separated one from the other: *'And the eyes of them both were opened, and they knew they were naked, and they sewed fig leaves together and made themselves aprons.'*

Freya fingers the leaf, turns it over once, twice, then lays it down on the shiny table, the spine of the big leaf at such a curvature that it seems to her then, as she places it back on the surgically white surface, that the leaf has become a human body, writhing in sharp, back-arching agony, frozen at this moment on the clean sheets of an indifferent bed.

'You know about figs?' she asks.

'I've learnt.'

Lily looks at Freya, waits until the younger woman has met her eyes, then fixes her as firmly as she can with her gaze. 'A mother wants to understand what it is that takes her son from her.'

Freya smiles, broadly, almost warmly, an energy coming off the conflict, entering her.

'It's okay, Lily,' she says, 'I'm no threat.'

Lily returns the smile and nods, not in agreement, but in understanding, and after a pause the tone of her voice changes, as if she is beginning a new conversation, open, light.

'How long have you been here, Freya dear?'

'Years.'

'I mean in this house, with Robbie. Twelve months?'

'Yes, something like that.'

'So you've been watching that tree for a year?' Lily says, pointing out over the railing at the fig.

Freya lets her continue.

'Let me ask you, in all that time have you ever seen it flower?'

The question penetrates. The answer is immediately, startlingly, unsettlingly, no. But rather than acknowledge that to this woman who has come for her, Freya continues to think, to try and recover some information, some comment Robbie might have made in passing which could explain this odd fact. Surely he must have told her this, surely he must have mentioned it. But there is nothing to retrieve. She doubts herself.

'They don't flower,' Lily says.

Twelve

Robbie asks about the bridge, working at the old man's memory like a needle probing skin for a splinter, asks him his name.

'Names don't matter when you get to my age. Belonging is what matters.'

'Tell me about the others, then. The names that have stuck to the bridge. The *Story* Bridge. *Kemp* Place. The *Bradfield* Highway. Did you know them — Story? Kemp? Bradfield?'

'Yes . . .' The old man weighs the word before speaking it — 'Bradfield.'

'The engineer who designed the bridge,' Robbie says.

'You know about him and the Sydney Harbour Bridge?' asks the old man.

Story

'He designed that too?'

'The public record has it that way, but not everyone says so.'

'What do you mean?'

'Another engineer – Ralph Freeman – also claimed credit for the designs. He was the consulting engineer, an Englishman with an English firm, Dorman Long and Co. They fought it out in the papers for years, he and Bradfield. For the right to say the Harbour Bridge was theirs.'

'What's the saying?' Robbie muses, '. . . about success having many fathers?'

The old man considers for a long time, then rather than answer he says to Robbie:

'Do you know who discovered the Brisbane River? The whites, I mean?'

'John Oxley,' Robbie says. 'Sent up here by Sir Thomas Brisbane, the Governor of New South Wales, his uncle.' Schoolboy history.

'Wrong. It was a couple of convicts. Not only that, lost convicts, castaways blown off course in a storm.'

Robbie shrugs his shoulders, turns up his palms.

'They pulled out of Sydney Town one fair April day in 1823, four of them. A few short days' sailing to collect cedar for the colony. But no sooner were they through the Heads than they were hit by a storm, a vicious one. Only when it ended, eleven days later, did they put up sail. So happens, they thought the storm and the current had taken them south. So happens, they thought they were off Tasmania – Van Diemen's Land. So happens, they couldn't have been more wrong. They weren't south of Sydney – they were north of it. But unawares, they chart a course north-west, and take it for near on three weeks sailing up-coast, sailing further and further *away*, further up-coast until, desperate and starving, half-mad from drinking seawater, they beach on Moreton Island. Believing, all along, they were still south of Sydney rather than seven hundred miles north.'

'Uh-huh,' says Robbie slowly, trying to work out what the old man is telling him.

'So they island-hopped – stealing canoes – till they reached the mainland. Then they skirted the bay on foot. They were beyond disorientation, they were. They were mad . . . Delirious. All but naked. Eventually they stumbled upon this big river, and worked their way up its south bank looking for somewhere to cross, or another canoe they could pinch. See, they were still committed to this idea that Sydney lay to the north. Amazing what belief can do, isn't it? The deceptive power of it.'

'And the river?' Robbie prompts as the old man seems to fade, seems to wander.

'The river? It was an obstacle to them . . . an obstacle. Almost did them in. Banks thick with trees, too. Eventually they crossed it, and soon after that they were found. By whites. Rescued, I mean. In the country north of the river. It was Oxley who found them, on his expedition.'

The old man draws breath, taps the table with his fingers, looking for something, his tapping growing more forceful, ever more urgent.

'But the fact remains, they beat Oxley to it. As discoveries go it was a shambles: unplanned, incompetent and unwanted. But it was them who discovered it, not Oxley.'

'I didn't know that.'

'Exactly.'

★

Story

Freya kneels before a bookcase. Scattered around her on the floor are volumes from the lowest shelves, Robbie's books on flora, his botanical resource books, the scientific works. She's searching out what she can about figs in the large pages of these heavy-bound texts. How can there be fruit without flowers? This question, chasing itself around the inside of her head.

She learns about Moreton Bay figs. Their taxonomy, *Moraceae* their family name. The etymology of their species name, *macrophylla:* from the Greek 'macros' large, and 'phyllon' a leaf. Too large, she thinks, for the first time. She sees diagrams sketched by careful, deliberate hands, of leaves and fruit, but no flowers. She learns about them, the scientific dissection of them: trunk, bark, branchlets, leaves, venation, fruit, habitat, distribution.

She discovers, slowly, that they are not flowerless – that is just how they seem. Their fruit, purple ripe and edible, is both fruit and flower, the flower both inflorescence and fruit. Rather than opening, expanding, and unveiling at bloom, the fig tree's flower is enclosed in the cavity of the fig. It grows in the dark, it blossoms in the dark, it is pollinated in the dark. It is an inwards-looking flower, a hidden flower, hundred-floreted.

You eat a fig, you are eating fruit and flower. Potent, intense, secretive.

Thirteen

It is morning in the apartment. His mother opens the door for him, and Robbie enters. Today, rather than pass it by as he usually would, he pauses before the shrine his mother has made to the Story Bridge, a different reflex at work in him. Lily continues into the kitchen to prepare breakfast, glancing at him as she goes, wondering.

Robbie touches a picture frame standing on the top shelf of the bookcase. He is exploring. Incompetent, yes. Unplanned? True. But he wants this now, wants to know. He picks up a china plate with the bridge painted on its face, turns it over, but does not understand the markings on its base, some coded stamp of ceramic authenticity.

His eyes rise above the bookcase to a framed sketch of the

Story

bridge, hanging on the wall. He sees it as if for the first time, this drawing that has always been there, hooked on a wall in his parents' home. The artist was sketching from the north side of the river, from the cliff, rather than from the southern bank, at river-height. The bridge crosses the page in deft pencil strokes, breaks where it is still unfinished, still unjoined, then recommences in criss-crossed girders which compress in perspective as the far end of the bridge shrinks away in the distance. The water sweeps underneath the bridge, then arcs around the tip of low-lying Kangaroo Point and continues its curve upriver. Its long graceful sweep strikes a contrast with the broken bridge. Robbie places the sketch in time. Late 1939.

Robbie lifts the sketch off the small nail driven so carefully into the plasterboard. There is no inscription on the back, nothing to help. Robbie takes it into the kitchen.

'Lily,' he says, 'who drew this?'

Lily looks around to her son.

'The bridge,' she says.

'Where did the drawing come from?'

'Your father gave it to me,' Lily answers.

'Did he draw it?'

'No – a friend of his did.'

'Who? It's unsigned.'

'A friend of your father's from his bridge days, love.'

'What was the friend's name?'

She pauses, and in the moment she turns back to continue slicing fruit for their breakfast she says:

'I think his name was Charlie Stahl.' Then, 'Love, do you want mango with your cereal?'

Robbie remounts the sketch, and reaches for the photograph album resting on the second shelf of the bookcase. He turns its leaves until he finds the photo he wants, then takes the album in to Lily. He stands beside her at the kitchen bench, and she pauses in her cutting, her son so close to her elbow, the old sepia image thrust into her line of vision.

It is a picture of his father and a dozen others on the bridge. In the centre of the photograph is a large steel upright. Men sit or stand on a platform around it, or they hang off it on either side, leaning out at angles like branches off a trunk. His father, hatless, is sitting centre-frame on the platform. Singlet and shorts. His left leg swings loosely over the platform, while the right is propped up, the foot on the platform itself. His father's elbow rests casually on his right knee, while his left arm is swung back, opening his chest to the camera. There is ease and there is strength in him.

'Which is Charlie Stahl?'

Robbie hears his mother take an awkward breath of air, a gulp which bottoms out. Lily clutches for another breath.

'I think that's him, Robbie,' she says, pointing to a man standing close to the girder. 'That's Charlie.'

Robbie sees a man in a short-sleeved shirt and beret. A man of average height and build. An open face with the forehead wide and the beret sitting high on his head. Robbie can't discern the man's finer features – the image is too small, the resolution of the photo too crude. Robbie peers hard, then lets go.

Out of his mother's sight, Robbie takes the photo from its sleeve then replaces the album in the bookcase. He slides the photo under his shirt and feels its cool surface against the skin of his stomach. Robbie sits to breakfast.

Story

'Don't you want the binoculars, love?'
'There's nothing more to see out there, Lily.'

Another thing Freya learns is that each species of fig tree has its own species of pollinator wasp. For the Moreton Bay fig, it is *Pleistondontes froggatti*, minute and unlikely, but without which the Moreton Bay fig is inconceivable. Nothing else, no other insect, no other wasp, will pollinate it. The great tree and the tiny wasp, the symbiosis of them, tight and infallible. So many revelations, Freya thinks.

When the fig is ready to be pollinated, a foundress – a pollen-bearing, egg-laden female wasp – enters the cavity through a tiny pore in the skin of the fruit, and burrows deep inside. Once there, enclosed in the dark, the foundress has two tasks, one for the fig, one for herself. She brings grains of pollen with her, from her previous fruit, and these she leaves on the stigma of the fig flower, fertilising it. But she also deposits her eggs on the ovules of the flowers. As each larva grows, it will eat a developing fig seed, obtaining from the seed the nourishment it needs to survive. As a wasp grows, a seed is consumed. Each developing wasp is one less fig seed. But figs have so many seeds, and when the fruit is mature, the wasps emerge from their galls. Still surrounded by the walls of the fig, their universe, the wingless males seek out females in the dark, often their sisters. They mate. And only then do the female wasps leave their birth fig, loaded with pollen, emerging through a tunnel in the fig-wall cut by the males, seeking out a new fig which will receive their eggs.

Freya pictures it: wingless males, the entirety of their existence lived inside the dark of the fig, and females that fly.

★

Robbie says, 'Can you show me your bridge sketches again?'

The old man picks up the cardboard cylinder at his feet – it accompanies him everywhere.

'Clear the decks.'

Robbie moves the glasses of beer and the ashtray to another table, then runs his forearm across the table, using his shirt sleeve to wipe off the condensation left from the cold glasses.

The old man peels back the prints Robbie saw when he first met him in the camp under the bridge. Streeton and Roberts and Nolan and the others.

'The nation-building artists,' says Robbie as the old man lifts them back, one by one, 'the myth-makers.'

'I never did get to see much of the country,' the old man murmurs. 'They did it for me.'

He lifts the prints away until he reaches the sketches, drawn by the same hand as the one Robbie examined this morning in his mother's apartment.

'Is your name Charlie Stahl?' Robbie asks.

The old man does not react.

'Is this you?'

Robbie takes out the photo, slips it from a folder he's brought, turns it around so the old man is looking at the group of men. So he is looking at the bereted one. 'Is this you?' Robbie says again, pointing.

The old man does not blink. He looks up and then straight ahead to a point somewhere on Robbie's chest. His eyes begin to water, but still he does not shift his gaze, locked on some arbitrary place where Robbie's shirt opens onto his chest.

'Hey ... Old Man River,' Robbie says as gently as he can, ' ... are you Charlie Stahl?'

The question hangs between them, long and heavy.

'Why do you want to know?' the old man says eventually, his gaze unmoved still.

'I'm trying to piece this all together.'

'Piece what?'

'The sketches,' Robbie says. 'My parents have one hanging on a wall.'

'Your father has one of the sketches?'

'Yes.'

'Of Stahl's? Of the bridge?'

'Yes.'

'The shameless bastard.'

'So who was Charlie Stahl?'

The old man rolls a smoke, each movement deliberate, each component of this ritual magnified by the silence: opening the pouch, sliding a paper from the Tally-Ho packet, taking a pinch of tobacco between forefinger and thumb and dropping the dried leaf onto the white paper. Robbie waits while the gnarled tobacco leaf is teased along the strip of paper. The man raises the paper and leaf with both hands cradled beneath it and rolls a thin white cylinder which he lifts to his tongue to seal.

'Stahl was a friend, your father's best mate. He died on the bridge, and your father and I were responsible.' Then after a pause, 'In our own ways.'

He watches these first words reach Robbie and, when he is sure they have arrived, strikes a match, its head bursting into flame as he raises it to the cigarette between his lips. He draws breath so the tobacco catches. Inhales, and resumes talking, smoke and words swelling from between his lips. The old man speaks rhythmically, in incantation, as if his revelation and the ceremony of smoking are the same thing.

'It was a crazy theory. Mine. I have to own that. It was madness, looking back, and if there's any explanation it's because it was after another mate, Billy Hodges, had died. We were young, we were angry, we needed someone to blame. We got this idea that the engineers could measure how dangerous it was, that they knew precisely how many deaths it would take to build the bridge. Precisely. And that therefore we were just pawns to be disposed of. Once the theory got a hold, it couldn't be dislodged, and your father wanted proof. Owed it to Billy, he said.

'The steel engineer was a Canadian – our perfect scapegoat, looking back ... It's funny how quick we are to do that. How feeble we really are. Though it shouldn't be a surprise ... human nature being what it is. So, Jack and Charlie worked out a way of getting into the engineer's house, to read the construction notes ... and the tender papers, if they could find them. Jack and Charlie would find the papers – that was the plan. They'd find the proof. And I was the getaway. When they had what they needed, they'd meet me at the river and I'd row them back across to the other side.

'But only Jack got to the boat. Something had happened. The police were after them. There were sirens going and police cars everywhere. Jack, well he continued on to the boat as arranged, but Charlie got left ...

'The next I saw of Charlie he was above us on the bridge. It had just been linked, and it wasn't safe, not at night. In fact it was dangerous as hell. So while I rowed Jack across to safety – *chauffeuring* him – Charlie was up there on the bridge with the police on his tail.'

Old man Carleton shakes his head to himself.

'We were still on the water when Charlie fell.'

He looks at Robbie through liquid eyes, watering now from the cigarette smoke as much as age and memory.

Robbie nods, thinks he understands.

'Your father and I made a pact that night,' Carleton goes on, '... or more accurately, he got my agreement. "Not a word to anyone," Jack said. "Not a word" – your father said that, and I went along with it. We didn't want to lose our jobs, we didn't want to get involved with the police. And it was, after all, an accident. So *not a word* during the police investigation, not a word at the coroner's inquest, not a word to Charlie's parents, not a word to his girl. Not a word.'

Carleton has unconsciously lifted his forefinger to his lips, hushing his imaginary self, *not a word, not a word*. As if he is whispering to a child. Hush, hush. He becomes aware of the gesture, and drops his hand back to the table. So much silence for so many years.

'We also never said another word about it to each other. In fact, we never spoke again. Never. I don't think we trusted ourselves. We kept away from each other in the months we finished off the bridge. Then we just went our different ways. He worked in the Evans Deakin shipyards, building ships for the war. Then he enlisted and went up to New Guinea or the Pacific or wherever he went. I worked the ferries. I saw him from a distance once or twice over the years. When he was passing through town. And some of the boys give you bits of information. You hear things. But not another word passed between us.'

'And ... Stahl?' Robbie says.

'Charlie was gone two days. For two days the water police dragged the river. For two days the police launch hung on the water. Like a drifting headstone, it was. Charlie rose eventually. You know, I thought he might have survived . . .

'Anyway, it was midday on the third day . . . always the third day . . . when Charlie floated to the surface. Bloated and fish-eaten, he was. Recognisable only from the clothes – his tweed trousers and plaited leather belt. His shirt was gone – ripped clean off by the current. And one oil-stained sandshoe, with mud thick between his foot and his shoe. I was the first to see him – just a dark shape below the surface of the brown river. Then the tide turned him over and his shoulder rolled out of the water, and I knew it was him. He was too heavy to drag up alone, so I ran a rope under his arms, tight around his chest, and rowed him in to the bank. Towed him in like I was a bloody tugboat.'

A neon light flickers on outside the hotel, and Robbie sees the man lit up now by coloured flashes, his old face throbbing strangely pink and green and alternating blue.

'We grappled him ashore at the bank – an ungainly thing to do. You ever dragged a man out of the water? They don't want to come. But we pulled him out. And when we'd lifted him out there was something I had to find out. I slipped my hand into his trouser pocket when no one could see. And you know, there it was.'

He reaches into his own pocket and pulls it out, the rivet. A piece of five-inch steel sixty years old, but rubbed smooth from where he's handled it day after day, year after year.

'There was nothing special about it. It was just any old rivet, but it was a talisman for him.'

'And for you, since then?'

Carleton considers this, grunts in response, a huff, short but open.

'Maybe not,' he says finally, this piece of the bridge resting in his palm. 'Either way, I've no need for it now.'

He tosses it then to Robbie, lobs it the short distance between them so it turns over itself in the air as it flies, floats and drops into Robbie's hands.

'It's yours.'

That night Robbie lies awake, turning the conversations with the old man over in his head, piecing events together, fitting his life into history.

'Frey?'

She is awake.

'I was right about him. I was right all along,' Robbie whispers to her in the dark.

'About what?'

'My father. And what he did, the hollowness of it. The bastard built his career after the Story Bridge on the death of his best friend.'

'What do you mean?' she asks, croak-voiced, tired.

'He basically killed his best mate.'

'The old man told you this?'

'Near enough. That he was responsible for it.'

Freya listens to Robbie's version, waterlogged and, she thinks, swollen out of shape. She is growing tired of the bridge – and all it is responsible for, all the distortions – and its place between them.

'Every bridge he built, every dam, every viaduct, every bloody tunnel – it cost him his best mate to learn that the engineers weren't what he'd imagined, and then he bloody well became one! ... The path of his career passes over the grave of his best friend.'

'You think so?'

'Lily moved him to that apartment overlooking the bridge after he had his stroke. I think she wanted it to be a comfort to him ... But I wonder now if it was a torment – there'd be justice in it, if it was.'

Freya whispers the word to herself, *comfort*. Thinks, that's all I want, that's all I'm asking for. Not your bridge, not your father, not your figs. Is it so much?

Fourteen

There is chattering in the darkness – night-feeding birds and bats and the insects which smell him or feel the warmth he radiates. In the bedroom Freya is tossing feverishly. Robbie fetches an empty seed sack from beneath the house and finds a torch. He slides down the banks of the gully till he is at the base of the fig tree. With the torch light he picks out the familiar route up the fig's trunk and into its branches. He climbs in the dark, the flesh of the fig cool under the palms of his hands. Robbie settles in the crook of a large branch, and picks leaves from the tree, depositing them into his hessian sack. White sap runs from the base of each leaf as he breaks it off its twig. Robbie interrupts his work at intervals to wipe the milky sap off his hands. He fills the hessian sack, leaf by leaf, and when he is done descends the tree, climbs the gully slope and takes the stairs up to the house.

In the house he lights a beeswax candle and tips the sackful of fig leaves onto the long hoop-pine table. He spreads the leaves out across the table, ordering them in lines according to size. Moreton Bay fig leaves: big and broad with their glossy surface and rust-red underside. Base to tip, base to tip, each leaf placed so it overlaps the one before it, the glossy surfaces of the leaves face up, until the table is covered with a pattern of overlapping leaves.

Robbie settles himself into a chair at the table, and begins to sew the leaves together. He passes a needle threaded with dark twine through the back of one leaf and then through the next. The needle pierces the flesh of the leaf and the leaf-membranes stay intact; the leaf holds its shape. He sews two leaves together. Then he adds a third and then a fourth, and he continues like this, adding one leaf at a time as he builds his leaf tapestry, leaf by leaf, row by row. Even from here he can still hear Freya crying out in her sleep.

The candle stump burns down. He replaces it with a fresh candle and continues his work. From time to time he tests that the blanket will hold, that there are no weaknesses and that the thread will not tear through the leaves from the growing weight. He must be gentle.

At some stage in the night, when Freya calls out again in her sleep, Robbie thinks he hears his name and pauses in his sewing to rise and check on her. She groans as he enters the room, and Robbie makes out a furrow deep in her forehead as her eyes fight against her dream. In one continuous motion she groans again, turns over and settles beneath the cotton sheet, her back to the doorway and to Robbie watching. It was merely a cry – no audible word.

He returns to the table and his work. His sewing fills the night.

Closer to dawn, there are stirrings. Creatures waking, others returning from their night's odyssey. It is dark still as Robbie completes the fig-leaf blanket, the night not yet doused. When he is done, Robbie folds the blanket once, twice on the table, and then over his forearm. He carries it into the bedroom where Freya sleeps, the sheet pulled up to her chin against the chilled hour before dawn. He rests his night's work at the foot of the bed and then, section by section, gently unfolds it over her sleeping body, the cool glossy surface of the leaf-blanket face down on the bed, so as he unfolds its final portion, the leaves fall against the skin of her shoulder.

Freya stirs with the strange, cool sensation. She rolls over, so that her back is no longer to the door, and her body moves under the leaf-blanket, under its weight. She wakes and her eyes find him, standing beside her.

'What?' she murmurs.

She feels strangely uncomfortable under his gaze. He remains silent, and even in the fog of her sleep she understands there is something here that he wants her to discover, some wish, a revelation perhaps. Freya feels she does not have the strength to feed his desire.

She closes her eyes again and is aware of the unfamiliar weight upon her, heavier than the thin cotton sheet, the balance of the weight different. She draws her arms up, lifting them out and over the fig-leaf blanket. She feels its roughness with her forearms, the ridges of leaf and stalk against her skin. She shudders.

She resists the instinct to shake off this foreignness, to toss it all off with a single violent shake. She is awake enough for that.

She knows what this is. She knows the leaves. His talismanic fig. *His* fig. *His* leaves. He is suffocating her.

'Do you like it?' he says.

She is more tired than she can ever recall. 'It's heavy, Robbie.'

'The tree of truth, remember?'

She doesn't respond.

'Remember – the Moreton Bay fig leaf – the leaf of truth?' his voice rising with anxiety.

'I know.' Her voice distant and sad.

'Don't you like it?' he says to her.

Even as she shrinks away from him, she realises that he too is desperate.

'It's heavy, Robbie,' she says again.

No longer able to contain herself, she turns her back to him, sinks her face in her pillow, and sobs.

Fifteen

In the early evening, when Robbie enters the empty house, there is no lamplight in the front room. The bedroom door is open and somehow sags on its hinge. From the front door, with the street behind him and the echo of the pub and the old man's voice fading, it is the silence of the house he hears.

He knows. He knows immediately. But still there's the shock of it.

He goes through the motions. He enters the bedroom to nothing. There is enough streetlight coming through the still-open front door to show him the empty, made bed. Robbie walks the corridor to the living room and the kitchen. He flicks lights on. Nothing. Despite himself he calls out – 'Freya,

Frey?' – and searches each room of the house. Then he is back in the bedroom.

Her clothes are gone from her drawers, her backpack removed from above the wardrobe. On the chair in the corner of the room is the fig-leaf blanket he sewed for her the night before. It is neatly folded in four. It glimmers where the street-light slides off the glossy leaves.

He slumps on the bed, hollowed out.

Freya had waited for him to go to work before packing. Before taking a taxi out to the airport, before walking down the long aisle of the plane to find her seat, before dropping into it, before trying to make herself comfortable.

It was late in the afternoon when her plane lifted from the tarmac and rose over the river's estuary. A layer of cloud hung above the city and the bay. She looked back as the plane began its curve out to the ocean. The sun in the west below her lit up the river in an orange blaze, as though a drunken trail of petrol had been splashed across the city and then torched. Her fingers tingled as if it was she who might still be holding the match. The river burned as she watched, burned with fire and light like a tear across the city, flaming. And in the burning river's glow she found the house she had just left, dwarfed by the quiet, dark fig in the gully behind it. The house where she had been broken, by whatever thing it is one gives up when one tries to love. Then the plane angle altered and the river-fire was drawn from her vision, doused.

She has begun her long flight home. This decision she has

Story

taken. An act of faith. That there will be a home, that you can't simply make one, you must find it.

She is gone. He is not sure what he does next. At some point he looks for a note but finds none. He spends the long night waiting for her to return. Each sound in the street is Freya making her way back. Each sound in the street is a hope dashed. He gets snatches of sleep, careful to leave her side of the bed free should she slip back into the house while he is dozing. Light rain falls during the early hours. A dull dawn arrives with the sound of pigeons cooing on the roof of the house next door. He hears a crow landing on his own corrugated-iron roof, and the beat of wings as the pigeons take to the air. The crow's claws scratch against the iron sheeting as the bird jumps and slides down the pitch of the roof. Robbie waits for it to take to the air again, but the scratching sound continues as the bird moves around above him, picking out food in the roof-guttering. It begins to caw in short bursts in answer to another crow across a gully of houses.

Robbie rises from the bed. The front door is wide open, and he realises he forgot to close it the night before. He descends the front steps, damp from the overnight rain. In the middle of the street he looks back at the house and the black bird perched on the roof. It caws again and Robbie hisses at the bird. Then, '*Garn*,' he yells, throwing his arms at the crow. The opaque sky looses itself once more and a shower of rain begins to fall. Robbie feels the first drops on his forearms. '*Garn*,' he hisses and the crow takes to the air with slow wing-beats.

He rings the airlines, but they will give him no information. The bus companies have no record of her. He calls Bec. She hasn't heard from Freya since she rang about the protest. 'Is she alright?' Bec asks. Robbie hangs up, unable to answer.

Robbie waits out the day in the house. There are no phone calls. No one visits. He wanders the rooms and things come to him. He notices the depth of the stain in the white ceramic teapot Freya always used. How the different-sized drinking glasses have been ordered in the cupboard. Which recipe book she last used. He notices that Freya has cropped the herbs in the garden. In the fridge the freshly cut herbs are tied into bundles with rubber bands, and line an entire shelf: basil and dill and parsley and lemongrass. He notices the way postcards have been arranged on the kitchen sill. How, beside them, in an old jam jar, stand two Moreton Bay fig leaves, drying in the afternoon sun.

He sleeps that night in the depression Freya's body has made in the bed.

Sixteen

Robbie wakes again without her, and finally realises she is gone. It is early, but he dresses, a new force in him, the shock turned to anger. What more could he have done? What more could he have given? For the first time in a year he leaves the house without having to worry about waking her, the sound of his boots sharp on the floorboards, as if each bootfall is deliberately struck.

Pigeons stir when Robbie climbs the ladder to the roof of the pub, and it is the movement of the birds which wakes the old man, their disturbed fluttering, their short, panicked warbling. Robbie apologises, but the sound of his voice is swamped by the bridge traffic. He says it again, louder – *sorry* – and as the old man sits upright on his couch Robbie passes him a loaf of warm bread from a West End bakery.

'You said you heard that my father had married my mother?' Robbie almost yells the question above the traffic noise.

'Lily, yes.'

'You said you were surprised. Why?'

The old man reaches for his smoke tin. To slow Robbie down, as much as because he needs one.

'Couldn't believe it,' he says eventually. 'Jack had been away for twenty-odd years, and then he comes back and marries Lily. Just like that. Couldn't believe it when I heard.'

'But why not?'

The old man, Old Man River, Peter Carleton, takes Robbie into his eyes now, and it dawns on him. It comes to him in rolling waves of sorrow and sadness and sympathy.

'You know who Lily is?' Carleton says gently, as gently as he can.

Robbie feels an unease rise from his stomach.

'My mother? Of course I know.'

Carleton begins the story again, tells Robbie the thing the old man thought he already knew.

'Charlie Stahl had a girl when he died – a sweetheart. He ... he *loved* this girl. You could see it. He loved her. You understand?'

Robbie does not. He feels sick. The only thing he knows is that the old man is looking at him with an intensity he can't meet. He realises it is pity. He feels Carleton wanting him to understand, forcing him to understand, but he can't think for the tightening in his gut, the dread spreading like roots through his body.

'Evelyn was her name.'

The old man looks for recognition, but it is not there. He continues, slow and patient.

'Evelyn was the Canadian engineer's daughter.'

Robbie's face remains blank.

'She was young – still at school, though she was older than that. Older than that in here.'

Carleton touches his heart with his hand. Once, twice, three times.

'And here,' he says, lowering his head slightly and pressing his finger against his forehead. 'You could tell it here too.'

Carleton keeps tapping his forehead, looking at Robbie at an odd angle, as if to say, you got it yet, do you understand?

'Evelyn was pregnant when Charlie died,' the old man goes on. 'She had a little girl. She called her –'

'Lily,' finishes Robbie.

Seventeen

'Charlie Stahl, Lily.'

She doesn't turn, the morning light on her face, Robbie at her back, her hips pressed against the kitchen bench and her hands suspended now from whatever morning task has been obliterated by the name.

'Charlie Stahl,' Robbie says again.

Does she turn to face her son? And if she does, then what? She thinks of God's wrath, and searches for guidance. But her Old Testament stories, her beloved stories, deny her at this moment. Was it God, or Lot himself, who forbade the turning back? She simply can't recall, her mind dizzy with the name and the engulfing past.

'Charlie Stahl.'

Story

'Yes, love,' she says, and looks at him now.

'Charlie Stahl was your father,' Robbie says to her.

'Yes, love.'

'Charlie Stahl was Jack's best mate.'

'Yes, love.'

'You married your father's best mate.'

'Yes.'

His family story falls away and another rushes to replace it.

'Jack has always been here, he's always been part of my life, Robbie. He supported us – my mother Evelyn and me – after I was born. After Charlie had died. He sent us money year after year, he cabled it to Mother from all over the world. And once a year, sometimes more, he'd visit. I got to know him from those visits. Twenty-five years of visits. Regular as the seasons, Jack was. He was committed to us, Robbie. He was always part of my life.'

He lets her explain.

'Then, after Mother died – How do these things happen, Robbie? . . . I don't know.'

She answers herself: 'I fell in love with Jack, but that happened a long time before I married him. Maybe even when I was still a child. Probably . . . Mother used to call me her "water lily", her "river lily", her "Brisbane River Lily" – Jack liked that . . . Anyway, after Mother died we got married.'

'Her dying gave you permission, did it?' he asks, the question folded over its own sharpened edge.

'He was fine, Robbie –' Lily catches herself – '*is* fine. The sketch of the bridge that Charlie did, the one you asked about – well, Jack gave that to me. And he gave it to me to remember Charlie, my father. I don't have my own memories of him, but I've got that. And it helps. Maybe only a little, but it helps. I think of my father sitting in front of the bridge, observing it, studying it, then sketching it out. The drawing helps. It tells a story. And it was also a gift from Jack, it doubled as that.'

'There's another story, Lily.'

'What do you mean?' she says, her voice subdued.

'Your father falling off the bridge to his death, your husband with him when it happened. Your husband abandoning your father to the police. The police pursuing your father off the bridge, pursuing him to his death. And your husband silent about it.'

'Abandoned?' Lily raises her voice. 'Where did you get that from? Jack didn't *abandon* anyone, love. You think I don't know what happened? Look, Robbie, I know about my father's death. Abandoned!'

She shakes her head, shudders at the thought, preposterous. 'My father wasn't abandoned. He was leading the police away from Jack!'

Lily calms.

'But that doesn't mean Jack didn't feel guilty about it, didn't feel he owed my father. I knew when I married him that he felt he was responsible. It was a guilt that would never leave him, Robbie. It's haunted him. It drove him from the city ... from the country. I tried to persuade him, to convince him that history would forgive him, that he didn't need to flee ... But when a thing happens it leaves its imprint on you. Things don't go away. Never.'

'The bridge was a curse then.'

'No, Robbie, it was a *gift*.' Fiercely, 'A gift, always a gift. And Jack is only half of it. There's more of the bridge in me than there is in Jack – my father worked the bridge too, and my mother was the steel engineer's daughter. I reckon that makes me bridge blue-blood, Robbie,' she tries to laugh, old and full of sorrow. Then she adds, 'Without that, you wouldn't be here.'

'But why didn't he tell me? Why didn't *anyone* tell me?'

'Guilt.'

'*Pah!*' Robbie nearly spits it out, dismissing her, matching her ferocity, a different question swelling inside his brain now: Why didn't *you* tell me?

Lily continues:

'You don't know guilt, Robbie – the hold of it. Jack was riddled with it. He was guilty Charlie had died, guilty he'd kept quiet about it, guilty my mother was alone, guilty I didn't have a father.'

'Guilt's no basis for marriage, Lily,' Robbie says, soft, cold, hard.

'Guilty he couldn't give you a clean, straight history,' she continues, choking now.

'Don't,' he says, unrelenting, 'don't bring me into it.'

'Oh Robbie!' Lily cries. She wilts into her chair and drops her head into her hands, sobbing.

He almost leaves then. Having hurt her, satisfied, he is a moment from walking out the apartment into the corridor, the lift, the street. But something keeps him. Something touches him. A hollowing of the air beyond the apartment as the morning breeze changes direction, a crow's echo falling through the sky outside, the muffling of the dawn light as a cloud passes low across the sun.

He stays. He watches her weeping, watches the great chafing

sobs, the shaking of his mother's small shoulders, the bowed head. Something enters him, small.

He begins to see his mother. A small woman, an only child, a fatherless child. A woman who dedicated herself to looking after others: her own mother, her husband, her son, her husband once again now he is an invalid. A woman who subjugated herself time and again, who made herself small at every opportunity, the better to cling to her place in things. Keeper and carer. A woman who brought her husband to this apartment with its Story Bridge views as a comfort to him, and, he now realises, as a comfort to herself.

Lily looks up at him, her eyes shot with red, and says, sobbing still:

'It was so unfair.'

'What was?'

'It was unfair Lot's wife was turned to salt.'

Robbie is confused at first, then remembers. He remembers the story from the *Old Testament Picture Book* his mother would read to him as a child, recalls the look of terror on the woman's face as she stands on that desolate biblical plain, her city and its people in ruins, her feet and legs a thickening column of salt, the knowledge of her eternal metamorphosis captured somehow in her eyes — doomed.

'What was unfair about it, Lily?'

'That she was damned for turning back to look at the city she loved . . . the people she loved . . . all destroyed. Sometimes . . . sometimes you've got no choice, sometimes you've got to look back at where you came from. The bridge, out there . . . It's unfair to damn a person for that.'

They look at each other.

Story

'Why these ones, Lily?' he asks after a while. 'Why the Old Testament stories, never the New?'

She looks away, thinks.

'It's where you find history,' she says eventually, 'King David ... Moses ... Abraham ... it's where things happened, where events unfolded and where life was lived, all of it. It's where people wrote their names into history.'

'Is that what you've been doing, Lily?'

'Oh no!' she almost cries it out. 'No, Robbie! I've just been looking after the names of others. I've been shepherding others into history.'

'Or protecting them from it,' he says quietly.

Robbie looks out through the windows of the apartment at the bridge, with its two great grey-steeled shoulders strong and enduring.

'I'm sorry, Lily,' he says.

Eighteen

The corner of something hangs from the front slot in the letterbox. Robbie reaches for it, his hand disappearing for a moment before emerging with a postcard. In the fading light he sees Freya's sure handwriting. The stamp is Canadian, the postmark a place-name in French. There is no return address.

He reads:

Robbie, there was too much we didn't know about each other, too much we didn't understand. It would never have worked, Robbie, figs or not. At least, it wouldn't have worked for me. It was too much your life. I'd forgotten mine. I'm okay. It was the right thing to come back. I'm just sorry it was so abrupt. Good luck. I hope this card helps. I care for you (did I ever tell you that?). Freya.

Story

He reads it again, shrugs his shoulders and lifts his eyes to the trees and the sky and the sun and the clouds, and shakes his head. 'Too much we didn't know?' he says to himself, aloud.

He turns the card over and looks at the photo. It's the Story Bridge with its cantilevered shoulders and the rise and fall of its lines, the K-shaped steel links, the suspended span, the white concrete arches and its stretch across the river. Something jars inside him. He thinks: Why is she sending me this?

For long moments Robbie sees only what he knows. But something's not quite right. As he looks at the bridge he feels heat gathering near the top of his skull. His memory shudders as if malfunctioning, waves of something begin to pound in his brain and suddenly there is a flash of darkness and Robbie is blinded, dizzy, as if the very flow of his blood has been cut. He grasps the letterbox to steady himself, holds on till the visible world returns.

He looks again at the bridge, and it is no longer the one seared into his memory. Robbie flicks the postcard back over to read the description, and it says, *Jacques Cartier Bridge, Montreal.*

'Those plans that Jack and your father were after when they –' Robbie begins.

'I've got them,' Lily interrupts quietly.

Robbie is incredulous. 'You've got them?'

'Every way I look at it I think I'm entitled to them. After all, they were my grandfather's before my husband took them.'

Lily smiles wryly, the relationships broken open now.

Lily leaves the living room for some minutes. When she returns she hands him a bound booklet, the soft brown leather worn around the edges, its finish discoloured into a light tan where it is scuffed from use. The front cover of the booklet is also marked, with superficial fingernail scratches criss-crossing the aged leather. Imprinted on the cover in gold lettering are the words, MONTREAL HARBOUR BRIDGE, and under them, *The Superstructure*.

As he opens the booklet Robbie knows what he will find. A photo of the bridge spanning a river is on the frontispiece. But the river is different from the one he knows. Where *his* river runs its short winding distance from the Great Dividing Range to the bay, this one sweeps vast miles, and strange seasons, freezes and thaws as it goes, parts and rejoins. This much can be seen even from the photos. And the bridge across it has been built by the *Dominion Bridge Company* rather than Brisbane's Evans-Hornibrook consortium. The date of construction is 1930. Robbie turns the pages and a story takes shape, leaf by leaf.

He is looking at a ghost. There are the diagrams of the bridge, mapping out a northern approach and a southern approach, anchor spans, a main span. Diagrams showing the construction of the bridge stage by stage. Then photos – the same series of photos he had seen as a child, but transposed now onto a different landscape: the same bridge shape, the same arches, the bridge's two halves growing together in the same way, across a river, in a photo-series. The same wedge mechanism used for the final linking. Then an account by the engineer-in-charge of the bridge's construction. The engineer was A.L.R. Lawrence, his mother's grandfather.

'It's the same bridge.'

'Yes,' says Lily.

'You knew.'

'Yes, love.'

'A thousand times Jack said the Story Bridge was "Queensland designed, Queensland built".'

'It wasn't just your father who said that, love. Everyone did.'

'But you knew all along that it was a replica of a bridge in Montreal?'

'It's not that simple. And anyway, there are so many stories you could tell. How do you know which is the right one?'

Nineteen

Summer wilts. March arrives, limping. Robbie wants to be angry but can't hold it. Freya is slipping further away, and his father has shrunk. Or the world has grown.

One evening Bec calls. It is nearly midnight, and the phone's ringing startles him awake.

'Can you spare an hour?' she asks. 'Can you come now?'

Robbie arrives at the Normanby Fiveways. It is surreal, ghostly. The figs on the Kelvin Grove Road median strip, which rises steeply to the intersection, are lit by fierce white spotlights projecting upwards into the canopy. The blinding lights beat colour from the trunks, the branches, the underside of the leaves, all leeched and dimensionless.

In the centre of the lit area, bleached like the trees, is a crowd of people, fifty, a hundred, swirling around the trunks. They are agitated, chanting, the object of their excitement three men with chainsaws standing not far from the figs. The men are gloved, the orange reflective stripes on their vests crossed in a way that reminds him of the armour of crusader knights. He looks at their faces, and recognises the men from other jobs over the years: fellings and cuttings, trimmings and plantings. They are anxious now, their work suspended, their chainsaws swinging loose from their hands, the crowd, baying, too hostile.

Robbie finds Bec among them – the leader now Freya has gone – and waits until she finishes speaking with a journalist from one of the television stations. Waits until the camera crew has swung away from her, and has begun to film the men with chainsaws.

'It's not bad, is it?' Bec says, gesturing to the crowd. Robbie notices more of Freya's friends with placards, and loudhailers. 'It took us less than an hour to get this group together after we got wind of what they were doing.'

'What *is* it that they're doing?'

'They're about to fell the figs. They say they're only trimming them. Do you believe it! Trimming! They would say that – they would've been told to. But of course they're cutting them down. In the middle of the night, so no one's the wiser. So it's too late to do anything. It's happened before. Remember Cloudland.'

He doesn't, but he knows what she means. The Cloudland Ballroom, part of the city's memory, knocked down by bulldozers while the city slept. *Cloudland*, the word a code for all the heritage buildings lost in the 1970s and 80s: Cloudland, the Bellevue Hotel, the Hoffnungs Building, the Queensland Trustees

The Comfort of Figs

Building, the ANZ Bank on Queen and Wharf. Cloudland, a call to arms.

'They want to cut them down, Robbie.'

Robbie looks across at the three men, distorted by the light.

'They might, but not today, Bec.'

'What do you mean?'

He points to the nearest fig, a number of grey branches already sawn from it and lying loose on the ground beneath.

'The figs are stressed, look at their leaves.'

She follows the direction of his finger.

'Now look at the chainsaws. You don't cut down a tree as large as this with a saw that small. If they say they're just removing dead branches, they probably are. To conserve them, to stimulate growth. Sometimes you have to prune them to save them.'

She is dubious, disbelieving.

'It's the middle of the night, Robbie!'

As if this is proof of guilt, as if this alone makes it a trespass, fatal.

'That's the best time to lop big branches.' Robbie nods to the closed lane and the line of orange witches' hats shaping the route of the merging cars. 'There's not the interruption to traffic.'

'Nooooo,' she says, to herself, a long note sounded, to give herself time to think.

'The figs can't help you, I'm afraid,' Robbie says.

Bec stands there for a while, shaking her head, trying to understand. Then she says – looking at him, trying to fathom him, her friend Freya's boyfriend, Freya's discarded boyfriend – 'Stuff you.'

'Huh?' Robbie is startled by the vehemence, the sharpness of the judgment. Its finality.

'"The figs can't help",' she repeats, capturing an echo of his voice, falling short of mimicry. 'But what about you, then? Are you going to help?'

'With what?'

'Listen to you, Robbie. Listen to yourself,' Bec says. 'Pathetic.'

'Wha . . . what?'

'Your figs help no one, do they? Never do. Never did. They sure as hell did nothing for Freya.'

'That's not fair,' Robbie says.

'Robbie,' Bec says, turning on him, hard, grinding, 'what did you ever give her? Really? What did you have to give?'

'You've got no right, Bec.'

'Right? I'll tell you what's right. It was right that she left you, Robbie. She had to leave. What else could she do? You damn-well drove her away.'

'That's just not fair.'

'Take your bloody figs, Robbie. Take them.'

Robbie turns, stumbles and goes, a quick erratic walk, head-bowed, as if pushing into something, through it. He stops when he gets to the Normanby Hotel at the corner, puffing from the hill. His heart is thumping as he looks back at the figs and the spotlights, and the swirling bleached figures of the protesters. *Protesters*. He remembers saying the word to Freya. *Believers*, she had countered. He sits down on the footpath, his back resting against the tiled wall of the hotel. He pulls his knees to his chest, wraps his arms around them, and watches. There is the cluster of Freya's friends. The thought occurs to him then, a question: What part of her did they know that he never did? Bec knew her in Canada, Bec was the one she followed to Brisbane. Bec, he realises, has lost a friend.

Another camera crew arrives. The crowd of Freya's friends respond, they raise their placards, grow louder. He thinks of one of the Bible stories his mother told him as a child, Moses in battle, holding a staff above his head. As long as Moses held the staff aloft, the Israelites would be victorious, but the moment he tired and lowered it, the battle would swing in the enemy's favour. But how do you know which battles to fight?

Though he tries, Robbie can't remember the name of the tribe the Israelites were fighting. There is a wild screech overhead. Robbie looks up at the flying fox landing in the high branches, the branches and their sound as they take its weight. But the flying fox is unable to settle, caught too in the outer reaches of the spotlights.

Robbie gets up. He walks back down the slope and through the swathe of light to the arborists, in their tight, anxious group of three, Bec watching him as he crosses over to them.

'Attracted quite a crowd, mate,' Robbie says to one of the men, the largest, the one with the woodsman's physique, the thick sprawling beard.

'It's a bloody joke, mate, a bloody joke.'

'Yeah — you don't get an audience like this every day.'

'Bloody ridiculous,' the man says — then, suddenly suspicious: 'What are you doing here? Are you with them or something?'

'Nah,' Robbie answers, 'passing by.'

The two men stand there for a while, unspeaking in the blinding light. The man shifts on his feet, scanning the crowd, keeping watch.

Story

'What are you going to do?' Robbie asks.

'Well, we can't continue like this, not in these conditions. Not without protection. We're getting out of here as soon as we get the word.'

Robbie nods.

'Mind if I take a piece, mate?' Robbie asks him, pointing to a freshly sawn limb.

'Go ahead, we'd just mulch it otherwise.'

Robbie lifts one of the fig branches to his shoulder, measures its weight and its length, balances it before stepping away.

'Careful you don't get lynched.'

He approaches Bec. She folds her arms against him.

'Well?' she says.

'You're right, Bec,' he replies. 'You're right. They're not going to cut them down. They wouldn't dare. They've got the message. Even if they were thinking of it before, they'll have got the message tonight.'

Robbie trims the branch, sets it aside for a few days. Then he cuts it into lengths, selects one, mounts the block on the lathe under the house. Still green, but he can't wait. He flicks a switch and the block of wood begins to turn, to spin, fast and dizzying on the lathe. Robbie leans forward and raises a chisel blade to the turning timber. It disappears in shavings of fig-wood blasting in shifting arcs of dust. Shrouding him in its delicate castings.

At last he lifts his goggles, releases the work from the lathe, and feels the weight of a fig-wood bowl in his hands.

He takes it upstairs to the long hoop-pine table, where his

gifts to Freya rest in the jacaranda bowl he'd turned years before. He puts the fig bowl down, places the new beside the old. Then, item by item, he transfers the things he'd given her, weighing them carefully in his hands as he does, lifting each close to his eyes, inspecting them all, each one. Remembering. Carefully. Laying to rest, as best he can.

Twenty

It's still dark and a koel is calling, even now, in March. *Coo-ee, coo-ee, coo-ee.* A series of high rising notes that hang in the air, unfinished. A storm bird, his father had called it, but it was not prophetic in that way. Its song had never heralded a storm, in the way that long thin lines of ants signalled impending rain – though as a child Robbie believed it and after hearing the koel call in the morning would wait all day for a storm to arrive, only to go to bed disappointed. It was not a storm bird but a summer bird, with its blood memory of monsoon weather patterns, and its summer migration to the branches high in Brisbane's trees to escape the rains of Asia.

    The koel calls again, a distinctive pre-dawn cry from a thick-leaved fig or old camphor laurel. *Coo-ee, coo-ee, coo-ee.* A strange, out-of-season call. The migrant koel should be returning home to the north. Is it lost? Robbie wonders. Disorientated? The cry again, rising with each succeeding note. Or is it lingering, tired of being an eternal visitor?

Robbie lies in bed as the dawn breaks, listening to birdsong. Koel, crow, pigeon, then, as the day brightens, magpie and mickey-bird and currawong.

The house begins to warm and Robbie rises. Sunlight streams in, as if it has accepted the invitation of each window to enter and now explores the house at will.

Jack O'Hara sits in his favourite armchair. The sun swallows the windows in front of him, dissolving the glass. Though the sunlight falls evenly when it reaches him, his body receives it in patches, arbitrary and pitiless. His right side is paralysed and feels nothing. His right leg has atrophied and hangs limp, a shape without mass. Jack looks at the sun falling on the back of his numb right hand, folded gently into his lap, and feels nothing of its warmth. He looks at it and observes the way the light illuminates his papery skin, as if it is someone else's hand.

The stroke has not destroyed his left side as it has his right. He sometimes feels he is split in two, that there are two halves of him. Jack feels the sunlight tickling the skin on the back of his left hand, still alive to him.

The stroke has taken much. He forgets much. He forgets sometimes that Lily has brought him breakfast. Sometimes he will eat it, spooning his cereal slowly into his mouth with his left hand, and half an hour after he has finished and Lily has cleared his plate he will signal to her to bring him his breakfast again. He needs Lily. She nurses him, prepares his meals, dresses him, trims his thinning hair. She moves him, supports him as he stands with his weight on his left leg and swings his body from one chair into another, or into his plastic shower seat, or into bed. He has given up trying to speak. The months of rehabilitation gave him sound, but no words. He can summon groans and grunts, the primeval noises, but nothing as complicated as speech.

Much has changed, so very much. Jack O'Hara weeps often now. He weeps through frustration. He weeps through pity. He weeps when he thinks of Lily's love for him. He is a different man, this man who weeps.

But Jack does not cry when Lily tells him Robbie has rung and wants to see him.

'Do you want to see him too?' she asks, sitting across from him in their bedroom. Jack is still for a long while, so long Lily wonders if she has lost him. For so long now Lily has kept Jack in the bedroom whenever Robbie visited. Each morning Jack has listened to his son's footsteps from behind the closed door of the bedroom. He has heard Robbie arrive, has heard snatches of voice – Robbie's, or Lily's. Has endured these humiliations. This has been their arrangement. That Robbie would visit his mother, and Jack would stay in the bedroom until Robbie left.

'Robbie's on his way over, Jack dear. He wants to see you. Do you want to see him?'

Eventually Jack groans, a low, pained assent.

There is no time for Lily to change him. She washes his face, wets his hair, combs it, wheels him from the bedroom to the living room and then shuffles him into the armchair with its large rolled arms. It is too low, and the springs in the old chair creak as they take Jack's falling weight, but the chair has been with them since he shipped it back from one of his overseas jobs as a gift for her. It's his chair now. She fluffs a fresh sheet and a rug over him as he sits facing the apartment window, the morning light on his stroke-ravaged face, waiting for the son who has not seen him for three years.

Jack hears knocking at the door and voices at the top of the corridor. He hears the sound of Robbie's footsteps approaching – his son's gait, calmed these last years, but still his son. He closes his eyes. The sunlight strikes his eyelids and he waits. His mind drifts. There is time enough to forget, remember, forget again.

Robbie kisses his mother. From the corridor he sees the back of his father's head where Lily has placed him in the centre of the living room. His father and the chair he is sitting in are pointed towards the window and the view over the river and the bridge, and light is pouring in upon them from outside.

Robbie enters the open living room and approaches the figure of his father. The chair and the silhouette of his father's head cast a single elongated shadow on the carpet, man and chair cutting a strange dark shape out of the sun's rays. As the distance between them shortens, Robbie's perspective changes, and he begins to make out detail. His father is dressed in pyjamas, and Robbie sees the clean light illuminate a floral pattern in the sheet which sheathes the bony crook of the old elbow.

Robbie moves closer. He can almost touch the back of the armchair, the crown of his father's head, his shoulders.

Story

He pauses, the dawn glare suddenly dizzying. Perhaps it is the flashing sunlight reflecting off the windscreens of cars which startles him – glints of light appearing and disappearing then appearing again behind the steelwork of the bridge. He turns to face the reflections, like hundreds of unsynchronised lighthouse beams flickering wildly out from the bridge. And it too is pulsating, afire. The glowing bridge looks like interlocking brand-irons freshly removed from a furnace.

He turns away from the bridge, to collect himself. By chance, or by habit, his eyes fall upon the canopy of a single fig across the river, solid, outstretched, emphatic. It also is lit by sun, but as he steadies his gaze to rest upon it, the image of the bridge, freshly burnt on his eyes, imposes itself in pulsating flashes upon the tree.

'Hello, Jack,' he says.

Jack opens his eyes and there is Robbie, standing in front of him.

From his pocket Robbie produces the gift Carleton had given him.

'Here you go – a memento from your Story Bridge days. Charlie had this in his pocket when he fell.'

The broken man squints, then blinks, a flutter, as of butterfly wings. His eyes open and close, hard and rapid, before he surrenders and begins to weep. Robbie steps back, as this father of his sheds strange, uncontrollable tears. He sees the contorted face, the thinning hair, the loose skin around his father's neck, the scars where cancers have been burnt from his scalp. His father in illumination, old, remarkable.

Robbie leans forward and places the rivet in his father's upturned left hand, where the dark lines chiselled into his palm branch out like a ragged canopy, entire.

Author's Note

This is a work of fiction. Some events and anecdotes in this work were inspired by historical incidents, however no character is intended to depict an actual person and all episodes and dialogues between characters are fictional. I nevertheless drew from a variety of sources in researching the novel, including Marc Serge Riviere's *Discovery of the Brisbane River, 1823 Oxley, Uniacke and Pamphlet 175 Years in Retrospect;* Richard Raxworthy's *From Footbridge to Harbour Bridge;* Pat and Sim Symond's *Bush Heritage;* L.R. Wilson's *Montreal Harbour Bridge – The Superstructure;* James Holt's *Story Bridge, Brisbane* in 'Transactions of the Institution', Vol XX, 1939, an excerpt from which was adapted on p. 125; archival material at the State Library of Queensland relating to the Story Bridge; and the papers of John Job Crew

Bradfield held at the National Library of Australia, including excerpts from Bradfield's speeches and correspondence, quoted on pp. 127 and 128.

Acknowledgment is made to the estate of Berton Braley, for use of excerpts from the previously published poem 'The Thinker', which also appeared in *The Story Bridge Commemorative Book on the occasion of the opening of the Story Bridge, 1940.*

My great thanks to Steve Foley, Peter Jensen, Justin Malbon, Victoria Marles and Maureen See, who all gave their time to comment on early drafts of the manuscript.

My appreciation to Arts Queensland, the Premier's Literary Awards, the Queensland Writers Centre, Madonna Duffy and Rob Cullinan at University of Queensland Press, and to Judith Lukin-Amundsen to whom I am especially grateful.

Finally, I thank my grandmother, Helen Margaret 'Peg' Barry, who was there at the start of this, and who has been so encouraging throughout.